10/21

SO MANY BEGINNINGS

SO MANY BEGINNINGS

A LITTLE WOMEN REMIX

BETHANY C. MORROW

FEIWEL AND FRIENDS
New York

A Feiwel and Friends Book
An imprint of Macmillan Publishing Group, LLC
120 Broadway, New York, NY 10271

fiercereads.com

Our books may be purchased in bulk for promotional, educational, or
business use. Please contact your local bookseller or the Macmillan Corporate
and Premium Sales Department at (800) 221-7945 ext. 5442 or by email at
MacmillanSpecialMarkets@macmillan.com.

Library of Congress Cataloging-in-Publication Data is available.
First edition, 2021
Book design by Michelle Gengaro-Kokmen
Printed in the United States of America by LSC Communications,
Harrisonburg, Virginia

Feiwel and Friends logo designed by Filomena Tuosto
ISBN 978-1-250-76121-7 (hardcover)
1 3 5 7 9 10 8 6 4 2

For Ana, JenJen, and Tonya.

PART I

I

AT FOURTEEN, AMETHYST MARCH HAD TERRIBLY SMALL feet. That meant that the brown leather, scallop-top boots that laced up the front, which had been issued to her by whichever Union officer oversaw such things this season, had very little wear. Amy had never owned anything with very little wear, though until she had her brown boots, she also hadn't known that. It naturally caused her to ponder the child from whom she'd inherited them.

Whatever child had first been in possession of her brown boots before their family escaped Roanoke Island ahead of the battle—or quite possibly evacuated afterward rather than watch the soldiers confiscate their lands, harvest, and cattle—must have owned more than one pair. That or they didn't share their shoes with siblings at the very least, and perhaps didn't have to walk far, when they weren't in a grand house with even flooring.

The floor was even enough here, and it belonged to her. Amy's father had built the house on the corner of 4th Street. If she understood what she'd eavesdropped, the honor of owning one of the first homes in the colony meant he'd proven himself of some importance, and in wartime, important men were rarely at home. He'd had his pick of the lots, Mammy said, and he'd chosen well. Amy was certain he couldn't have done otherwise, since in the old life—which was what the March family had taken to calling everything that came before the circumstance of war had freed them—there had scarcely been enough cover over their heads. Near the fields, her whole family had been able to count the stars between the feeble slats meant to constitute a roof. She was young—as her family reminded her all too frequently because they'd decided to guard it as a precious thing—but Amethyst was already on her second lifetime, and in this one, Papa had built a roof that was whole.

This house on Roanoke Island faced Lincoln, one of three avenues in the village, and that meant that despite it being too hot to amuse herself outdoors, Amy could at least watch the others as they came and went. She saw her eldest sister hustle up the avenue and then cross the street, the young woman's skirt in her hands as she acknowledged a salutation from a colonist Amy couldn't see. When Meg was nearer, Amy opened the door before her sister's hand could take hold of the knob.

"Amethyst March, how dare you!" Meg pressed her sister

out of view of the street, and rushed to close the door. "In nothing but a chemise and boots? Where's your sense?"

"Meg, your hat," the girl said, mimicking her sister's disapproving stance, though she didn't actually care.

"Oh, I know," Meg said apologetically. And then as though recalling why she'd come back to the house, she hurried past her little sister without unpinning and removing her straw bonnet. "I've only come back for a moment."

Amy placed the toe of an unblemished leather boot behind the opposite heel so that she could swivel slowly to watch Meg move through the room, down the hall, past Mammy and Papa's room on the right and the room their four daughters shared on the left, and into the kitchen at the far end of the long house.

"That was nearly perfect," she shouted down the hall when she was finished. "I've taught myself to do it just like the dancer in that music box we had to leave behind! Meg, come and see!"

"I have to get back to school, Amy," the eldest replied, returning with full hands and her face glistening. "It's so hot now, I've had to start shortening the lessons just like the missionary teachers do. Four hours for the early class, and four this afternoon, but at least I had time to come home when I realized I'd forgotten my lunch."

"Cornbread and an apple is hardly lunch."

"Don't pout, it's unbecoming."

"And who have I got to be becoming for?"

Meg forced herself to slow a moment and looked down into her sister's face.

"Amy," she said, and smiled. "For yourself, of course."

"I like myself just fine, thank you."

"All right," Meg answered with a laugh. "I like yourself, too. If you get dressed in a hurry, you can walk me back."

Amy's large dark brown eyes brightened, her cheekbones leaping up to meet them, and her sister immediately regretted the invitation.

"Only if I can stay and take my lessons properly, like everyone else."

"Oh, Amy," Meg began, her shoulders sinking at the start of a familiar discussion for which she had no time. "We've been over this. More than one hundred new freedpeople arrive to this colony every other day, and most of them have never had a single lesson until now. We simply can't spare the space, not when you can already read, and I can teach you fine when I'm home. Try to be reasonable."

When her sister crossed her arms, Meg continued: "If I had my way and a too-warm day to pass, I'd go to the edge of the village and lie underneath the cypress trees. Doesn't that sound angelic?"

"I'll stand outside a window—"

"The missionary teachers have the buildings. I teach in a tent."

"I'll stay outside the flaps!"

"Amy, I must get back, dear one," Meg cried. Amy's only solace was in the breeze created when the door swung open and shut again, after which she stomped around the front room in her lovely brown boots until someone else came bursting in.

"Mammy, what a lovely surprise!" Amy threw her arms wide, and when her mother created a new breeze, it was as she swept past her youngest child, whose forehead she fell just shy of kissing in her haste. "Is it hot enough that the officers are finished dictating their letters and they've sent you home?"

"Wouldn't that be delightful, my love." The woman's voice carried from her bedroom, into which Amy followed her with a disappointed trudge. "Fan Mammy's neck a moment."

The young girl retrieved her mother's fan from the dresser, admiring the pink ribbon that trimmed the woven straw and wrapped around the handle. It had seen better days, and now only half the ribbon clung to the handle, the rest dangling dejectedly.

"Amy, please!"

Finally the girl fanned her mother, while Mammy pushed her rolled hair up from her damp neck.

"I have to get back," she said after a time. "I only thought your sister might have come here. She wasn't at the school-house."

"Meg teaches from a tent, Mammy," Amy reminded her. "She isn't a missionary teacher, after all."

"I can't imagine where else she'd be. It isn't like her to be unpredictable . . ."

Amy didn't say it aloud, but she knew that Mammy meant

5

her eldest daughter could be a dreadful bore. Everyone knew it, though she'd gotten in trouble on more than one occasion for saying so.

"She came home and went back again," Amy said.

Mammy sucked her teeth. "Well then, I must have just missed her."

"Whatever you needed done, perhaps I could do it!"

"Thank you, Amy, but it's nothing like that. I've invited someone to supper, and I didn't want it to be a surprise." Mammy kissed her on the forehead successfully this time and then swept back out through the front room; Amy hurried to follow. "I'll send word to her somehow, but don't you go bothering her at school, do you hear me?"

And before Amy could argue that whether or not she was allowed to deliver the news, she should at least know it for herself, her mother was out the door.

She collapsed onto the floor, though there was no one to see or pity her. It was just as well; someone would have made her get up, and it turned out lying on the floor was slightly cooler than all that moving around.

Amy was bored—dreadfully, in fact—but if it meant she'd have to wear heavy skirts to make up for the lack of a hoop, she was glad at least that she didn't have to do important work like Mammy and Meg. Joanna, the second oldest, worked alongside the freedmen charged with building more houses, and no one chided her for wearing the kind of flat skirts one might wear on a plantation in the old life. Bethlehem, the third-born March girl, was a celebrated seamstress;

no one minded what she wore so much as what she made for them.

Still lying on the floor of the front room, Amy closed her eyes and willed her other two sisters to come home, too. When the door flew open for the third time, she sat up so quickly she felt light-headed, but still managed to blurt out, "Mammy's invited someone to supper!"

"Has she?" Beth came just inside the door and dumped an armful of uniforms on the floor.

"Isn't that unpatriotic?" Amy asked as her sister rushed to retrieve something from their bedroom.

Beth was sixteen, and the nearest to Amy in age. Along with her calm manner, this made her feel most like her younger sister's equal, and *that* made Amy feel certain she was the leader of the two.

"I don't think so," Beth answered breathlessly when she returned, because it wouldn't occur to her not to, however silly the question. "I think something must be intentionally unpatriotic, or it isn't at all." She spread the thin throw blanket she'd collected onto the floor beside the pile, then transferred the uniforms onto it before tying the ends to create a cumbersome-looking bundle. "You haven't told me who Mammy invited to supper."

"Oh. I don't know." Amy hated to admit that. She lit up like a spark at recalling something important that she *did* know. "It's got something to do with Meg, though."

Beth stood up, wayward strands of her very dark hair swaying with the motion. Whether from the heat or from

7

hustling around, or from a headwrap not properly secured the night before, her thick hair was puffy at the root, so that the two once-neat flat braids looked too swollen to fit beneath anything but a cloth bonnet. Amy grew warmer just looking at it; it was a familiar occurrence in the summer, and it made her scalp swelter and steam like a pot of crabs.

"I hope she'll enjoy it then," Beth said, and smiled a bit. It was enough to produce her charming dimples, which Amy couldn't help but envy because Papa had never seen his daughter's dimples appear without marveling at them. Mammy said it was because Beth had gotten them from his mother.

It didn't seem fair, since Amy hadn't been born a March and couldn't have gotten any adorable feature from her parents, let alone their parents. Beth was at a distinct advantage, and pretending not to know it only made her more insufferable, though no one seemed to know that but Amy.

She was the youngest, at least. Smart, which Meg informed the family, otherwise Amy would have had to; pretty enough that it shouldn't have bothered anyone how much she hated having her hair managed. Hers wasn't as thick as Beth's, and so there were always hats to cover it.

She wished it'd been Joanna to come home next. Whatever distraction had sent her into the house, at least *she* was curious and inventive enough that at news of a supper guest and Mammy's search for Meg, Jo would've concocted an entire conspiracy to explain it. A story anyway, which was Jo's one talent.

Amy huffed. Enough of this wretched house, and her boredom. It would be stiflingly hot out in the sun, but she'd put on the limpest skirt allowed and a blouse with eyelets so her skin could breathe. She'd walk at a reasonable pace, quickly enough that the inevitable sweat would produce a momentary chill, if she was lucky. Jo would be at the build, and there were only ever one or two builds ongoing, as there were only enough builders to construct one or two new houses at a time. Whichever lot they were on, it was a good bet they'd be along Lincoln Avenue—or visible from it, at least. There were only three avenues in the colony's village—Lincoln, Roanoke, and Burnside—and very few homes so far. Amy would be able to spot them, even if they were clear on the other side.

Jo would have something interesting to say about this new development, and she wouldn't scurry back to her task once her imagination was captured. She might even insist on going to Meg's school tent—and if she did, Amy couldn't be chastised for accompanying her older sister.

She'd made up her mind, until Beth's dimples reappeared.

"I don't suppose you'd like to take the ferry back to the mainland with me?"

"Bethlehem," Amy said suspiciously. "It isn't like you to suggest mischief."

"It isn't. I've gotten Mammy's permission, for whenever I need to use the sewing machine. And I could use an extra set of hands, if you're willing to work just a little."

Amy leapt up on her toes.

"I have an impeccable work ethic," she exclaimed, constantly annoyed of the "freedom" that made Mammy insist the youngest child shouldn't have toil.

For Beth's part, she smiled and rolled her eyes. "Come on, then. A soldier's been instructed to take us to the shore." Then she raised her finger, as though to halt Amy's excitement. "But we'll be walking from Manns Harbor to the big house, and this bundle must be carried."

"I'll get a blanket of my own, and we'll halve the burden," Amy said, not waiting for a reply before dashing off to find one.

"That's very good thinking," Beth told her.

"I know," Amy called back from the bedroom. "Meg says I'm the smartest of us all."

II

THE NORTHERN REPORTER HAD TAKEN UP THE WHOLE DAY'S conversation among the boys at the build, and by the time Jo made it home and cleaned herself up, she was impatient for someone else to arrive so she could relay the news to her sisters. Mammy likely already knew of the gentleman's assignment, working for the Union officers as she did, since he had come to report on the success of the colony in order to drum up donations from wealthy Northern abolitionists.

There was someone else she was anxious to tell the family about, though, and she expected a much more engaged response to news of a handsome, young Black man, also from up North. This one she hadn't simply heard about. Joseph Williams was his name, and despite that Jo wasn't in the habit of considering marriage prospects herself, she'd felt immediately that Meg—who thought of little but teaching and marriage—would find the nearest broom to jump at the sight of him.

Jo hadn't had much chance to acquaint herself with the man, though he'd come to watch some of the construction—and just to be in their company, as far as she could tell. It *had* occurred to her that perhaps they were a kind of novelty when she learned that Joseph Williams was a free man visiting from Pennsylvania, and had no old life.

Whatever the newly arrived young man might have called it, Jo couldn't imagine what it must be like—to not know the time before. Before the freedpeople colonies and villages, and the pilgrimages in between, when the big houses of the North Carolina islands were still inhabited by white families who thought they could own another human being. Before those white families had run off—either to fight to keep Black folk captive or to escape the judgment brought by the veritable sea of Union soldiers who so handily conquered the area—they had done abominable things.

The truth was that if there'd never been violence, the writing of a person's name on a piece of paper that said they belonged to someone else would have been horror enough. There was no better or worse when the condition was enslavement. There were no good and bad masters when there were masters at all. Be they young or old, man or woman, ill-tempered or applauded for their mild manner, they were all heathen beasts who should have expected they'd be held to account. That they hadn't expected it—or at least that they hadn't expected to lose—only proved they were not what they claimed to be.

They were not superior, Jo had always known. They couldn't be, when they were so bewilderingly ignorant.

Because Jo knew all this at a young age, she'd trained herself not to speak. Unless she was alone with Papa and Mammy, or Meg and Beth, she'd rarely said a word as a child. She certainly didn't speak to white people. They mostly assumed her mute as a result, and thought very little of poor Meg—whom they'd made keep their daughter company during lessons—pretending to teach those lessons to her younger sister, who was clearly incapable of learning.

What a revelation they would have received, could they have witnessed what really went on inside Jo's head. Not speaking aloud had been her act of intentional self-preservation, but what she began because of it was a wonderful surprise. Sentences she was not yet permitted to write down, beautifully crafted with words lovingly chosen. All day, she'd knit them together in her mind the way Beth would learn to stitch fabric, taking something most anyone could use and making from it something only she could conceive.

She developed a formidable memory, waiting as she was forced to until much later in each day, when her family returned for the night to what the white people generously called a cabin. Then she would recite everything she'd composed that day, and even if it wasn't a story, which Meg and Beth liked best, and was instead a scathing indictment of this land and its crimes, Papa and Mammy would let her recite it. They would huddle close, in a circle so tight that their knees and shoulders knocked against each other, and sometimes their foreheads, too.

But the old life was over. It had been for several years now. She wasn't a child anymore; she was seventeen, and Jo spoke as often as she had a mind to. She spoke freely because that's what she was.

Free.

She still didn't make a habit of speaking to white people. It could be reasonably avoided, now that the family had found their way to the colony. There were so many people around all the time, and if she stayed in the village, which she almost always chose to do, all those people were Black like her. It was glorious, a stunning sight, to look in every direction and see brown-skinned people building houses of their own, or coming and going. When she did see a white person, they were missionary teachers who'd come south to teach the newly free, or they were wearing Union uniforms. That didn't make Jo trust them, but at least it meant they were on the right side.

She hadn't meant to think all of that just because of meeting Joseph Williams and finding out that he had no old life of his own. She'd been so caught up in her thoughts and memories that she was halfway to slathering sweet butter over the deep cuts she'd made in the shad fish she'd brought home. She was ready to put the first collection of them in the skillet she'd set on the wood burner when she finally heard the front door open.

"Meg?" she cried, leaping back so she could look down the hall and into the front room. "Meg, are you home?"

"Joanna, it's Mammy."

Jo felt guilty at the way her shoulders sank. It was lovely to have a Mammy, especially the one she had. And especially because Papa was away.

"Come and sit near me while I cook, Mammy. You must be tired."

"If I must be, then so must you," the woman said, beginning to unpin her hair now that she was home for good.

She moved much slower now and Joanna smiled, though she could not help bristling immediately after at something her mother had once told her. There were no soldiers or officers to demand things of the woman here, and so while it was safe to take a restful posture in the comfort of her home, and despite that this was not a plantation, in the office Mammy dared not appear affected by the heat or the hours spent briskly at a dozen tasks—no matter how many times she was forced by some officer's error to rewrite a letter or document. On any such occasion, they freely berated her, intimating that she was a lazy cow if she didn't work twice as fast as they had to.

Though few outside the family would say so, in the March house, Jo was known for her passionate character, and so Mammy had not been surprised by her daughter's outrage. Joanna had raged that she hadn't been there when one of the Union men had had the audacity to say such a thing to Mammy, who had for her entire life done more work before sundown than many a white man, and never for a day's wage or the lavish congratulations they all seemed to require for the slightest effort.

But of course that hadn't even been the reason Mammy took issue with their complaints. It was that none of them had children to mind in the morning. She'd said that before she could even think of helping a white man sort his correspondences or make a list of supplies or men or the wounded, she had to make sure her daughters were well. She had to know they were fed, even if one of the blessed dears had taken it upon themselves to prepare or set out the food. She had to see them, lay her hands on them, to know that they were all still here.

Few things could silence Joanna March, but that had succeeded. It stilled her to hear her mother admit that daily she had to be convinced anew that the colony wasn't a dream, and that no one had come in the night to snatch them back. She had to hear her children, she'd said, while Jo held her breath to ensure she didn't interrupt. More than that, Mammy had told her, she had to remind her daughters that they could be heard. She had to listen to her Jo, whatever her second born wanted to say, because it was a blessing that the girl spoke at all. She had to make sure her children knew they were her treasure. And, like people who knew something of respect and consideration, her four daughters didn't mind if she moved at a reasonable pace, she'd finished with a smile.

Today, Mammy made it to Jo's side in her own time. She had a metal pin between her teeth, which she removed before wrapping an arm around the girl's waist. She kissed her cheek four times, because the other three girls weren't there to kiss, and then Mammy let her head rest on her daughter's shoulder and breathed a full and restful sigh—which was when she smelled the skillet and the fish and the butter.

"Oh, Joanna, no!"

"What's the matter?"

"Not shad, when we're having a gentleman guest!"

"You love shad fish, Mammy," Jo contested before turning with a start. "And how was I to know there'd be a gentleman guest?"

The newly arrived Joseph Williams sprang back to mind, but it was too great a coincidence to imagine.

"We'll either spend half the night picking bones out of our mouths, or choke on them, there are so many." Mammy sighed again, only this time, it was heavy with agitation.

"How lucky that Mary Pollack came by the build today, then, or we wouldn't have enough of anything to offer your guest."

"We have cornbread and smoked fish, and plenty of fruit," Mammy said, looking around as though to confirm her stock.

"And you'd rather feed a gentleman something hot, even in the dead of June, Mammy."

That was true.

"I don't care at all," Jo added, turning the fish once more. "But I know you do."

"I do," Mammy agreed before sighing again. "Thank you, Joanna."

"Thank Mary Pollack—haven't you been listening? The boys and I are nearly finished building her house, and she's so pleased to have been next on the list that she went by the fishery and brought us each a feast of them."

"I'll thank Mary tomorrow . . . if none of us choke on shad bones tonight."

Jo laughed as Mammy retreated to her bedroom to store the handful of pins she'd fished out of her rolled hair. The night was still warm, so she would no doubt braid and cover it with a crocheted snood so that it stayed off her neck but still looked becoming for their guest.

"It smells wonderful," Meg said in salutation before anyone knew she'd come home. "But I couldn't bear to stand before a stove in this heat."

On her way out to the yard, Meg poked her younger sister in the ribs, and then she was back outside. Jo heard her working the pump and then giving a quiet prayer of thanks when she brought the cool water to wet her face and neck.

Jo smiled. "We're all lucky I had the conviction, since Mammy's invited someone home."

Meg reentered the house. "Oh?"

"Meg, you're home!" their mother exclaimed when she returned to the kitchen. "I meant to send word to you at the school, but I couldn't get away again, and now he'll arrive at any moment. And with Beth and Amy still not back!" She was speaking excitedly, and though she'd seemed tired before, now Jo could guess at the prayers her mother might have said throughout the day.

"You have high hopes for this gentleman, whoever he is," she said, somewhat incredulously.

"Gentleman?" Meg wrapped one arm around her own waist and straightened.

"She's invited someone to supper and hasn't even told us his name," Jo explained, "but he must have impressed you, Mammy. You sound ready to commission Meg's wedding gown."

Now both of Meg's arms tensed at her sides, and if Jo noticed, at least she didn't make a show of it. It would be embarrassing to find it common knowledge how distracted Meg had become this past year, wondering when she'd marry, and whom. She was nineteen, and Mammy assured her it would be several years before anyone wondered why she wasn't. It was meant to put her at ease, but the problem was that Meg wished to be courting and couldn't help being disappointed not to be. Worse, men poured into the colony on almost a daily basis, but few were prospects. They were too young, or else they came with wives already or women they intended to marry. Others were concerned with the war, and when they would be allowed to enlist in the Union; they had no head for romance, and Meg had every desire to be a wife, but none to be made a war widow.

"Don't be dramatic, Jo," Mammy said, but then she covered her mouth with her hand, and both her daughters knew that Joanna had been right.

"I thought I was the only one desperate to find me a husband," Meg said, doing only slightly better at seeming calm. "Well. At least tell us who he is."

19

Mammy looked between her two eldest daughters, whose eyes were wide and expecting, one with nervous anxiety, the other with curious excitement.

"If ever I were going to make a perfect husband for you, Meg, it would be him," she said, taking her eldest daughter's hand. "He's the kind of man Papa would adore; I know it. That's the first thing I thought when we met."

"Which was only this afternoon," Jo said with a smirk that made Mammy drop her chin a bit, as though embarrassed.

"That's true. I shouldn't have let my imagination get away from me. It matters more what Meg thinks of Joseph than your father or me."

"Joseph?" Jo asked incredulously. "Joseph Williams?"

"That's right."

Now it was Meg whose attention volleyed between the other two women.

"Will someone please tell me who this Joseph Williams is?"

In reply, Jo grabbed her sister's wrist from Mammy's hand, and pulled her from the kitchen and toward their bedroom.

"It turns out Mammy might be right, Meg," Jo explained, closing the door behind them and pushing her older sister backward until she had no choice but to drop onto the bed they shared. Then she opened the trunk where Beth kept all the lovely pieces she fashioned for her sisters, among the scraps that were not yet completed.

"You know something of this Joseph Williams, too?" Meg asked, unbuttoning the blouse she'd worn all that very hot day.

Mammy burst into the bedroom with a tin wash basin and a rag thrown over her shoulder, both of which she placed on the stand between the two beds where all four of her children slept.

"I'll see to supper, Jo," she said, submerging the rag before wringing it and handing it to Meg to wash her face and neck. When she left, she closed the door behind her, and at the sound of the front door opening, both Meg and Jo froze. They waited and listened, but soon they heard their youngest sister shriek in telling Mammy about her day. Relieved, they set back to the task of beautifying Meg.

"Put this one on," Jo said, tossing a delicate blouse onto the bed before taking the rag and submerging it again. "But wash under your arms first."

She wiped her damp hands on her skirt and went back to the trunk for a belt, and then knelt down and felt underneath Amy's pillow before retrieving something wrapped in lace.

Meg was nearly put back together now. She stretched her neck to see around Jo's shoulder at the contents of the lace bundle.

"I hope she won't mind," she said, smiling at the revealed hair comb.

"If she does, she'll mend."

Jo came back to their bed, and Meg turned so that the comb could be fitted into her hair. It was lovely and ornate, with seven long teeth, and a scrolling floral design hand carved into its metal. It was also not the kind of thing any of them would have owned before finding shelter at the abandoned big house en route to the colony. There had been so many treasures there, left behind when the previous residents fled. The best had been hidden for safekeeping, as though someone intended to return one day. It had become a daily pastime while the March family sheltered there, the girls searching for nooks and crannies where something else might be tucked away.

Amy had come upon the hair comb beneath a loose bit of flooring in the largest bedroom, and claimed it as her own. It was fair that she should consider it hers, but they were sisters, Jo thought, and she shouldn't be bothered to share things.

"How do I look?" Meg asked when they were finished.

"Like you haven't been standing on your feet all day in a tent, teaching freedpeople their letters despite the heat, because you know how important it will be that we all know how to make our marks."

The two held each other's arms, cradling elbows, and smiled.

"Although I think Mr. Williams should know," Jo added. "How else will he understand how lucky he'd be to win your attention?"

"If by some miracle he doesn't, I trust my Joanna to set him straight."

They each took in a deep breath, and then reopened the bedroom door.

"Mammy wouldn't let me go inside my own bedroom," Amy huffed as she barreled past them. Surely she had no need to occupy it, but was offended at the restriction.

22

Beth, on the other hand, had two heavy bundles to stow—one she held in her arms, and the other she pushed with her foot down the hall before nudging it into the room.

"Do you like the blouse, Meg?" she asked. "It's the thinnest material, I was worried I'd ruin it."

"It came out perfectly, Bethlehem. It's refreshing to wear in this weather."

Everyone milled about, at their various tasks and rarely in the same room, but kept up several conversations at once, as they always did.

"Come and help clear the table so we can set it," Mammy said to whomever had free hands, and Amy came bounding out of the bedroom where she had flounced on her bed and watched Beth organize what they'd brought home.

"Where did this come from?" Jo exclaimed, coming down the hall with a pie in her hands.

Meg leaned close to smell it. "Is that molasses apple?"

"Florence at the big house made it to thank Beth for the way she mended a dress that must've belonged to the master's wife," Amy replied.

It was only that that caused the house to quiet, three of the sisters and Mammy halting and looking at each other before looking back at Amethyst. Jo put the pie on the table and then held the youngest's hands. No one else was ready to speak, or else would need too many moments to decide how best to redress the conversation, so it came to Jo.

"I know that's what we called them, Amy. But not now. Words are so terribly important, you know I think so. And it matters what we call each other, and what we call everyone else." Her usually excitable baby sister looked small with her eyes wide and wondering, as though she weren't certain whether she was being chastised, but Jo was only correcting her. Jo spoke gently now so that the young girl wasn't confused into thinking she'd done anything wrong. "No one was ever a master, dear heart. They were only enslavers, and they aren't now. Not anymore, and never again."

"But they might be," Amy replied. It was more timid than her usual nature, and her eyes roamed a bit without landing on anyone too long. "The war's not over."

It was just like her to say something that no one else dared, but it didn't mean she was the only one to think it. In the front room of this home built just for them—before there were groups of men young and not so young organized to do it, and while the five had still been living as refugees on the mainland in an abandoned big house with nearly a hundred others—the March women huddled closer without thinking to. Arms wound around waists and hands landed on shoulders after touching a cheek or a coil of hair.

Jo knelt down, even though it meant that the youngest was above her now. She kept Amy's hands in hers.

"It is here," she said. "Here, and New Bern, and as far as Corinth, Mississippi, where Papa's gone, the war's been won."

She felt Beth, Meg, and Mammy close behind her, and she nodded up at Amy.

"This is a freedpeople's colony. That's what they call it, all over the country. They know about us and this place, and what we're building. Everybody knows we're free now." She smiled so she wouldn't cry. That wouldn't do. Her sister would be confused and think she was telling one of her tales, meant to pacify the young ones but not meant to be true. And this *was*. "That's the way it'll stay, Amethyst. I give you my word."

It was quiet after that, Jo on her knees, and Amy's hands in hers, the other three standing close enough to share a breath. It was still enough to hear an angel pass overhead, until there came a knock at the door.

They'd all but forgotten Mr. Joseph Williams, and now a guest felt almost like an intrusion.

"Well," Mammy said, breaking the spell, after which everyone breathed again and stood a little ways apart. "Bethlehem, would you see to the door? And Amy, help Joanna in the kitchen."

They dispersed at her command, except for Meg, who wove her fingers through her mother's.

When Bethlehem invited him in, Joseph Williams took off his hat before entering, and Meg March was already smitten.

III

IF JOSEPH WILLIAMS HAD HEARD TELL OF THE GENTEEL
nature of Southern women, the Marches did not dissuade
him of its validity. They ate so carefully and hardly spoke,
even though they made polite expressions to mask the way
they ran their tongues along their teeth to clear the shad
bones. Only Amy reached into her mouth before Beth tapped
her sister's leg under the table to bring her to her senses. The
young man was the gentleman Mammy had promised—he
pretended not to notice, though he almost immediately
begged their pardon before doing the same. That made Amy
and Beth exchange smiles, and caused Meg to wistfully sigh.

Beneath the jacket he'd worn to supper, Joseph had
square shoulders, despite which he also had long arms and
soft hands. There were no marks on the back of them and
few calluses on the front, which every sister noticed, from
youngest to eldest. It was a strangeness they couldn't have

predicted, because until him, they'd only ever met Black men with workmen's hands. He was no more handsome because he'd been born free, but the clay-brown skin of his face and neck had fewer lines. He hadn't spent every day of his life at the mercy of the weather, as far as they could tell.

Amy, Beth, Jo, and Meg all studied him while he spoke—which he seemed fond of doing, or at least he was accustomed to a rapt audience—and he was able to tell them of his journey from Philadelphia to North Carolina in great detail, sharing anecdotes about Brigadier General Edward Wild, in whose company he'd come to explore the island and now the colony.

"This General Wild," Meg began, finally interrupting Joseph's storytelling. The glimmer in her eye was now notably dimmed.

"Yes, Miss Meg," he answered, and there was perhaps the beginning of a glimmer in his—or at least two of the women at the supper table hoped.

"What's his business in a freedpeople's colony?" she asked. "There are so many officers here already, it's intriguing to have another come from such a distance. And in the company of a free Black man brought all the way from the North?"

"It sounds," Joseph answered with a handsome smile, "like you might be asking what *my* business is, Miss Meg."

"If your business is the same," she said, and now the worry was evident.

The young man must have been prepared for it. Jo could tell as much when instead of sighing, he drew in a breath, as though to steady himself, and squared his already distracting shoulders.

"We hope to enlist good freedmen to the cause." He was afraid to leave too long a silence, because he barreled on at the sight of Meg's disappointment. "There are some up north who question the abilities of negro soldiers, but General Wild is devout in his faith in our value."

"I wouldn't think that would need confirming," Jo said, because it seemed Meg and Mammy wouldn't. "We were valuable enough to be napped from our original lands, after all. And valuable enough to spark a war."

"Of course you're right," Joseph said, inclining his head toward Joanna as though she were the schoolmarm, and he'd been warned to watch his p's and q's. "And it is our fight. It's *our* freedom, after all."

"I thought you were born free," Amy chimed in. She'd been watching the molasses apple pie ever since Beth finished her last bite of fish, wondering when it would be cut and distributed, or whether it was simply to be table dressing.

"No one is free until we all are," he answered, and around the table there was unanimous approval. There were sounds like something between a sigh of relief and an involuntary hum, and the glimmer snuck back into Meg's eye.

"My husband is away, in Mississippi," Mammy said when the moment was done. At her remark, her daughters' heads bowed slightly, as though in reverence. It only took a moment to say a prayer for their father, and they'd gotten into the habit of doing so at least a hundred times a day. "There's work to be done, making this place a colony and not just another camp, and in Corinth they're further along. He's gone to learn how they've done it, because you see, Mr. Williams, there's more to it than forcing white folks to leave off our chains. We must build alliances, dependencies. We must be allowed to know our Black neighbors, the way we weren't before, so that we can get along without the Union. There's plenty of resistance, even to that. You must understand that we who needed this war to become free already know it's our fight, whether we see battle on a field or only every day."

"Yes, ma'am," Joseph said, which was the only appropriate response.

The conversation settled there for a while, and Mammy elected Amy to help her retrieve the kettle and tea strainers from the kitchen, if only because the girl could not be trusted so close to the pie unsupervised. For the few moments they were gone, those who remained around the table said nothing, Meg exchanging a timid glance with Joseph before seeing that both Joanna's and Bethlehem's eyes were on her, too. She was relieved when her mother came back . . . until she saw the tea leaves she brought.

"I'm sure you've never had yaupon tea, Mr. Williams," Meg said, a flush warming her cheeks.

"I'm sure I've never heard of it, Miss Meg," he said, and his curiosity was unfortunately piqued. "I must confess I tend to depend on coffee, though, and not tea, which may account for my ignorance."

"Oh no," she answered, with a slight shake of her head.

"You'll not have heard of it because folks don't tend to drink it unless they must." She thought of the missionary teachers who seemed prepared for a great many sacrifices—until they could not procure what food staples they'd taken for granted back home. Being reduced to drinking tea made from holly leaves seemed one injustice too many for several of them, and they complained about it often.

Probably when they felt unable to voice other less tasteful concerns, Meg thought.

"You'll be grateful we're not serving you what passes for coffee," Jo quipped. "Believe me."

"I'm aware of the many substitutions Southerners must acclimate to, and I've found I'm quite partial to sweet potato coffee," he said. "Thus far I've been served coffee made of okra seeds, peanuts, and once—if memory serves—dandelion root."

"And you tried them all?" Amy asked, while her sisters and Mammy laughed in a kind of relieved amusement. She bounced forward so that she was perched on the edge of her seat, one leg bent beneath her and her elbows landing on the table with a careless thud.

"We Northerners aren't as heralded for our manners as you, but wartime requires a measure of graciousness. Beside which, when I'm a guest, I always eat what I'm given." He looked then at Meg. "I will be delighted to try this yaupon tea."

Mammy placed one of their two tea strainers atop Joseph's cup and filled it with the dried and torn leaves of the yaupon holly. "Speaking of the war," she began, pouring the piping hot water over it, "How many of our good men does your general intend to recruit?"

"General Wild has been authorized by President Lincoln to recruit four regiments from North Carolina, to contribute to an entire African brigade," Joseph answered, his shoulders squared again, this time as though with pride.

"Four," Meg said as frailly as if the wind had escaped her.

"What's so awful about four?" Amy whispered.

"A regiment has ten companies," Beth answered, leaning toward her younger sister so that their heads nearly touched. "And in each company, there are one hundred men." She'd tried to speak as quietly as possible, but the rest of the table was silent and everyone heard.

"So Mr. Williams has come to take four thousand of our men," Jo said without looking away from the young man who perhaps wished he did not strike such an imposing figure just then.

"We haven't got four thousand men." Once she'd spoken, Meg seemed the only March who could look elsewhere. In an effort to steady her hands, she stood abruptly and began cutting the molasses apple pie. When she'd finished, she seemed to remember that the supper plates hadn't been cleared, and with Mr. Williams taking her father's place at the head of the table, every available plate was in use. They would have to be cleaned before the pie could be served.

Beth stood next, taking hers and Amy's plates, and followed Meg toward the kitchen. Amy grabbed the utensils left behind and went next. Jo took Joseph Williams's plate and utensils, placing them on hers, and collected Mammy's, too, before joining her sisters.

Mammy didn't leave their guest. It was the benefit of having four daughters. One of them anyway. They consoled each other when one needed it. Whoever was downtrodden, she had three sisters to set her right again.

If it was Amy, they would shower her with attention, giving her an undistracted audience while she danced or sang. If Beth was feeling low, they would ask her opinion on a frock that perhaps was best tossed out, knowing she would have a host of remedies for making the thing seem new. When Jo was upset, her sisters told her stories that they made up on the spot, and which she would inevitably improve, or else be too amused by their intentionally awful telling. Tonight, it was Meg whose mood had soured, and that meant her sisters would mostly be silent, but they would help her in whatever task she undertook.

The worst times were when all four of her daughters were heartsore. That was when only a Mammy would do. She'd invite them all into her bed, even though there were beds enough for all of them now. Still, there was something about cuddling together, everyone held by someone, and all in the same place. It was the way they'd had to sleep in the old life, and then immediately after, at the confiscated big house. The family had taken refuge there, but the place had been stocked beyond capacity by all those looking for a safe haven now that they were free. It hadn't been comfortable there, either, but it had been wonderful.

"You don't know quite what it's like, Mr. Williams," Mammy said. "The moment after enslavement, because you have always been free. Don't think that we are uninvested in this war because we don't want someone coming and selecting the best stock. We're only too accustomed to that around here."

"I'm beginning to realize," Joseph began, "that there were many thoughts that hadn't occurred to me before coming south. I thought, of course, of all I'd be giving up."

"Perhaps you didn't think *we* had anything to lose."

"Yes," he admitted. "I'm ashamed to admit you might be right."

"Your General Wild, and General Burnside, and all the others—they think *they* are building this colony. That because they commission the leveling of trees, and exchange letters with the president, and permit missionary teachers to come, that this is *their* doing. But *we* pilgrimaged here." Mammy placed her palm flat against the supper table. She used no force, and it made no sound, but it lifted her chin, and it caused Joseph to straighten in his seat. "We came from all directions, making those commissions and correspondences necessary at all. We had schools and churches before they designated any building, or permitted any white schoolmarms. We have constructed this place, and its community, as the founders built thriving colonies and then a nation. We are doing the same, Mr. Williams. And we need our men for that—free, of course, and alive."

"It is something to behold, Mrs. March, and that's the

truth. I daresay I never saw a place I liked better than Roanoke Island." When he said it, Joseph Williams was looking past Mammy, at the procession of young March women coming back down from the kitchen, carrying clean plates and cutlery. The first of them was Meg, and Joseph stood at her coming, and could not help but smile.

"What a strange day," Meg whispered.

Jo hadn't fallen asleep, though she could hear the soft snoring coming from Beth and Amy's bed. She'd known Meg was still awake by the occasional sighing.

"It seems Joseph Williams came out of nowhere, doesn't it?"

"It seems he came out of Pennsylvania to me."

"You know what I mean."

"Will you marry him and get it over with?"

"Joanna!" Meg exclaimed in a scratchy whisper. "Don't be silly." But even as she stared at the ceiling of their little house, she couldn't help what she imagined. "I'm as boring as Amy says I am, aren't I?"

"Amy says you're *dread*fully boring."

"She's right. I want to teach, and marry, and that's all. But to me, it seems like the world."

Jo turned on her other side so that she was facing her sister. "Then it is the world."

Meg turned, too. "Just like that?" she asked.

"Why should it need to be harder? We've had more than

our share of difficulty in this country. You should pursue it, when you know what would satisfy you."

"But you wouldn't be so easily satisfied," Meg whispered. Though they'd been speaking hushedly all along, with this whisper, she sounded almost ashamed.

"And you wouldn't be tempestuous. And Beth would never be unkind. Nor Amy undramatic. We're sisters, Meg; we aren't twins. Why should you be what I am?"

"Is tempestuous what you think you are, Jo?"

There was only room for one sister to lay on her back at a time, so when Jo turned, Meg stayed on her side, watching the outline of her sister's face.

"Only I know what I'm like inside," Jo answered finally. "Finding all the right words in all the right order doesn't calm the storm. Memorizing them isn't enough anymore, and reciting them is a spell that never seems to last long enough these days."

"I think that means you're growing up, when what once satisfied doesn't."

"Maybe," she replied softly, but her eyes didn't stop searching the darkness.

"What about the building? You must enjoy that," Meg said. "It's the work you chose."

"More women will have to choose it if General Wild and Joseph Williams get the African brigade they're after. The freedpeople need proper homes, if we're to be permanently settled."

Meg didn't answer that, and her eyes fell away from the

shadow of her sister's face for a moment. She wanted to remember the young man's shoulders and his unblemished face. She wanted to think about his manners, and the feel of his soft hand when he took each of theirs to kiss goodnight and saved hers til last. She would always remember what he'd told Mammy at the table, while looking her in the eye—that he had never seen a place he liked better than here. Meg was sure he'd meant it had something to do with her, and she didn't think she was being proud.

His one blemish—the thing she wished to forget—was why he'd come at all.

"Perhaps my unrest *is* just growing up," Jo carried on, unaware of where her sister's mind had gone. "Then what do I do?"

Meg thought on that for a few minutes, welcoming the redirection. She could think of a way to help her sister, if she couldn't help herself. The answer that came to her might not have if she weren't a teacher, and the thought made her smile when she put her head on Joanna's shoulder.

"I think now you must try writing your words down."

"Will that make a difference?"

"Words committed to paper can be shared beyond the five of us. They can challenge the ideas of people you might never otherwise meet. Create tempests in their minds to match the one in yours." Meg poked Jo in the ribs, a broad smile on her lips. "I think it's a brilliant idea."

"Or would be," Jo said, helpless to escape her sister's

repeatedly poking finger in the small bed they shared. "If paper were in grand supply."

"The soldiers and the missionary teachers have a limitless store, and Mammy uses ledgers and notebooks every day. Just begin mentally composing your masterpiece; we'll keep you in parchment and ink."

"So begins the criminal second act of the March women."

"I thought Amy was the dramatic one."

"Please be considerate of others trying to sleep," croaked the just-mentioned younger sibling, in a voice still hoarse and thick with slumber that caused the older two to snicker amongst themselves.

"Speak of the dramatic devil," Joanna whispered, to Meg's delight, and then they calmed themselves enough to drift away into their respective dreams.

IV

MEG HAD ONLY ONE SLATE CHALKBOARD FOR USE IN HER teaching tent, and she stood looking down at it now because it was broken. She didn't rage or weep, because neither was her way. Instead she breathed evenly, blinking slowly, as someone accustomed to misfortune might. She would have this moment of calm lament and then adjust, as one accustomed also to making due, and she'd carry on with her lessons tomorrow without chalkboards despite that in an apparent show of camaraderie, a missionary teacher had gifted her two—both of which were gone now.

The gifts had been considerate, emblems of good faith meant to signify that the missionary teachers didn't wish to replace the "devoted negro teachers." When asked directly, they insisted that "negro" teachers had their place, though *they* were women—and occasionally men—who'd been specially trained for the work of instruction.

She'd been specially trained, as well, Meg thought but didn't say. By a wealthy Southern child's governess. She couldn't know for certain, of course, but she doubted any of the missionary teachers had an upbringing like the girl she'd been made to shadow all her life, and—by forced attendance—the education Meg herself had received.

They hadn't been friends, she and the wealthy Southern child. Yes, Meg had been treated like a plaything, but one could grow a devoted affection for a doll, so she did not doubt that the girl believed she loved Her Meg. When she threw tantrums that resulted in Meg being forced to stay overnight with her or when she insisted Meg be retrieved from the little shack where she would otherwise have slept happily amongst her family, the wealthy Southern child—who was permitted to act like one well into her debutante years—cooed to her that she loved Meg more than almost anyone.

Meg sometimes felt she'd had the strangest old life of everyone. Her education extended far beyond letters, and as much Latin as the wealthy girl could be forced to memorize. For one thing, she'd learned that things did not have to break in that house for them to be replaced. The wealthy girl would often insist that something was "worn clean out" and without investigation her parents would send for another.

In her teaching tent, Meg wrapped the shards of slate in a kerchief. She didn't feel right disposing of it, when it was such a valuable thing. Perhaps the missionary teachers weren't very unlike the wealthy girl after all, and they'd send it away to be replaced.

She sighed, untying her bonnet and closing her eyes in relief when she uncovered her hair and what little air didn't hang thick in her tent touched the dampness on her skin. She'd better not get her hopes up with these Northern white people, she decided. They might be like their southern neighbors in more ways than she'd care to witness again. Because among the things Meg had learned as the living doll of a wealthy girl was what many genteel Southern women tried to disguise. Like their ownership of people. Their inheritance and profit of them. There must be things that Northern white women hid, too.

Meg's hand held the slate pieces wrapped in a kerchief, and she was standing in her teaching tent in the sweltering heat of a summer day in 1863, but it might as well have been a summer day years before. The wealthy girl held Meg's naked hands in hers, the fingerless lace gloves she wore prickly and damp with sweat.

"He's going to marry me, Meg," she'd said, her whole face pink with excitement. "I knew he would, aren't you envious?"

"Yes, ma'am," Meg had answered, because by now she knew that the girl only understood congratulations that mingled with sadness. Good news was only good news if it didn't apply to everyone. "Will it be a long engagement? Will you live here?"

The wealthy girl was pleased with Meg's questions, but only because she didn't know her captive as well as she presumed. In the cabins near the fields, a girl Meg's age had gotten married already. The wealthy girl's father didn't know, of course, but that didn't make it any less true. Meg had been surprised at the news, but Jo had told her that of course she wouldn't have known. She spent all of her time in the house with the wealthy girl, while young folk near the fields were stealing moments to spend together. She'd be lucky if they weren't all paired off by the time her wealthy girl was finally married and sent away, Jo thought—and soon Meg thought the same. She'd begun to worry, and so her enthusiasm about the wealthy girl's engagement had been genuine. It was months before the war would destabilize the area and the March family would take an opportunity none knew to suspect yet, months before they would steal away to real freedom—but Meg felt certain that she was soon to be free of her most suffocating captor. The wealthy girl was going to be married, and Meg was finally going to be free to do the same.

"But don't you worry, Meg," the girl had told her then, binding Meg's hands one on top of the other and then nearly crushing them both in her own. "You're my dearest family, and I haven't forgotten you."

The girl bit her lip and took a deep breath as though she could not sense that Meg held hers.

"What've you done?" Meg asked quietly, when she could wait no longer to have her fate sealed.

"You spoilsport, you have to be surprised!" The girl slapped Meg's face playfully, the way she often did. The sting didn't make Meg jump anymore, because it was meant to be a loving gesture, or so the wealthy girl said through tears when Meg's pained reaction hurt her feelings.

"I will be," Meg said sweetly, "but I can hardly stand the wait."

"I knew you'd be excited, Meg—we mean so much more to each other than people rightly know! I *told* Father you'd prefer to come with me, because we're family, and . . ." The wealthy Southern child bounced the way young Amy did so often by then. "You're mine!"

Meg stood stunned now, as though the girl had struck her face again.

"You're properly mine, on paper, as you should've been all along, Meg, and you shall come with me when I marry!"

She couldn't bring herself to move, let alone smile, though she knew there was a danger in not doing so. But Meg could not perform, not just then. Not in the moment when she was being delivered the most terrible news as though it was a dream come true.

"And I've done something wonderful for you, Meg, even though Father doesn't think I should. And I won't tell you what until you ask."

When she tried to speak, Meg's voice croaked as though she'd been parched. She had to clear her throat before she could try again.

"Please tell me what you've done for me," and Meg said the girl's name then, though she had not done so since, and intended never to again.

"I know that you have sisters," she said, and Meg culled her own breath sharply. "And don't get your hopes up—I've no use for gossiping ninnies who'll mind each other better than my home. But I've asked Father to let us take the mute one. Aren't I generous, Meg? Aren't you pleased?"

"You are. Generous." Meg pulled the corners of her lips up, though it felt like her skin might tear. "I'm so grateful, and pleased."

The girl had thrown her arms around Meg's neck then, and it had taken a heroic measure of strength to hug the girl back.

In her teaching tent, Meg still held the broken chalkboard in her hands.

She hadn't thought of that day in quite some time, and she hadn't meant to just now, either. Sometimes the old life intruded into her new one in a way she was beginning to suspect it always might, while she had to be so close to white people. While she still had to ask them for things, or depend on what they considered their generosity.

"I suppose I shouldn't be surprised, to find a young teacher so deep in her thoughts." Joseph Williams's voice snatched Meg back into the present, and when she turned to see him standing just inside the tent flaps, her chest rose despite where she'd been. "You must know a great many things worth devoting a quiet moment to."

"It's lovely to see you again," Meg said, and she was almost pleased with the way her painful memory made her steady and calm. After all, this was perhaps the first time in the day since he'd joined the March women for supper that she hadn't been thinking of Joseph.

He took a step deeper into the tent, his chin dipping as though asking for permission.

"Please," she said, extending her hand momentarily. "Come inside. If you can stand to be inside in this offensive heat."

"It is taking some getting used to," he confessed, and took a handkerchief from his pocket to dab the back of his neck. "I can't say I wasn't warned, but I don't think one can fully prepare for North Carolina's summer."

"Is the weather in Pennsylvania very pleasant?" Meg asked, sitting on a crude bench where the most punctual of her students perched during lessons. Joseph joined her, though he minded a respectable distance.

"By comparison, I must say. Although I doubt very much that your winters are quite as bitter."

The two fell into silence after that. Meg hoped he'd tell her more—of Pennsylvania, and how else it differed from North Carolina, and of the people he'd left there. There must be people. He wasn't married, of course, but even Northern folk were said to love their families, and having been born free, she thought it mustn't be a blessed miracle for him to know both his mother and his father. Of course, she wouldn't ask. Her wealthy Southern girl had received all manner of instruction on courting language and how best a lady should inspire conversation, which often was simply with an inviting openness that did not demand divulging.

Perhaps it was not unlike her role as polite plaything, though not nearly as stifling, and certainly not painful. She had learned to be available, though not insistent, and perhaps that patience would serve her well in getting to know Joseph Williams.

"I've enjoyed meeting you, Miss Meg," he said, turning his chin to look at her. He turned at the waist as well, as though he were opening up to her.

"I'm so glad," she replied, turning at the waist as well. She wanted to say more. That she'd worried, even after stealing free, that courtship and marriage had already passed her by. That she'd worried the chance had been stolen from her, even though she never moved away with her wealthy girl and the fiancé. She didn't even know whether the two ever got married. Perhaps the fiancé took up the Confederate uniform and went to fight instead. Maybe he'd fallen in battle already, and married or not, the wealthy girl's beautiful, certain life was already done. She didn't dare hope those things, she only wondered. She needn't, though, she realized, now that Joseph Williams was sitting next to her, saying that he'd enjoyed meeting her. Nothing had been taken, she was finding, she'd only needed to wait.

"I've come to ask if I might write to you," Joseph said. "When I leave."

Meg was still smiling, because he'd spoken too quickly, and it took another moment before she realized what he'd said.

"When you leave?" she asked.

"I'll be continuing my recruitment with General Wild," he said, and clearly he was still pleased at the prospect.

"You've only just arrived," Meg said, trying to hide the extent of her bewilderment. "Would you move on so soon?"

"War waits for no man, I'm afraid." As though he'd intended the words to land more lightly against her than they did, Joseph carried on. "But I'll remember Roanoke so fondly, Miss Meg. And yaupon tea."

She was meant to smile then, so she did.

"And I'd like to write to you, if you'll allow it," he said.

I'm being impossible, Meg chided herself. He wanted to write to her while he was away; she could at least take heart in that. It wasn't as though she could honestly have expected him to ask anything else just yet. And he was recruiting men for battle—he wasn't yet fighting in one himself. She wouldn't be a war widow, if Joseph Williams was the man she was meant to marry. He would be away, like Papa was, she thought to comfort herself. Distant, but not in danger, no more than they'd all always been.

"I'd like that very much, Mr. Williams," she said, and this time, her smile was sincere.

"Please, Miss Meg," he said, one of his hands falling over hers. "You must call me Joseph."

V

August 1863

BETHLEHEM MARCH WAS GENEROUS, OR SO OTHERS SAID OF
her. It would have seemed to disprove the claim if she made it
about herself, she thought. If anything, generosity was simply
a by-product of being considerate—something Beth was much
more comfortable attributing to herself because, she thought,
that quality was a by-product of being part of a family. Most
had it, if they loved the people around them.

Yes, she was currently the only one who knew how to
operate the sewing machine that had been abandoned at the
big house, but that didn't mean she had to keep it so. When
several still living there asked why she didn't take the thing
to the colony where she could access it more readily, she said
she wouldn't dare. Instead, when she wasn't doing the paid
work of darning soldiers' uniforms, or doing the passionate
work of repurposing extravagant material or clothing from

the family who'd lived there before, she gave lessons to any-one who wanted to learn.

"How thick-headed. What if the Union hires *them* once you've taught them everything you know?" Amy asked while ripping seams at her sister's feet one day in the sewing room.

"Then my friends will be paid, and I will be pleased."

"Yes, but *you* wouldn't be. They would do all the work before you had the chance, since the machine is here, with them."

"What would you have me do instead? Take the machine where only I can reach it, or refuse a skill to someone who wants to learn?"

"You've made both options seem selfish."

"Well, say them back to me, then, in a way that doesn't."

Beth kept at her task but glanced at her younger sister occasionally enough to see the skin between her brows furrow and fold. While quick to criticize, it seemed many of Amy's opinions were cobbled together from the opinions of others—though she was either too young to realize it or else too young to at least express the adopted convictions mildly until fully considered. Anyone else might have told her so, but Bethlehem had faith that Amy would wisen with time. She was too smart not to.

"Do what you like then," the young girl said with a small huff and a sharp rip.

"Careful," Beth told her. "I'd like to salvage the thread, if I can."

"But it goes so much faster this way."

"That's enough for now anyway."

At that, Amy hopped to her feet, the pile of garments she'd been charged with disassembling allowed to carelessly tumble to the bedroom floor.

"I'm going to help with the new baby," she said, twirling a time or two in the middle of the spacious room. It required a different technique to spin properly against the friction of the ingrain carpet, and Amy had a mind to master it, if only because of how outlandish it seemed to dance—or do anything really—in the big house. But she pressed her toe down hard against the rose color that covered the floor of the sewing room. Elsewhere in the house, the carpet was an ostentatious red, and many of the wide, high walls wore velvet wallpaper with damask patterns of equally obnoxious coloring. Whoever had lived here—and anyone unlucky enough to work inside the house—might well have gone blind.

"What new baby?" Beth asked her. "Did someone give birth?"

"No one here," Amy answered, pointing her toes and prancing toward the hall. In the doorway, she wrapped her hand around the frame, the rest of her tiptoeing into the hall, waiting to be released. When she was at the big house with Bethlehem, she'd promised Mammy to mind her, and that meant she required Beth's permission to wander the grounds. "New freedpeople passed through on their way to the colony, and one of them had an orphan baby. No one knows where the mother and father went. I heard someone say that one died before they could be free, and the other died getting here."

"But why leave the baby here?" Beth asked, without bothering to inquire how Amy always knew the details of things before any of the others knew there was a thing at all. Her sister had a skill for eavesdropping and, besides that, a sweet face that made older folks think her innocent and aloof. They always spoke freely around the girl, and she never forgot a word.

"They're afraid our colony is like the contraband camps," Amy said. She gave a convincingly knowing roll of her eyes, but then she added, "whatever that means."

Beth couldn't decide what to say.

She knew what it meant, or much of it anyway. She knew what it meant to fold a baby or small child into one's family and heart, because that was precisely what the Marches had done with Amethyst. Separately, she knew what it meant that most places where formerly enslaved people traveled and then gathered were ramshackle. People unwilling to stay on or near the grounds where they'd been brutalized gravitated toward Union encampments, for good and obvious reason, but in most places, there was rarely if ever any attention or resources given to making their conditions livable. Some had wagons or tents, and perhaps an animal or two, but most had nothing.

Beth knew what it meant when in those camps that sprouted up around the Union posts anything at all was offered, that it was for the benefit of the soldiers, not the freedpeople. It was to keep the army from falling ill or being otherwise encumbered by the freedpeople's presence. If they were given shelter, it was so that their tents and makeshift dwellings didn't litter the ground around the barracks, creating obstacles that might impact the soldiers' readiness.

The word *contraband* meant that even the soldiers and officers whose recent victories had won their freedom did not view them as people. Black folk were spoils of war, if they were more than a nuisance, and their greatest value was in not being available to serve the Confederacy. Jo said they had been confiscated, not liberated, and in those camps it felt palpably true. Anyone could guess it, by the shabby treatment many endured, being so near the soldiers, and by the fact that those who could be were made to do labor on the Union's behalf almost immediately. It wasn't slavery, the Union must have reasoned, if the people were promised pay. But in most camps, the coin never came, once all the rations and clothing were deducted, as well as the keep for those who could not work at all.

Beth was two years older than Amy, and a young woman. Those years hadn't meant much in the old life, when much the same could be expected of both of them. In that life, Amethyst had to know and understand a great many things more awful than the reality of contraband camps and the complicated allegiance any freedperson must feel to the Union—but this was not the old life.

In this life, Beth carried a heavy bundle and kicked along a second rather than ask her baby sister to help. In this life, her eldest sister, Meg, treated both girls preciously, touching them often, because a gentle touch was like a salve that might erase all the harsh ones that came before it.

In this life, Amy was allowed the privilege of boredom, of wiling away at least a few hours a day, because she was the youngest, and at least one of them should experience having been a child.

If she hadn't eavesdropped on enough conversations to understand everything a contraband camp meant, Beth would cherish not telling her.

"Perhaps we should take the baby to the colony," Amy exclaimed, bringing her sister out of her thoughts.

"The baby?"

"The orphan baby! Does no one listen to me?"

"We hardly have a choice," Beth was saying when she stood from the sewing table and collapsed down beside it.

"Beth!" Amy was beside her sister before Bethlehem could open her eyes. "Beth, what's happened? Why have you fainted? Are you pregnant?"

Bethlehem could hear her sister's absurd question, and would have laughed, if she had the energy. As it was, it seemed to have drained out of her feet as soon as she'd stood, funneling in a rush from her head and clear through her body so that she couldn't help but fall. Now before her eyes, colorful dots swelled and shrank, making it difficult at first even to tell that her vision was blurry.

"Beth, please!" Amy was crying now, which was not absurd at all. Were their positions reversed, Beth would have done the same. When she had the strength, she put her hand on Amy's arm and, eyes closed, nodded her head.

It was enough to quiet her sister, and the two stayed that way on the floor beside the sewing machine until Beth had her strength back.

"What happened?" Amy asked, silent tears still dangling from her eyelashes.

"I don't know," she answered, and if it frightened Amy, it frightened Beth more. "It's gone now," she said, trying to enliven her voice despite feeling thoroughly exhausted. "And you haven't introduced me to the new baby."

"Next time," Amy told her, helping her sister to her feet, and watching her fearfully. "Now I just want to get you home."

It was unlike Meg to storm into the house, but there had been no door on her tent to slam, and so the one at home needed to be. Having walked away, she returned and reopened it, so that she could slam it once more. She unpinned her straw bonnet and yanked it from her head, lacing the pin through the straw again with practiced ease before tossing the thing onto the table, and paced the naked wood floor in a straight line that she retraced on her way back. She'd always appreciated that the room was sparsely furnished, and now it easily accommodated her frustration. When she realized that anyone walking down Lincoln Avenue could see her, Meg slammed the window shutters, too.

"I am permitted a moment out of character," she informed the nonexistent detractors with gusto, though they might've clucked their tongues at this outburst just as readily as at the first.

A moment later she had returned to her senses and dropped into a chair. By the time Joanna came home, Meg had been biting her lip for several moments, and as soon as her sister closed the door, Meg demanded, "Will they always assume they know better than we do, what we need?"

Jo stood just inside the front room and searched it with her eyes as though expecting to find the intended recipient of her sister's abrupt question, or, Meg worried, as though where she'd paced she might have left a tread that everyone could see.

"And am I a horrible teacher for thinking there's nothing I might learn?" she asked, to call her sister's attention back, and because she honestly wanted to know.

"I'm going to have to insist you start at the beginning," Jo said. Instead of proceeding to the backyard and the pump to freshen up, she dropped down in the seat next to her sister. "You'll pardon the odor, if I have one."

"Oh, Jo, if?" Meg asked in alarm. "You might have set yourself down more delicately at the very least."

"Is it that bad?" Jo sniffed at herself, as though genuinely surprised. "It's hardly my fault that it's only gotten hotter this summer. The air's so thick and muggy, I can sit on a pine log and still feel as though I'm swimming. But I'm surrounded by men all day, and they smell so much worse."

"There's only you and I now, and you smell positively awful."

"Fine." Jo slapped her hands onto her knees and stood.

"No, no," Meg whined, grabbing her sister by the arm with both hands. "Stay with me."

"Women are so fickle," she concluded with a sigh, and did not wince when Meg swatted her for the remark. "What is there you might learn, so that you don't think yourself a horrible teacher?"

"To take the missionary teacher's instruction with good humor, and without judging every white person's motives."

"Given everything we've experienced at their hand, why *wouldn't* you judge them? It's a matter of survival, if you ask me."

"Some would still say it isn't Christian. Especially when there are so many fighting to undo what we've suffered, and to ensure it won't happen to anyone else."

"Fine, if you think it's too much like judging their hearts. Don't judge their motives. Judge their actions at least, and those of their neighbors, and how long they appeased the latter before taking action against them. Though please don't be so foolish as to think it's all on our behalf." Jo glanced at her sister and nodded in apology. "Continue."

"I was speaking with Miss Constance Evergreen this morning, before the afternoon lessons—"

"Which of the missionary teachers is she? Does it matter?"

"Not especially. She's kind, I think, and genuine. She gets very excited seeing freedpeople take to their lessons, especially the older ones. She's one of the missionary teachers who lead lessons at night, as well, for the adults who couldn't otherwise come, so I can't question her passion or her delight in doing what she does."

"And yet?"

"And yet," Meg repeated, reclaiming her earlier frustration, her fingers splayed, hands raised as though she might conjure something between them. "For all her confessions of *honest* abolitionism, of believing that *negroes* must be given equal status once the stain of slavery is really and truly purged from the fabric of this country—"

"Did she say precisely that?" Jo interjected through a snort.

"Of course she did! To *me*, as though *I* might need informing! And it shouldn't annoy me, except that we are so often surrounded by white folks with wrongheaded beliefs that when one stumbles upon sense and an honest adherence to scripture, they pause to be congratulated!"

Jo tossed back her head to laugh. She loved to hear her sister talk this way. She didn't mind that Meg was so mild, that she was prone to follow the prescribed route in life from a deep want of its structure and rewards. Her older sister had been pretending to be Mammy—or someone's mammy, at least—since she was a little girl. It was clear she would live a simple and quiet life given the chance, and Jo would be happy for it. Still, praise God, her sister wasn't mindless. Meg wanted what she wanted, not for lack of thought, but because having considered it, she approved. Jo could be forgiven for taking immense pleasure in the fact that Meg considered a great many other things and rejected them.

"Go on, go on," Jo prodded.

"Yes, I don't mean to be so passionate," Meg said, and took a calming breath. "Despite all her fervency on the matter of equality, she very clearly does not think the freedpeople can equip themselves. They admire that our own Martha Culling began our schools before the Union permitted missionary teachers to come, and applaud our self-determination. Yet now they expect us to adopt their style of teaching. They want to remake the South in the image of the Yankee, so that we do not persist in the ways of the slovenly slave master, as we so unfortunately have done."

"Another Constance Evergreen quote, I presume?"

"Not only hers, I'm afraid. Apparently it's the talk of the *American Missionary*, which all of those stationed here read. Have I mentioned that, according to it, we have not attained the status of freedpeople?"

"Oh?"

"We are presently 'colored refugees.'"

"But they'll inform us when we ascend, I hope."

"How else would we know?" Meg settled into her seat with a huff and made a muted shriek by screaming without opening her mouth.

"I'm inclined to agree," Jo said in response to the sound.

"I'm so conflicted all the time," Meg continued, and the strain in her voice confirmed it. "Even though considering us refugees is meant to indict their countrymen and remind them there is work to do to ensure our freedom. So why does it enrage me?"

"Because," Jo told her. "They're only ever speaking for us, and about us. Rarely *with* us. Even when they have our best interest in mind, how could they know it without our input? The person who believes they know best, still, in some small way and in some interior place they've yet to interrogate, does not truly comprehend equality. Yet they mean to deliver us to it."

Now when Meg sighed, her shoulders relaxed in a way they hadn't despite her many attempts. "Yes," she said. "That's why."

She turned to look at her sister in the seat beside her, noticing for the first time that their hands were clasped together on the arm rest.

"You see? Your words are an immediate refuge. Joanna, tell me you've been writing them down."

"Oh," Jo groaned.

"Jo!"

"I know! I'm trying to get accustomed to it. It still seems like such a needlessly complicated step when I can offer them immediately to you this way."

"But there are people outside this house who would benefit, Joanna. I know it."

That stilled Jo, and a gleam lit the dew in her eyes.

"Thank you, Meg," she said, placing her free hand atop the ones joined. "It's always pleasant to be believed in."

When Mammy came through the front door, she was warmed by the sight before her.

"What lovely little women," she said, collecting their smiles and waving at them to keep their seats. "Stay. I never tire of seeing my daughters adore each other. Your whole life, it'll be its own reward—but today I've got something for each of you."

"A letter for me?" Meg's eyes were impossibly bright.

"A letter for Meg," Mammy confirmed, even more happily when she placed the envelope in her eldest daughter's hand. "From Joseph Williams, of course."

"He hasn't forgotten me."

"Of course he hasn't."

Meg couldn't help holding it to her chest for a moment.

"It's the third, and it must mean something that he continues to write," she said, almost whimsically. "I'll bet he'll tell me more about his family in Pennsylvania, now that we've corresponded so many times."

"I'll bet the letter would tell you sooner, were it opened," Jo replied, and with a smile and sigh, Meg carefully began unsealing it.

While Jo watched her sister's progress, Mammy furnished her with a Boston newspaper. The wide publication covered her lap, the thick, black scrolling typeface of the title and headlines looking back at her. It wouldn't have mattered what it said; it was a gorgeous sight, Jo had to admit. Even the smell was pleasant, but she'd always thought so of ink.

"What's this?" she asked.

"You might've heard a reporter came to Roanoke this past June. I thought you might like to read what he had to say about our colony," Mammy answered, with an almost intentional innocence in her voice that made Joanna raise her eyebrow.

"Just me?" she asked, taking the newspaper in hand. With the whirlwind that had accompanied Joseph Williams's visit to their home, and the way her daily work building houses often consumed any energy not reserved for her family, Jo had all but forgotten the summer's other visitor of note. She'd never met or seen the fellow, to be fair, but now her interest was piqued anew, especially because Mammy seemed to have a purpose in showing it to her in particular. Still, her mother didn't stay to observe her, instead moving toward the kitchen to open the back door.

"One of you open the front window so we can pray for a cross breeze."

Both the girls were poring over what they'd been given, but Jo stood, her eyes scanning line by line. Her lips occasionally moved as she made her way to the window and, with one hand, unlatched the shutters before absently leaning against the wooden opening while she continued reading. The further she progressed, the straighter she stood, slowly shaking her head.

Meg might have asked what had been reported, were she not enthralled in letters of her own. "He talks of Roanoke Island so fondly," she murmured. "Yet he almost never mentions me."

"Didn't you think that must be his way of complimenting you, Meg?" Mammy asked. She'd returned from the kitchen to rest against the back of her daughter's chair.

"I had," Meg answered, and then let the pages fall against her lap. "Only I'm tired of supposing. If he can speak poetically about the brigade and the hundred-and-fifteen able-bodied men he charmed away from our colony alone, and how they're now in Charleston—as though I should be pleased despite that most of Jo's builders went with him and construction has come almost to a halt . . . If he can think to say all that, I think he could at least spare a plain word for me."

It wasn't unreasonable, Meg decided, without her mother or sister having to tell her so. She'd thought Joseph modest when at first he spoke of the island to speak of her, but now he spoke so much of so much else, she found that it had lost its charm.

"Wouldn't he want his intentions to be clear, if he had any?"

"Perhaps." Mammy didn't want to seem discouraged, and quickly added, "But he's from the North, and perhaps they express things differently there. Or take longer to broach them."

"I don't know." Meg didn't want to be discouraged, either, but she couldn't help it. "I don't know how he'd expect me to know why he can do one and not the other. He's told me nothing about Northern life and customs. I don't know why he'd bother writing, just to tell me military things, or what he misses of this place."

"Letters from the battlefield are more for the soldier than the receiver," Mammy said, more assuredly, because this she did understand. "Your father writes to me to remind himself we're here, that he built a home someplace and we're still safe in it. It's a kind of therapy, I think."

"That's different, Mammy. You're man and wife, and I'm sure on top of all the business he recounts to you, he still speaks of *you*." Mammy always read his letters aloud to the girls after she'd had a chance to read them once by herself, so Meg already knew it to be true. "Joseph and I are still perfect strangers, and he tells me nothing that would change that. He asks nothing but to write to him, not to tell him anything about me, but how the colony fares and how many men arrive each week, as though General Wild couldn't learn that from his fellow officers. I could probably have you write him back with the news, and it might suit him just the same."

She refolded the letter and placed it back inside its envelope. Many letters from the field hosted drawings of landscapes or flowers, the men dedicating time and attention to every inch of paper. Joseph's envelope was unembellished except to identify it as a soldier's letter, but she'd already given so many examples of her disappointment that she kept that one to herself. Recalling the lofty hopes she'd harbored the day Joseph Williams came to her teaching tent to ask if he might write to her, she only permitted herself one final thing in conclusion, and it was honest. "I enjoy his correspondence less and less."

"I'm sorry, darling," her mother said. Mammy had no

sons, and no way of knowing how she would comfort one whose heart was so visibly sore, but with daughters, there was always their hair. She'd begun gently detangling a quarter of Meg's hair with her fingers, and having worked through it with a mindful amount of tension and release, she began the same ritual on the next. "Will you still write to him? Perhaps if you do, he'll come back to the colony and something will have changed."

"I don't know what I'll do," Meg told her, looking out the open shutters at the still-bright sky of early evening while Mammy lulled her with hair-tending. "My heart leapt at the sight of his letter, so I suppose I haven't stopped hoping. I'm worried I don't know how."

"Running out of hope isn't a lesson I'd ever wish my children to learn," Mammy said softly as she began to braid. She wove her fingers slowly through her daughter's softened hair, knowing that the rhythm was a comfort that might not reach Meg's heart. "But I pray I haven't inspired you to link your hope to him. I spoke too highly of him too soon—I take the blame for that, but not because Joseph Williams is the prize. I'd never forgive myself if I didn't say plainly that the prize, Meg, is you."

She didn't reply, but let her mother's words fall over her. Eyes still on the powder-blue sky, only Meg's hand moved to wipe away a tear.

"Whatever you choose to do about Joseph . . . someday soon you'll be rich in the possession of a good man's heart. That I know for certain."

63

Mammy kissed her head, close to tears herself at the ache she could sense in her child. Meg was the oldest, and the hurt she felt now that she was a young woman, a mother could not always heal. Papa couldn't, either, but it was still made more difficult by his absence, if only because he could've held his wife.

"It is no simple thing," Mammy said as quietly as if aware now that perhaps the conversation should have been a private one. Joanna was nearby but absorbed in her own reading, but Mammy took measures in case Meg wished it to stay between the two of them, which—even in a lovely family—was allowed. "It's no simple thing, I mean, to parent a child old enough to want her own."

"I'm sorry, Mammy."

"No! No, no." She held her daughter's hair in her hands so that nothing would distract Meg from her reassurance. "That wasn't a chiding, dear one. I meant to acknowledge that you have a desire on your heart, and I'm not as useful as I once was. You're right to want what you want, Meg, and to want it purely, without blemish or need of settling. It's only difficult because now you have a desire I want for you, too, and when and how you get it isn't up to me."

Meg let her head tilt to one side so that Mammy opened her hand to cradle her eldest daughter's face, and while she did, Mammy said a quick prayer to all of their Heavenly Father before she carried on braiding.

As though the front room had somehow been divided into two stages on which very different productions were playing out, before the window, Jo whirled around to face her kin.

"The audacity!" Her hand closed, cinching the newspaper, which became a wide fan on either side of Jo's fist. "It's just as you said, Meg. They ceaselessly exchange glowing reports about the welfare and the progress of the Roanoke Island Freedpeople Colony without ever interviewing a freedperson!"

Meg was quite sure she'd said no such thing, but she simply nodded, wide-eyed, when her sister unclenched the paper and held it up, leaning toward her mother and sister so that they knew she was going to read aloud from it.

"The Roanoke Colony is one of the most important and one of the best managed experiments undertaken in behalf of the negroes."

Jo snatched the paper shut, crushing it in her hand again, her mouth and eyes wide with incredulity as though awaiting her family's reply, despite that they awaited hers.

"Experiment!" she finally exclaimed, and Mammy and Meg nodded vigorously. "Undertaken on our behalf! What's worse, I never once saw this so-called reporter speak to one of us, and he only calls by name members of the Union or the missionary teachers! As though mere observation is consideration enough of our opinions—as though the overseer never witnessed something he did not fully understand! They speak for us, and it never occurs to them that *we* might have something to say!"

When she'd reached the end of her outburst, Jo stood

65

wide-legged in front of the open shutters, the day bright behind her, a Northern newspaper with a national readership crumpled in her grasp, and her chest heaving.

"Well," Meg said.

"Well what?" Jo asked, breathing heavily.

"Write it down!"

Jo looked from Meg to Mammy, who tipped her head as though there was nothing more to say.

"Right."

"Right!" Meg insisted, adopting a contagiously wild expression despite her own woes.

"Right!" Jo echoed once more before the three fell into laughter.

There had been another letter in Mammy's possession, but that one she needed time alone with. When three of her daughters were cobbling together a satisfying supper that did not require a fire and Beth was napping in their bedroom, Mammy had slipped into her own. She hadn't closed the door, lest Amethyst immediately grow curious. Closed doors inspired that in the child. Instead, Mammy took to her rocking chair in one corner of the room, so that if anyone interrupted, she would have a moment to collect herself before their eyes found her.

The envelope she'd handed her eldest daughter had been almost bare, she'd noticed, though of course she hadn't drawn

Meg's attention to it. Perhaps the girl had thought her suitor lacked the time to embroider the white space with drawings, but Mammy knew that men in the field or on the road had precious little but time. Except for the brief and ugly inter-ludes that were their enlisted purpose, she heard they craved the escape, and the beauty—many discovering artistic abilities they might otherwise have never displayed. Thankfully, her dear husband was not away in battle, but still he devoted himself to sending her thoroughly embellished envelopes.

On this one, he'd left a white trim around the address, but everywhere else, he'd painstakingly drawn sassafras. Three-lobed leaves were arranged all over the paper, shaded beautifully so that despite the lack of color, she could almost smell the plant's lemony aroma. He'd even drawn the berries, perfect little orbs that outside of pictures were an alluring dark blue. He'd drawn five of the berries, of course, and nes-tled them on a bed of leaves in the right corner of the enve-lope, on the front, where his wife was sure to see them. She smiled when she did, hearing his voice, and the adoring way he might describe them.

Five sassafras berries, for my five girls.

Five wildflowers . . .

Five kisses . . .

Five huckleberries, he'd said once, *for my five sweet girls.* He'd presented a rather unamused wife with less than a handful of them, enlisting their youngest to keep the full tin hidden behind her back. Amy had waited until her mother was just about to ask if the two would like an imaginary pie, because there was nothing she could do with only five huckle-berries, and then bouncing, the girl had produced their harvest, some of which were jostled onto the kitchen floor. Mammy hadn't minded. Fallen fruit could be gathered and cleaned. Her husband and her child were pleased with their deception, and she was pleased he loved them so.

Now she looked back at the envelope in her hand and wondered why sassafras, when its berries weren't fit to eat. The thought stung, just a bit, like a pinprick in the tip of a finger, and she knew before she opened the letter that something sour weighed on her husband's mind.

After she'd read the letter, Mammy put it away. They would have dinner first, she decided, on the back porch, the way they did when they'd waited til sundown and the heat still hadn't abated. The girls would take turns rewetting their rags at the pump before replacing them on the backs of their necks, and Amy might eventually stick her whole head under the stream. She couldn't decide whether it was best to let them laugh together before she read their father's letter, or whether it was cruel to tell them so near to when they'd all retire to their room and be left with their thoughts as they tried to sleep. They wouldn't be alone, at least, two of them to a bed.

"Thank you, Lord, for four daughters," Mammy whispered her commonly expressed and genuinely felt gratitude. Tonight she meant it even more.

"Papa's sent a letter," she told her children when they were together on the back porch, and water was beading off of Amy's hair.

Four breaths caught, followed by excited chatter, as they gathered closer to their mother's skirt and sat down to hear.

"Dear wife, my darling Margaret, beloved Mammy," she read, amid happy sighs. They were each hearing it in their father's voice, she could tell, the way she always did when she read his letters.

"I will not bore you with missives detailing your beauty, as familiar with your own face, and the mahogany of your eyes, and the curve of your delicate chin as you are." The girls smiled and exchanged approving glances. Even Meg, who could not be blamed for being less enthusiastic about a letter that immediately extolled its author's adoration, having received such a different one in the same day. *"I will not tell you how often I say your name aloud, as though it might cause you to appear before me, or how frequently I am the subject of gentle ribbing for asking you a question you couldn't possibly hear."*

Mammy made a fragile laugh, but in the company of her daughters, no one could tell the way it tapered. Her eyes were wet now, but they must have thought her moved by their father's precious words.

"I will not ask if Meg is still a skilled and remarkable teacher, and whether the Union and the colony are lucky to have her. Nor whether Joanna builds houses as well as I—or as well as she builds pictures in our minds with the elegance of her words."

"No one will have a home as lovely as the one you built,

Papa," Jo said, as though the letter might capture her voice and transport it back to her father. She didn't say how few builders there were, or how few tools, and how even the Union officers were constantly pleading for supplies on their behalf, not to mention pay. There were probably worries enough in Corinth, or else Papa would have come home.

"*I will not ask after Bethlehem's latest masterpiece,*" Mammy continued reading, "*or whether she has recently spun gold from straw, as she is known to do. Nor whether Amethyst has been keeping the dust away by dancing on the wood floors I laid.*

"*I will not ask if you are keeping each other well, and whole, and happy, because I know you always do. No man has ever been luckier than I, and none has greater cause to take up the Union's banner, when it is finally offered.*"

Mammy's voice broke then. All four of her daughters noticed, and one by one, their faces slackened or stilled, and Meg's eyes fell. Mammy didn't return the three gazes that still held her. She was afraid they might be quivering as terribly as hers. She held the letter as though she were still reading, though now that paper trembled.

Jo had to take her father's letter, gingerly, and then one of her mother's hands while the woman cried quietly, and Jo read in her place.

"*I will only ask your forgiveness, Margaret, for thinking you would agree to this. That you would know I'd choose to fight, when I have so very much to fight for. I'll ask you to forgive me for leaving from Corinth without coming home first, because I couldn't. The officers in command would not allow it, and I would not have come, lest I lose my nerve at the sight of my five angels and decide to stay.*

"Know that it's not the Union's side I'm on, Margaret," Jo read through her own tears, "but yours. Always. My love to you, and then to our children. May God bless and keep us, Alcott Josiah March."

Joanna looked down at her mother, around whom all her sisters huddled, Amy almost entirely in her lap. She sank down to the porch to join them and wrapped her arms around Mammy's shoulders.

The sky had finally fallen dark, piercing bright stars gleaming throughout it. The humidity had broken, or else grief masked it. The March women could hardly feel the weather when they were occupied with the breaking of their hearts.

They should feel proud, someone like Joseph Williams might have told them. In their heartache, they should be buoyed by the courage their husband and father displayed, and know that whatever happened, he would be a hero. It didn't matter that to these five women, he was already so much more.

Mammy held her fourteen-year-old daughter curled in her lap, and thought of all she was privileged to know because of her work with the officers. There were dangers only a Black soldier faced, in addition to the terror of battle. In the short time since President Lincoln had begun allowing them to enlist, she'd heard more than one report about what befell their men who were captured by Confederates.

The Confederates' illegitimate President Davis ordered them delivered to the law officers in whichever state they were captured—only it rarely ever got that far. There would be few Black prisoners of war, even for the purpose of reenslavement. For daring to resist their oppressors, for having the audacity to fight as white men did, Black soldiers captured by the Confederacy were executed.

If Alcott March survived the battle, he might still not come home.

Mammy would not dare tell that to her children. She would keep it to herself, lodged in her throat like a hot stone rather than let it scald even the eldest two.

"Come on," she said, leaning down to kiss a still-crying Amy's cheek. "We might as well cry in bed."

Jo unwrapped herself, and then Meg, who had to help Beth to her feet. It was despair that weakened her just now, but Mammy saw the way Bethlehem winced. She'd done the same during supper, twisting away then so that her family might not see her face.

"I'll put Amy in bed with me, and then I'll be in to kiss you all goodnight."

Somehow they dispersed, shutting the kitchen door behind them and closing out the starlight.

As she promised, Mammy tucked Amethyst into her bed, and then came to sit first beside Bethlehem.

"How have you been feeling?" she asked quietly. Meg was sitting in her bloomers, her back against the wall, with Jo's head in her lap. Both girls were still, but Mammy could see from the look in their eyes that their thoughts and attention were miles and miles away.

"I'm all right, Mammy," Beth answered. "Only tired."

"You have been for days."

"I didn't want to worry you. It must be the summer's heat dealing harshly with me, and missing Papa all the time."

"No child who has ever tried has managed to spare their mother worry by hiding things from her," she said, stroking the hair Beth hadn't captured beneath her sleeping cap, before tucking it inside. "Tell me what's going on."

"I don't understand it," Beth said, barely above a whisper. "Pain, sometimes, in my chest. Aching behind my knees, and sometimes pain there, too. And dizziness, for no reason. As though I've been twirling with Amy, even when I haven't."

"And fatigue," Mammy added.

"Always. Sometimes I can't keep myself awake. I'll go to the big house expecting to work, and before I know it, I'll lie down on the carpet and hours will pass."

Mammy's brow creased, and she took her daughter's hand.

"What's happening?" Beth asked. "Am I ill?"

"I don't know." A fresh tear slipped down Mammy's face. She had questions of her own. Was the whole world coming undone? Was freedom to be just as fraught as the old life? It'd been miraculous to keep a family together back then, not to mention taking in a child whose mother had not been so blessed, but they'd done it. Now her husband—who was only meant to be gone another week or two, or until a migration of

Union soldiers made it safe to travel from Mississippi back to North Carolina—was going toward danger, rather than away from it. Now one of her children was unwell, and she didn't know with what.

Mammy stopped herself.

Beth was asleep already, praise God.

Praise God, that was what she would do. He'd brought them out of Egypt, and not into a desert but a paradise they would have a hand in cultivating. Roanoke Island was Canaan, and every time a little rain fell, she would not worry it might flood.

"Some of the missionary teachers have trained as nurses, haven't they?" she asked aloud.

When she turned, Meg and Jo were exactly as they'd been when she looked last. Her heart threatened to sink, but she straightened her shoulders and went to their bed.

"Meg," she said gently, sitting in the sliver of space that remained. She took her eldest daughter's face in her hand and waited while the girl's eyes slowly drifted to hers. She felt as if she could take no more of seeing her family hurt, but she'd lived a very different way not so long ago, and so had they; she knew all of them could manage much more than any one should be required. "I need to know which of the missionary teachers have nurse training. Beth isn't well."

Meg's eyes focused at that, and she turned toward her younger sisters' bed.

"She's sleeping now, but I'd like someone to come and see to her."

"Constance." Her voice rattled a bit, as though it'd sat on

a shelf for some time without use, instead of a matter of minutes. "Constance Evergreen was training to be a nursing missionary before they began recruiting teachers. I'll ask her to come between lessons tomorrow, if you don't mind her coming inside the house."

"We never had a say before," Mammy said when her daughter reminded her that now they did. "Everything was theirs, even the dirty mat and the floor where we laid our heads."

She looked around the room her daughters shared and tried to recall what she'd hoped for in the old life. Her imagination had been big enough to know that one day they'd be free. She'd known there'd be a house, but it had only been a word. The feeling of having her husband and her daughters near, with no threat of sale, had seemed more than enough. Even if she'd pictured a real homestead, she'd had no way of knowing there'd be any rooms but one. One would have seemed enough back then, with hanging sheets for privacy. Now here they were in a room just for her children. They slept in beds raised off the floor, built by their father, on a small plot of land that belonged to them, and it was up to her who came inside.

Praise God.

"Give Constance Evergreen my permission, and my thanks, if she'll come and see to Bethlehem."

VI

"Good day," Constance said when the door was opened a modest sliver. Amy's face was only visible in part, and the young woman tilted her head as though that would reveal the rest of the girl. "My name is Miss Constance Evergreen, and I've come to see about your sister."

"I know," Amy informed her, and then widened the opening without stepping back to let the woman in. "Mammy told me to expect you."

A quiet fell over the two of them, during which Constance was not sure what to say. Clearly she didn't know why she hadn't been invited into the home, as she'd already removed her hat. Amy gave her no assistance, standing uncharacteristically flat on her feet in her lovely brown boots and watching the young white woman flush in the hot day.

"May I come inside?" Constance asked at last, and Amy broke into a charming smile.

"Why, of course you may," she said cheerfully, and stepped back to let the woman in before twirling on her tiptoes farther into the room and extending one arm toward the hall. "Beth is resting in the room with the open door."

"Thank you," the missionary teacher told her, and went where she'd been directed. Amy carried on, performing a solo waltz before the open shutters.

A short time later, Constance reemerged from the bedroom, but went farther into the house, taking the jug from just inside the kitchen door. Amy heard the pump not long after, and then the woman reentered the house and made her way back to the bedroom.

Peeking around the doorframe, Amy watched Constance help her sister sit up with her to drink the water, and some of the lightness left her. One of her shoulders sank, and she nibbled the inside of her lip.

"Forgive me, Bethlehem," Constance said, "I don't mean to be indelicate, but have you been using the rag recently? You do bleed each month by now?"

Beth nodded her head as though if left to herself for a moment or two, she might fall immediately back to sleep.

"And has it come recently?"

Beth shook her head, and reached for the water jug again.

"And you haven't partaken in activities that might have interrupted it?"

"Do you mean with a man?"

"Oh!" Constance's cheeks blushed, but it looked to Amy like all her visible skin did. Her hair was brushed flat and pulled into a harsh bun, low against her neck. It wasn't very becoming on a woman only a few years older than Meg, though Amy thought it very much matched the teacher's name. It seemed a hairstyle that someone named Constance, or perhaps Prudence, would wear. Worse, around her hairline, Constance had very short and therefore unruly hairs that disrupted the desired sleekness. It seemed clear that they were the result of pulling her hair back too tightly, and they stood straight up despite that when the young woman was very concerned or in thought, she laid her hand against the sides or top of her hair as though to smooth it down. It looked dreadfully painful, and not only because Amy despised having her hair tied down at all, but because when Constance's pale skin brightened and rouged, it made it look like the tight hairstyle was to blame.

"No, no. I'm sorry, Bethlehem, I meant have your chores been too strenuous? When a woman is on the rag, doctors prescribe a bit more rest, and a lessening of work, so as not to interrupt it, which can make one ill."

"We were never given that option," Beth answered before adding, "but it isn't time this month."

"I see." The woman applied the back of her hand to Beth's forehead and then to her chest. "You are warm, but then it's August. You don't feel feverish. And you share this bed with your younger sister?"

Beth nodded, eyes closing.

"And she seems in good health."

Amy presented herself, fully, in the doorway, in case

Constance wanted to analyze her, but the woman only felt Beth's forehead again and sucked her teeth. She seemed genuinely concerned, at least.

"I'm sorry," Beth said, and scooted down to lie flat. "I'd like to go back to sleep, if that's all right."

"Of course."

Constance stood and leaned down as though she might help Beth, but there was no need, and she withdrew her hand without turning away. Instead, she lowered her head, closing her eyes. Her brow was heavy, and she must've said a series of fervent phrases to herself, because Amy heard none of the young woman's prayer.

When she was finished, Constance moved the jug of water closer to the bedside and then met Amy at the door. "I'd like to come again, with your family's permission. I'd like to ask Bethlehem more questions when she's awake enough to answer. In the meantime, I'm going to write to the Association, and to my former nursing instructor in Gloucester."

"Of course," Amy answered, nodding along.

"If there are illnesses I'm unaware of causing issue in other camps or colonies, they'll almost certainly make their way here. We're receiving hundreds by the day, and homes are built so slowly that the barracks overflow while they wait."

"My," Amy said quietly.

"Some have gone to stay with family on local plantations," Constance continued, as though she were a pump or faucet herself, that with the slightest bit of coaxing could not help but flow. "Or they try to make their way to colonies like

Corinth, I hear, which is said to be a bit further along, and profitable. But the deluge won't end, and we must be prepared to make *this* colony a safe enough stead."

"We must."

Now the young woman seemed to notice that it was a girl before her, and not another young woman, but instead of chastising her for eavesdropping or something else meant to draw attention away from the way adults forgot themselves, Constance smiled.

"I've got to get back to the school, I'm afraid," she said, and then she paused. "Do you attend?"

"Sadly, no. I would like to," Amy answered, seizing on the change of topic. "I've had lessons since long before the colony, but Meg teaches me at home, though I rarely have the benefit of her instruction."

"That's unfortunate."

"Her tent can only hold so many students, and perhaps she thinks a little sister a personal distraction," Amy said with a heavy sigh. She toed the floor and let her eyes fall to it.

"Crowding is an issue, but teaching is our ministry, and we'll find solutions for as many as we possibly can. Perhaps you could come to my class instead. There's such a benefit to learning among other pupils, and I'd hate for your curiosity to be extinguished because it languished too long alone."

"It does sound like an awful fate."

"Perhaps if I spoke to her," Constance said after a moment. "Today, after this afternoon's lessons. We could have you with us by tomorrow, and it wouldn't hurt to have you out of this house, being minded."

Amy kept her smile, though it snagged a bit. She hoped the young woman wasn't planning to say that last bit to her sister. Amethyst liked Constance Evergreen, and it would be a shame for the missionary teacher to find that, however things went in Massachusetts, in North Carolina, even a young woman as polite as Meg March might tan someone's hide without a switch. Every Northerner she'd ever met—however few—seemed to think they had manners and decorum, but then they easily tromped into impolite territory, such as instructing strangers how best to raise their kin.

She *did* want to attend the schoolhouse, though, so Amy nodded and clasped her hands in front of her chest.

"I would be in your debt, Miss Constance," she said, at which the missionary teacher looked full to overflowing.

"Bless your gentle heart, child." At the door, she turned while fastening her hat into place. "Would you keep the water jug full for Bethlehem?"

"I will."

"Good day, child."

There was nothing for Jo to do at the site but wait. A boy called Yannick waited with her, rather than wandering off toward the fishery or the shore to find other work. He wore a straw hat with a brim so wide it cast a shadow over his shoulders and chest, which were barely clothed otherwise, his shirt was so threadbare.

"That hat would never have fit yesterday," Jo remarked, swatting at a pest. It had been too quick for her previous attempts to clap it between her hands. "You had hair as thick as midnight last time I saw you. Where's it gone?"

"Sold," Yannick said, swatting at something himself without looking away from his whittling work.

"For what? For netting? It'd make a fine brand of tulle, I imagine." She barely gave attention to her own jest, glancing around to see that there were no missionaries or white men milling around the village before hiking her skirt to rest above her bent knees so that her legs could breathe.

White folks had little need to be in view, since there were so few homes built yet in the village, and no buildings for their purposes. It separated the colony in Jo's mind. There was the town, which included the barracks and the buildings confiscated from the Confederates or from white islanders who'd lived near enough for their property to be useful, and in town there were always white and Black people around. Too many, in fact, and people seemed to be stacking one on top of the other. Then there was the village, where the tall trees and shrubs and overgrowth had been before the Union got permission to level them. Even those without a plot assigned to them walked the grid of streets and avenues, and where there was grass, small children played before or after their lessons, and usually en route to their next task.

Here in the village, there was usually only brown skin and uncovered, coily hair.

"If they had to see us during the day, or if they made us come into the house, we had to cover our hair," Jo said. "Did you know that?"

"I did. Back home, too." He let Jo take the hat off his head when she stood, and run her hand over his shorn scalp, glancing up at her with one eye, the other squinted shut to keep the sun from blinding him.

"Back home where?"

"Louisiane," he answered, sweat pearling above his lip.

Jo didn't mean for her hand to stay so long, but Yannick's scalp almost looked discolored, pale when the rest of his skin was a plum brown.

"Louisiana?"

"Louisiana," he repeated with a nod, his attention back on the small square of wood in one hand, and the whittling knife in the other. "It was law there. I thought here, too."

"It may as well have been," Jo said, sitting back down on the stack of wood intended for the home they were supposed to be building. She scratched absently at her scalp, as though the subject required it, and to reach it, she had to dig through the kerchief holding her hair off her neck like a cloth snood. "They were always either tugging at it, as though they'd never seen anything like it—despite the many of us constantly around—or they were feigning disgust, and declaring it unkempt."

"Feigning," Yannick repeated, as he did when he wanted a word defined.

"Pretending."

"What makes you think they pretend?"

"Their insistence on having an opinion at all, I suppose. White people ponder us constantly, with a fixed attention I can hardly muster for anything that doesn't bring me delight. I certainly wouldn't have reason to give their hair such consideration when it has nothing to do with the quality of my life."

"Yes, I see. Well," Yannick said with a shrug. "Perhaps they feign, but now they pay for it."

"*They* paid for your hair? Whatever for?"

"Wigs, for their actors."

Jo opened her mouth to scoff, or to screed, she hadn't decided which, but in the end she made a considering sound. "They'll pay us for it now. What did I tell you? Feigned disgust. Well. If the heat won't relent, I might just sell them mine. They'll have enough for beards, and tufts, and anything else they can think to fashion."

Yannick gave an amused snort and bobbed his head a few times to signal he'd like his straw hat put back, which Joanna did.

"Are the Carter brothers planning to bring back the nails today?" she said in exasperation after she and her friend had waited another half hour at least.

"They're not coming," Yannick answered matter-of-factly, as though he'd always known.

"What do you mean? That's what we're waiting for, isn't it?"

"We're waiting in case Madame Armentrout or one of her

six comes to see about our progress. So they'll know we are at our post, only the soldiers don't give us what we need."

Jo slumped, letting her back curve unbecomingly because neither Meg nor Mammy would bemoan what they did not see.

"I could be writing, if there are no more nails to be delivered and everyone else has gone to some other task."

Yannick blew the dust and bits from his wood, and then took one of Jo's hands and held it so he could see her discolored fingertips.

"It's ink," he said, as though she were unaware.

"Of course it's ink," she answered, yanking out of his grasp while he grinned.

"Wisdom and Honor thought you'd taken up berry picking. I told them no."

"The Carters' names proved too high a calling, and they've settled for making them satire instead."

"I'll tell them you think so."

"No, you won't."

"No. Your English is too elegant to remember."

"You can tell them in French, if you like."

"They make fun."

"Dullards," Jo said, and Yannick grunted in agreement. After that the two sat in silence for a moment, too beset by the sun to speak too elegantly too often, in either language. "I fear I'll die of heatstroke."

"Let's swim."

"What about Madame Armentrout and her six children?"

"They have no house today. We'll wait some more tomorrow, if it pleases them. We'll curse the Union together tonight."

"What's tonight?"

"The reception, at your big house."

"It isn't—" Jo gave up explaining to Yannick that the big house had been a stop on their way to the Roanoke Colony, and not the site on which she and her family had lived their old life. Like the Carter boys, she only spoke one language, and not always well enough to clarify things to someone who spoke two. "What kind of reception?"

"A wedding. A man and woman arrived and they had only been married on a plantation, until they became free and met a vicar."

"That's lovely," Jo said.

"You don't care for marriage," Yannick said, wiping the gleam from his broad nose.

"Perhaps not for myself," she conceded, "but I care very much for those who cherish it. I'm glad they've been properly married, if they wanted to be."

"Come," he said, nudging her with his elbow.

"I don't know them."

"You know the big house. Anyway, they have no family, and they want many guests. Bring your sisters who *do* want to marry," he said, and then laughed good-naturedly. "There are many new arrivals to the mainland on their way to this island, or as far as Ocracoke."

Meg would like a party, Jo thought. If nothing else, it might distract her while she decided how to proceed with Joseph

Williams. There was no question that Amy would love to dance, and it might lift Beth's spirits, too.

"They've been cooking for at least a day," Yannick remarked. "So come at least to eat. Food tastes better when it's shared."

"That sounds like something a brilliant mother makes small children believe when there's not enough to go around."

"My mother was brilliant, this is true."

"It's true what she taught you about food, too," Jo said, and the two laughed. When they set out for the shore to swim, they ran to spite the sun.

"We shouldn't attend parties when our father is at war," Meg said firmly enough that it sounded like truth even to her excited sisters. They settled, and the sound of their giggling quickly turning to silence stung her. She had no desire to be the thing that stifled her sisters' happiness, but she could not help the way she felt. "How can we celebrate when he is putting himself in harm's way for our freedom?"

She'd voiced some opposition when Jo first told the family of the wedding reception, and had only grown more certain while putting on one of the petticoats Beth had discovered and repaired at the big house.

"Meg, it's not as dire as all that. Try not to work yourself up."

"This feels positively decadent, Mammy," she replied, thrusting her arms out as though to showcase the puffed sleeves. "It doesn't remind you of the elegant trappings the wealthy girl used to dress me up in? It's worse, in fact. Wearing the clothes a woman probably lorded over her slaves in, as beautifully restored and creatively improved as Bethlehem's work always is." There were tears welling in her eyes, and they made the other March women heartsore and attentive.

"Whatever that girl dressed you in, you were always you, Meg. They took so much from us, why should wearing their clothes *now* bother you?" Jo asked, taking her sister's elbow in hand.

"All of it does. Papa fighting on the side of men who only want to free us to cripple their southern neighbors, and who still abuse us in their own ways. All the Black men who come and then follow him and Joseph and General Wild to the front before they've had a chance to think what they might want from their newfound freedom. Everyone behaving as though it's a privilege, when none of it seems fair! And us! Living in a house of our own when so few are being built, and so slowly, and my students huddle in barracks and tents, and if anyone is ill, it spreads like fire. Wearing beautiful clothes when there are fewer and fewer decent coverings for the Union to issue because of how many freedpeople there are, and so few proper colonies to host them."

She would have gone on that way, perhaps all night, if Mammy hadn't taken Meg's face in her hands. They weren't soft. Margaret March had known the field before her daughter taught her how to write years ago. She'd worked land before she kept records and wrote correspondences, as she was now paid to do. But had her hands been soft, her daughter might not have recognized their touch.

"You're hurting because you're a good woman, Meg," Mammy said, looking her eldest in the eye and not leaving space enough for her to unravel any further. "That's why you feel this way, so I won't try and change your mind about some of it."

Jo, Amy, and Beth looked on, having given their mother space to intervene, but curious what answer she could give.

"There's space enough in this house for more people, to start with. We've enjoyed it on our own for a time, and your father would be pleased, but you're right. There are so few homes, and too few tools to build them quickly. We can't take them all in, but if I come into your room, there's room for another family, at least." Mammy lowered her chin, as though asking Meg what she thought of the suggestion.

"At least," Meg answered between breaths still quicker than normal but that began to even.

"How exciting!" Amy exclaimed when she couldn't wait any longer, and Meg's lips caught her smile briefly.

"But Papa," Meg began again.

"Papa has chosen to fight," Mammy said, touching her face again. "And we must honor his decision, the way he honors ours. And we must go on enjoying the freedom that made him choose it. We mustn't feel guilty when we feel beautiful, though I know that is a struggle you uniquely know. We mustn't feel guilty, either, when we find ourselves laughing. Even in the old life, we confounded our captors with our spirit, with the joy we made together. Not because we approved of our enslavement, but because we are resilient people. We hide light in the darkest place, and when others think embers extinguished, we know how to breathe them back to life. And now we're free." Mammy's chest expanded, and all her daughters found theirs doing the same. "Should we despair? Should Amy never dance?"

At the question, Amethyst bounced onto her toes and gave a twirl.

"Of course she should," Meg said with a smile that lingered now.

"Should Beth not sew, and should you not teach? Should you both let talents that others profited by wither in disuse to prove you love your people? Should Jo not write her words down now that it is safe to, and now that you are teaching so many how to read them?"

"You said I must," Jo said. "And you were right. And I've made a decision. If a reporter can solicit donations from the North with his writing, then I can do the same. Instead of waiting for the Union to provide us tools—and those often only being the ones they are willing to spare—I can start a newsletter of my own. *I* can write of life on Roanoke, in the Freedpeople Colony, and I can ask those true abolitionists to donate directly to the freedpeople, for the building of our homes."

"Jo, that's a wonderful idea!" Meg exclaimed.

"Then be excited," she pleaded. "Let's all of us be, at the

ways we can help, and the life we're living. It doesn't mean we've forgotten Papa. We couldn't. But we must be allowed to be excited, if we're to make this country what it's meant to be."

"I'm excited," Beth said. It was her first interjection, and it gathered her family's attention. "I know I've caused you worry, not knowing why I've felt so poorly, but this is the best I've felt in weeks. I'm afraid I must insist on going with or without the rest of you."

"Bethlehem!" Meg exclaimed.

"I'm going with you," Amy said, and laced her arm through Beth's.

"I'm going as well." Jo laced her arm through the other.

"And me," Mammy declared, taking Amy's hand, and then they all stared back at the eldest daughter, knowing they wouldn't leave her behind.

"Well, I won't be left out," she said to a collection of exclamations and praise. "Let us celebrate a stranger's marriage as a family!"

VII

BUT FOR THE YOUNGEST TWO, THE MARCH WOMEN RARELY crossed the Croatan Sound. Manns Harbor was on the other side, opposite Roanoke, and could usually be seen not long after casting off in one of the many shallow draft vessels. These were manned by anyone who'd salvaged or built one, be they fisherman or folks as young as Amy. The night of the party, the sound was alight with half a dozen ferries at a time, each with its own lantern, held by a passenger or attached to a long stick. For all they knew, it looked very much like a flotilla determined to take the mainland, or the way the Union might have looked bombarding Roanoke Island—except that laughter bubbled up from each vessel. The partygoers' mirth sounded quite at home on the water, which always sounded so cheerful when parted and churned by nets or oars or rudders. Once ashore, some were met with carts or horses, but more set out on foot, as the March family did.

The big house could be seen for a mile at least. The lanterns that bordered the property, and those that trimmed the walking paths, had all been lit, and light shone out of every window from the bottom to the top of the place.

From a distance, it would've been impossible to tell that this was a confiscated home. Tonight it looked alive, as though the house had drifted back in time. It shone with merry life in a way it might not have since the previous inhabitants' own parties. Those parties had been decadent and had surely overwhelmed the nearby fragment of woods with laughter and music as well.

Neither was a sign of civilized society, the March women well knew. People could laugh and curse in the same breath. They could dance and brandish a whip in the same night, and the one activity did not always interrupt the other for long. It made walking toward the house feel like foolishness, and that feeling, when they knew that there was no captor here, that they were going to celebrate their own, made them feel as though there were more chains than those the eye could see. It made the oldest among them wonder whether or not freedom was something that could be declared, or whether it would have to be learned and practiced, like one of Meg's lessons.

It was the songs that gave the partygoers away. Whatever familiar discomfort the March women felt as they drew nearer to the stately manor that night, the unconfessed hesitation that fluttered inside their chests like fragile wings, it dissipated when they heard the hollers.

There was dancing around a bonfire on the big house lawn, and every so often a call would start from one side, someone hollering out a phrase, and the rest giving a unified response, and throughout, whoops and laughter and shouts that carried bits of story in them. As always, part of it was a song they'd heard before, and the other part was being written here, tonight, by those in attendance.

Any memories of another big house they'd known from the old life, where the lanterns were lit for the captor's guests, melted away. This was the place where they'd found rest on their way to the colony, and these were their own people, lighting lanterns to illuminate the night for their own amusement and not someone else's.

Amy's and Beth's steps quickened first, until they were several paces ahead, glancing back as though to ask Mammy's approval. She smiled to spur them on, and in a moment they were absorbed, zipping among the clusters of partygoers and around the crackling fire that lapped at the night sky.

Meg and Jo were too old to dash away excitedly, nor could they have while holding a cast iron cooking pot between them. It'd been filled that afternoon with crawfish after Jo and Yannick's swimming excursion, and now the women would have to find the cooking fire before anything else.

Partygoers shouted in salutation when Mammy, Meg, and Jo were nearer, and they smiled or waved in reply. Some faces were familiar—from the colony, or their time living in the big house—and others weren't, but they were pleasant and inviting just the same. Eventually, there were bolder sorts, children or young men who came right up to the pot to peek inside and survey its contents, one boy calling back over his shoulder.

"They brought mud bugs!" he announced, to a swell of approval. Jo appreciated the nosiness much more when it resulted in the boy and one other relieving her and her sister of the pot, and carrying it the rest of the way themselves.

"I'll follow," Mammy said. "You girls enjoy the festivities, and see that your sisters do as well."

"We will, Mammy."

They watched her for a moment, slipping into the young men's wake, inclining her head when she was greeted, a smile visible on her face every time she turned at a new sound, despite that her daughters were behind her. Then Jo linked her arm with Meg's.

"What shall we do first?"

"Well," Meg said, drawing in a deep breath as though she were preparing to submerge herself in water. "I suppose I should ask each one whether they have learned their letters, how to read and how to write them, and invite the ones who haven't to the colony to learn."

"What?" Jo recoiled. "Meg," she began to protest before recognizing the glint of amusement in her sister's eye. "I see. Well, never let it be said you haven't got a sense of humor."

"Honestly, Jo, you must think me as boring as Amy does, you very nearly believed me," she said as the two strolled around the fire a second time, taking stock of who surrounded it.

When the bonfire snapped, the women's shoulders cinched up toward their necks momentarily, and turning to ensure it stayed where it was meant to, they noticed for the first time what had been used for kindling.

When the March family first arrived, there had been a grand portrait in the entryway of the big house, a painting of a white man and someone assumed to be his sister or his wife—there was no way to tell. Behind them, but still purposely included in the portrait, was a brown-skinned child holding the man's riding crop. The child looked well and was dressed in fine clothing, though unlike the other two models he did not smile or wear a soft expression.

It was upsetting all the same.

More than once a new inhabitant of the big house would be found standing before the portrait, staring into it, arrested by everything the painting meant. It was not lost on them, nor was it possible to ignore, what it was meant to convey. Worse, and what would often ensnare those who'd simply meant to pass by the display, was the understanding of the efforts taken to produce the portrait in the first place.

Often it was the consideration of the many intentional steps planned and executed that made something sinister, where it might otherwise have seemed unfortunate at best. But a child had been selected—or was readily and constantly on hand—and he was made to stand within reach, in clothing that set him apart from his friends or even his family, since the clothes he wore looked almost royal. After all of that, he was given something to hold, something that clearly had not belonged to him. It was not something any enslaved person would have laid hands on without express instruction and permission, since it was as likely to be used on their back as on a horse's hindquarters. That he'd been made to hold it filled the observer's guts with a curdling, sour air, and eventually someone in the big house, long after the pictured man and woman had fled, graciously draped a length of material over it.

Jo hadn't approved—not of the portrait, and not of the decision to obscure it. It had become a haunt, whispering from behind its veil, impressing the picture onto one's mind when they passed, since they refused to look at it anymore. If something was worth covering, it was worth taking down, she'd decided, and that was what she had done. Because of what it was, and because of what her sister had suffered, she'd taken the heavy, cumbersome thing down, turned it toward the wall and on its side beside the staircase, removing it from its hallowed place by enough distance that soon it was possible not to know what the disgraced art piece pictured.

Now she returned to the property to find the portrait roaring in the fire beside them, and Jo smiled, satisfied and warm.

"There's music," Meg said. She'd drifted away without her sister noticing, and now came back to retrieve her. "Inside the house, they're dancing."

"I want no part of that," Jo said.

"But I do," Meg replied, and, taking her sister's hand, rushed across the lawn with the others excited to join the revelry.

They could only take a step or two inside the wide front door. Just beyond it, the floor was being trampled and stomped by men and women circling each other, entangling and then freeing themselves, exchanging sides, and lacing together before twirling apart. Beneath where the offending portrait had hung, there stood a fiddler, a banjo player, and an over-turned pot made into a drum. The house thrummed with the vibrations both of the instruments and of the onlookers who didn't dance but stomped a foot or clapped in time.

Before they could be crushed, Jo dragged Meg to the foot of the staircase, though it took some effort. Meg's eyes were wide and wanting, and she craned her neck as though there was some aspect of the dance she could not, but must, see. Her lips parted each time she tried to hold them closed, and when a man hoisted a woman into the air and the whole room gave a high-pitched exclamation, Meg's chest inflated so that Jo thought she was going to float away.

And then she did, happily, when a young man dashed to the stairs and offered his hand, the same sort of wide smile gleaming on his face. Before she could snatch her sister back from Wisdom Carter, who was as tall and daft as his brother, but objectively more handsome, Meg was gone.

That was enough for Jo to know the foot of the staircase was unsafe. She would not wait for another young man to be encouraged by Wisdom's success, especially when his brother Honor was never far behind him. Joanna March had no desire to be swept into the churning sea of dancers, dragged to her death, most likely stomped should she miss an unspoken cue and fall underfoot. She was even less interested in being flung to everyone's delight. So she climbed all the way to the landing and settled in between others too amused to take part or too engaged in conversation. Below, she watched her sister spin, the decadent dress that Beth had restored looking as though it'd been made for just this occasion.

"Safe enough to smile now," a voice beside her said.

Jo snapped her head to the side to see who was standing so close that his breath had grazed her face.

Whoever he was, he'd been smart enough to pull back and give her space to regard him. He wasn't smiling, not exactly. When Jo narrowed her eyes at him, something happened in the dark eyes before her that made her think he must be smiling somewhere unseen. That annoyed her.

"Don't let yourself be bothered," she told him, and turned her attention back to her sister in the bustling foyer below.

"You aren't a bother," he replied, alerting her that he was still there.

"You're becoming one."

"Am I?" Now he grinned freely. It was a handsome one, and that annoyed Jo more.

"Did you watch me? You must've if you knew precisely when I started smiling."

"It's romantic, isn't it? To be noticed from afar? That's what I've gleaned from books."

"What sort of books are you reading then?" Jo asked before forcing herself to look away from the young man and back at the dancing.

"The kind with romance in them, naturally."

She tried to ignore him, or at least to seem distracted enough to convey aloofness. She failed because every other moment, her eyes slid back to find him, lest she miss whatever he did next.

"What are you doing here?" she demanded, and his eyes widened a bit, his shoulder pulling back.

"Do I in particular require a reason outside the reception, or do you plan on questioning everyone this way?"

"Only the ones who intrude on me."

"I don't think anyone else will have the nerve, don't worry. I could've thought you unfriendly before your uncharacteristic smile."

"Oh, could you have?" she asked. "And how would you know what's characteristic of me and what isn't?"

Jo could hear her voice rising and knew her brow was furrowed. He must have observed it, too, yet his eyes were still bright. That did *not* annoy Jo. In fact, it worked to undo some of the perhaps exaggerated annoyance she'd felt before, since outside her family she had often been cautioned that a temperate manner was the only one acceptable in young women, lest gentlemen be driven away.

"I think we're probably quite alike," the young man said.

"And why, complete stranger, would you think such a thing?"

"Because we're both seeking solitude at the top of the staircase, content to observe, but not so disinterested that it doesn't make us happy to see them all so happy." He looked at her a moment longer before turning to rest his forearms on the banister, leaning over it as though the conversation was done. If Jo waited long enough, it would be like they'd never spoken at all, his attention was so clearly transferred back to the party.

"I used to live in this house," she blurted.

"I live in this house now," he answered, and turned back to her with a smile. "You see? Alike."

She snorted amusedly.

"You must have gone on to the colony," he said.

"We did. My sisters, and Mammy. Papa built us a home before he left."

"Has he gone to help the war effort?" the young man asked, sober for the first time.

"Yes. And, yes, I know—we must be proud."

"I wasn't going to say that. You must feel any way you like about the call to arms. We each must."

"You haven't enlisted?" she asked.

"No one's convinced me freedom needs earning. It's owed, and I will have it, whether here or abroad."

"Abroad," she repeated, and he must have assumed she was taken aback by the mere thought. In fact, it was at hearing anyone so near the famous colony speak as though there might be a whole world to see, or as though if there *was* life outside the Outer Banks, it could be anywhere but the American North. "Not to Boston?"

"No indeed," he answered. "Though I might consider visiting Chicago, if it suits me."

"What's in Chicago?" Jo asked. "From what I read, most of Europe's decided to settle there, and while they're quite unwelcome, *they* also tend to be quite unwelcoming to Black folk."

"Oh, I've no intention of staying. I only want to go long enough to visit Camp Douglas and see where they keep the Confederate prisoners of war."

"Oh, well. That's quite an attraction. I wouldn't mind seeing it myself."

"Two tickets then," he said. "We'll make a day of it."

The two stood firm-footed now, facing each other and away from the rail. He was tall, and somewhat slight. He didn't have the shoulders Meg sometimes described of Joseph Williams. This boy somehow towered but did not take up too much space. He wasn't imposing, except when he stood too close and whispered observations to strange young women. His clothes were neat, but not extraordinary. He wore a white blouse tucked into trousers, and a simple vest atop it. The vest lay open, as it had no buttons, and it made him seem rakish and gregarious in the way Jo already knew he was.

"Did your mother give you a name, young man?"

"She gave me one, and I gave myself another."

"Tell me both."

"What for?"

"So I can decide which of you was right, of course."

"She called me Loren," he said with a smile that caught Jo's lips as well. "But I prefer Lore."

"I'm sure your mother's a wonderful woman, but I didn't expect her to be wrong."

"Then you agree with me," he said, raising one brow.

"No, I just assumed you'd be wrong, so it didn't surprise me."

"And you know better?"

"I do."

"Then, please. Have mercy on me."

She reached up and took his chin between her finger and thumb, turning his head first one way and then the other.

"Mm. You're a Lorie, that's certain."

"So I am," he said, comfortable in her hold.

"You're easily persuaded."

"Only of what's right."

Jo released him, and Lorie followed when she walked away from the staircase and into what had once only been a library. Now there were pallets where families cuddled together, what furniture hadn't been claimed and taken elsewhere pushed against the wall to leave the floor clear for bedding. Whoever slept here was elsewhere just now, and Jo and Lorie navigated the room alone, first admiring the wallpaper whose blue and white pattern depicted several pastoral scenes. Without communicating the game to each other, they determined where the pattern began, and how many times it repeated in an arbitrarily observed space before moving on.

There were few books remaining, and Jo had seen them all when she lived here, but she ran her finger down their spines because it was lavish to have even these few, and to have a place specially to house them. She pulled a tome from the shelf and opened it to press her nose between the pages. When she glanced at Lorie, he was watching her as docilely as he had before. It was an undemanding kind of gaze, one that did not seem to require any performance or self-consciousness on her part, and one that she had never experienced outside her family. Jo offered the open book to him, and he stepped closer, bending his head to do as she had done before nodding his approval.

When they walked around, making slow progress around the frame of the room and back to the door, Jo felt him behind her somehow, even when he was a pace or two away. She'd never been in his company before, and she couldn't help thinking there was something uncommon about the way it felt to be. It was more an absence of unfamiliarity rather than the active presence of comfort, but perhaps it shouldn't feel like anything. Perhaps it should be the way it was with Yannick, and others. The way she could sense something just outside herself, as though it emanated from them. It was like an invitation, and she was aware of it, but it never quite reached her, and she was comfortable ignoring it until it dulled or dimmed, as long as they were.

She tried to make sense of why she felt differently with this young man she'd just met. *It must mean something*, she felt her mind insisting, despite that the rest of her made no such demand. Her heart didn't skip a beat the way she'd heard Meg describe, and while it would have alarmed her if it had, that it didn't was equally confounding. It made it difficult to know what was happening, except to know that *some*thing was.

On their silent circuit around the library, Jo wondered what Lorie might be thinking, and whether his thoughts matched or explained hers. When she turned slightly, she couldn't read his mind, but she saw that he held his hands behind his back just as she did, and she found that she was unsurprised. She bit back a smile, turning again and unlacing her fingers. She crossed her arms in front of her and walked past the closed door without opening it. If Lorie felt their silent constitutional drawing to an end, he must've hoped it wouldn't, because he followed her when she cut across the room and returned to the windows.

There were more in this one room than in her entire home, and these were not merely openings with shutters to close out the weather. These had glass, and panes, and some still had drapes. Above one window, there were framed silhouettes, and when she stood beneath them, her chin tilted high, Lorie did the same. To her quiet amusement, his arms had somehow entangled at his chest the way hers were.

Lorie was either very strange, or he'd been telling the truth that they two were remarkably alike, in a way Jo had never experienced. She found that she didn't mind which was the case; how could she when it felt so still to stand beside him? It was like standing next to a mirror, and though the theory needed no further testing, she let one of her arms fall forward without uncrossing the other. It wasn't exactly a natural pose, and she didn't expect the young man to match it precisely, but after a moment he did straighten one arm, placing the hand in the pocket of his trousers.

"Do you have brothers or sisters?" she asked him while he studied the silhouettes.

"No. I always wished I did." He looked down at her. "Have you?"

"Three sisters," she said.

"Who are they?" he asked, and she found the question pleasing because he hadn't merely asked after their names. He sounded as though he very honestly wanted to know them, as anyone with the opportunity should.

"There's Meg, the eldest, and she's nineteen."

"So am I," Lorie interrupted, his voice a bit excited with recognition.

"Yes, well, she's much older at heart, I must say," Jo said quickly. "She's a teacher, and if she has her way, by morning she'll be a wife and mother."

"I see." His eyes had widened a bit, but they recovered. "She'll be proposed to soon enough, if the young man who asked her to dance and the others who didn't get the chance have anything to say about it."

"Were you watching her, too?" Jo asked, and then smiled to hide the sharpness in her tone.

"Only because she was beside you." He nodded when she did, though the gesture had been involuntary. "And the other girls?"

"Bethlehem," she said. "And Amethyst. Sixteen and fourteen. One is an angel, and the other is mischief, and they adore each other. Beth is an artist with a needle and thread, and Amy cannot be contained, so she dances."

"The way they do downstairs?"

"No, no. She needs no music, and no partner. She makes the melody."

Jo had been looking wistfully out the window while she listed her sisters, and when she glanced back at the boy beside her, he was looking down at her as though she'd told him much more than a brief summary.

"And which are you?" he asked with a still expression that she matched without meaning to.

"I'm Joanna. Jo."

"Jo," he repeated. "The sister who makes her melodies with words."

"That's right," she said. It wasn't a compliment she would ever have given herself, but acknowledging it didn't feel too proud. She hadn't told him she wrote them down, or that they mattered dearly to her. If he knew, it was because he was meant to. "Where did you come from?"

"You came," he said. "I was here."

"Fine," she said, waving away his intentionally literal reply. "But this is strange, isn't it? How did you know we were alike?"

"I saw you." Now he shrugged a little, his eyes arching over her head as though he had to look slightly away to think. "The way you responded to the room and the people, and your sister's admirer—"

"The way I moved away? My unfriendliness and my disinterest?"

"The way you know what you want for yourself, and you still want for your sister what she wants, too," he said, quieting her. "You aren't unfriendly, Jo. I knew that right away, and well enough to know I should speak."

"How could you see all that? Who observes that well?"

He shrugged again, and smiled.

"I don't think I felt alone," she began slowly, but not out of caution. "Not with my sisters in the world. But I must've felt strange. Because I feel less so right now."

"I'm glad you do," he told her, and she smiled, too.

"So am I."

The newlyweds were headed for Corinth. The Roanoke Colony was there, almost in their backyard, but the wife had family among the freedpeople in Mississippi, or so she'd heard, and Corinth after all was the model whose likeness many in Roanoke hoped to emulate.

"You'll be well," Mammy assured them when they were making their last rounds through the party and receiving well wishes both from folks they knew and folks they'd never seen. "My husband was there, not long ago, and the colony is thriving. It's a wonderful place to start a life together."

"And if my people aren't there?" the bride said, somewhat quietly, though her groom squeezed her to his side so that Mammy knew it wasn't a sudden or unweighted concern.

"It might take some time to find them," she acknowledged.

There was no use or comfort in denying what many Black folk already knew. There was a lasting impact to the forcible separations they'd endured, and some cruelties would take longer to heal from than others. Skin closed, though scarred, and even amputations numbed. The familial severing that enslaved people had suffered was a different kind of wound, and Margaret March did not know of a salve potent enough to stop its ache. She did know that if it existed, it must be very much like hope, with which she was intimately familiar.

"There's such a thing as family you're not born to," she told the bride. "There's family you find. When you lose the ones you know, you praise God that you still don't have to be alone. And, if you need to, you come right back to Roanoke."

The two women stood with hands clasped together, close enough for their foreheads to almost touch. They hadn't known each other before tonight. Mammy had followed the boys who took her pot, and made herself useful with the others organizing the food before making first plates for the bride and groom, and making their acquaintance.

It was her mother the bride was searching for, Mammy knew. It had to be. A heaping plate had been all the incentive the young woman required to roll her shoulders forward as though to burrow at the slightest invitation into Mammy's chest, and when welcomed, the young woman had asked a half dozen questions about marriage and children while Mammy pressed her to eat.

Mammy recognized the girl's nervous energy. She remembered it. Even in the old life, where there would be nothing to follow the celebration but the same toil that filled every day, even when there would be no house, and no new life, deciding to take Alcott as her husband still felt like an exciting and uncertain new undertaking. Despite the circumstances, it felt like it could change everything, and it made everything new—even when there were very few choices to make, and they'd only had a ceremony to begin with because the man who enslaved them thought it good for the moral community to allow folks to marry.

She couldn't imagine everything marriage must mean now. What she had learned was difficult enough, and it was that white men still found a way to tear Black families apart, though now it was out of obligation. The Roanoke Colony spoke of caring for a Black soldier's family while they were away fighting for the Union, but elsewhere, in places still more like contraband camps, a man's labor wasn't paid in full as long as he had a family or children. Deductions were taken until some realized they were still performing slave labor. They would never be paid as long as Black families stayed together. And so, many left. The women and children were still given rations and clothing, though now it was the women working with a promise of pay that rarely came, and the untethered men were not only paid but mobile, which must have felt truly free.

She didn't speak any of this to the young bride and her husband, nor did she voice her worry that after slavery, all their people—the very idea of their families—would still be under attack. Perhaps it wasn't true, after all. Mammy was a woman and a mother, and she survived sometimes by her intuition, but she wasn't the Lord. Sometimes a worry was just a worry, woman or not, and she was a woman with four daughters. She would choose hope as long as she lived, if it meant that everything hideous–like slavery, like family destruction, like torture and torment and watching helplessly while someone with the same color skin was made to bleed– might end. She chose to believe it would end first for this young bride, and for everyone who came after.

When Mammy and the couple finally parted ways, they were on the landing. The two proceeded farther up in search of the attic room that the big house's inhabitants had agreed should be specially theirs the night before they departed, and Mammy leaned against the banister a moment to look around.

So many people lingered, though the music had ended an hour ago. The dancing in the foyer was done, and folks huddled together in couples or groups, reclining on the staircase, or letting the wall hold them up as they sat on the hardwood floor. Their conversations were soft now with the late hour, and the satisfaction that came with having full stomachs and having exerted themselves in activities that pleased them.

The hushed voices rose up to Mammy, meeting her at the top of the staircase like the comforting sound of a sleeping child's gentle breathing, and, as always, she wished to find her children. It was the same at the end of every long day, but tonight, it was to see that they were full and satisfied and happily exerted, too–and perhaps a little because the bride had reminded her that now Black folk would be free to come and go as they pleased. She had to squeeze her daughters while she could.

She turned at the sound of a door opening and saw Jo and a tall young man emerge, exchanging places with people on their way in.

"Mammy!" Jo exclaimed, as though she hadn't noticed the quiet. "Where have you been?"

"Where have I been? All over. It's a party, isn't it?" She glanced around again. "Or it was, not long ago."

"Did you dance?" Jo asked, still not introducing her companion, who stood just behind her left shoulder rather patiently.

"A bit. And I ate, and I talked, and I found your sisters and lost them again," Mammy said, then opened her mouth again to ask for an introduction but didn't get the chance.

"Mammy, can we stay the night?" Amy said, trudging up the staircase toward them with Bethlehem in tow. "My feet hurt."

"I think her boots are pinching, but she refuses to take them off," Beth said with a yawn. Each of her loved ones managed to look her way without their gazes lingering too long. Her illness had passed. It was natural to be tired after such an extravagant night, and each of them was as well.

"My boots are perfect," Amy replied before she realized the person standing close by wasn't passing. "Who are you?"

"I'm Jo's Lorie," the handsome young man told her, and offered her the palm of his hand while he bowed slightly.

"Jo's Lorie?" Amy asked, but she gave him her hand anyway, because he was handsome and tall, and he didn't have a mustache like so many attending the party had.

"He belongs to me," Joanna said, laughing over her shoulder with him. "I've laid claim. It's been decided."

Between Mammy, Beth, and Amy, the youngest seemed the only one capable of a reply.

"Have you two had too much to drink?"

"Amethyst, hush. We haven't had anything. We haven't eaten at all, in fact—we passed the entire night in the library, talking."

"You didn't see Yannick, then, and the rest of your boys?" Beth asked.

"There are others?" Lorie said quietly, and he and Jo giggled again.

Beth could've hidden her face in her hands at the insinuation. "I didn't mean that."

"Of course you didn't," Jo said, taking her sister in her arms and kissing her cheek. "You never would. Lorie knows all about my sisters, and he knows only to take offense at the things Amy has to say."

When the youngest sucked her teeth, annoyed that she would be so disgraced in front of a man who—despite his and Jo's ridiculous claims—was in fact a stranger, she was ignored.

"How are you?" Jo asked Beth. "Did *you* eat?"

"I did. I had the crawfish you caught, and greens, and a bit of anything that wasn't too sweet."

"On top of everything, she doesn't even have the decency to indulge a sweet tooth?" Lorie asked, as though insisting on maintaining a private exchange with Joanna despite the presence of company.

"I told you," Jo said with a broad smile that she turned from Lorie and shone on Beth. "She's our saint, perfect because she is, not because she tries to be."

"You're embarrassing her," Mammy said, reaching between the two to save Beth from the directness of their attention. "Come on, girls. Let's find Meg and our pot and start home."

"I can't, unless one of you carries me," Amy said, alert again at the prospect of walking the distance even back to the sound, now that the excitement would be behind and not before her. "Have your Lorie carry me, Jo!"

"He isn't a mule, Amy," Jo said, taking him by the wrist and heading down the staircase. "And he lives here on the mainland, he isn't coming to Roanoke."

At the sound of Amy's disappointment, and careful not to trip while being dragged down the steps, Lorie spun around to catch her gaze.

"I do have a cart, though," he said, pretending to whisper. "And I promise I'll take you to the ferry." He winked at her, and all was forgiven.

"Mammy, you rest here," Jo called from the foyer, disturbing those who'd begun to fall asleep along the walls and in the corners, some with their legs outstretched so that others could rest their heads on them. "We'll find our pot, and our Meg, and his cart, and then we shall be whisked away home!"

With that, the two disappeared out the front door, leaving more than a bit of confusion.

"My word," Mammy said at last, slowly lowering herself

down upon the top step. Her two youngest folded down beside her.

"That was rather interesting," Beth agreed.

"I suppose this means Jo's fallen in love." Mammy had to pause, despite that she'd spoken the words and shouldn't be surprised at them. "I wasn't sure I'd see the day."

"For my part, I'm not sure I like it," Amy said through a yawn.

"Joanna's the only one who must, I suppose." Mammy petted her youngest daughter's hair, and then pulled her toward her chest, coaxing her to rest. "But I do wonder how Meg might feel."

"Why only Meg, and not me?" Amy asked, sitting erect again, before Mammy repeated the gesture and had her back inside the hold of one arm.

"You're too young to understand."

"I'm as hurt as Meg will be!"

"All right, darling. There, there, you poor dear."

Beth covered her smile, leaning against Mammy's other shoulder while her eyes drooped, closing longer and longer each time she blinked. "I love him for Joanna, if only because he has a cart," she said. "But I won't assume she's in love until she tells me so."

"That's much more reasonable than I've been," Mammy agreed. "I could learn to be more careful from you, Beth. I'd hate to incite another daughter to trust in something that might not be."

She didn't have to say that she meant Joseph Williams and

Meg, and she wouldn't have, when her eldest daughter came through the front door and smiled up at her family.

"Wasn't tonight the loveliest night?" Meg asked, coming to lay both hands over the decorative finial atop the post at the base of the staircase. It was extravagant, as so many things in the big house were, shaved into the shape of a pineapple or something similarly kingly when painted bronze. Meg's fingers held it as though the thing were as delicate as she, and it looked more regal in her hands. In the gown repaired by Bethlehem, and with her thick hair in dozens of soft twists and then wrapped around and around each other, she looked like this house might be hers if they all lived long enough for a third life.

"You danced as much as I did," Amy said. "And with twice as many partners."

"I did no such thing," Meg replied, her brown skin flushing around her eyes.

"I danced with Beth, which is one partner, and you danced with two young men. Isn't two twice as many as one?"

"It's too late to bicker," Mammy interjected, and hushed Amethyst until she laid against her a third time.

"And I only danced with Honor Carter because he asked."

"But you danced with Wisdom first," Beth said, eyes closed but not out of disinterest.

"I danced with Wisdom because I wanted to," Meg answered with a smile. She bit her lip as though to keep from saying more, and laid her cheek against the pineapple finial with a sigh.

"You see, Mammy?" Amy said. "Meg won't even be as hurt as I am that Jo's in love with Lorie, now that she's danced with a Carter boy."

The whimsical expression Meg wore settled.

"How can Jo be in love?" she asked, straightening and letting her hands slide down the post until they were at her side. "And who is Lorie?"

As though conjured by her interest, the door opened and the two in question stood in its frame together. They looked winded, but more amused and far more awake than anyone who'd come to the party. Behind them, folks trudged either to a nearby encampment, or else toward the cabins none had been willing to use until the big house itself was sufficiently crowded. The cabins had been for the enslaved of the estate, and there were people who would sleep beneath the stars before they'd huddle inside. Tonight, fatigue won some over, and at least a few would find things felt quite different when done by choice.

Jo and Lorie were a stark contrast to everything around them, it seemed, and before Meg was given any explanation, she understood. They looked a little wild, as though they'd raced around the property, collecting the pot, Lorie's cart, and a blanket to cushion the back for her family. They hadn't danced—Meg knew because she would have seen them—but without music or memorized steps, they stood as close now as she'd gotten to Wisdom Carter, and they looked as though they'd done so since well before tonight. They couldn't have because Jo would never be the type to hide a boy from her sisters—and she'd never shown an interest in hiding one at all.

While they bundled her mother and sisters onto the cart, and then when Lorie helped her up, too, Meg accepted something she'd worried over before: It was better to be adventurous and passionate than it was to be measured or smart. Jo was most of those things anyway. She wasn't measured, but she was the rest, while Meg was only dreadfully boring. It wasn't any wonder that neither Carter brother had ever taken notice of her until she'd worn a dress Beth had improved, and let her mother style her hair. She tried to keep her hair as still and tidy as the missionary teachers much of the time, and often beneath a straw bonnet, despite that it made her look older than she was. Stodgier, at the very least.

The cart jostled her, but neither the bumpy ride nor her sister's free-flowing laugh from the front seat could rearrange her thoughts tonight.

There was a reason Joseph Williams hadn't written poetry or embroidered his envelopes with care and calligraphy.

Meg March would make a good wife and mother, but she was not the kind of girl who sparked a man's imagination. She'd never made someone laugh the way Jo did right now.

When a tear slid down one cheek, she pinned her chin to the side so only the darkness outside the cart could see.

VIII

AFTER THE RECEPTION, JO TOOK TO ACCOMPANYING BETH and Amy across the sound to the mainland on occasion, and Lorie took to meeting the March women on the shore with his cart even when she didn't. It became clear that though Beth had never complained of it, there were often times she meant to take a ferry to Manns Harbor but couldn't, as anyone with a skiff or the like was on the water hoping to earn a wage or transporting soldiers, and a young woman or two was no one's priority.

"It's also that Beth doesn't let them know she's there," Amy informed Lorie and Jo, while he charioted them to the big house one day near the summer's end. "She'll sit by the shore with her scraps and her pile of clothing, and she'll begin disassembling it right there, so that anyone who *might* ferry her across thinks she's only there to admire the water while she works!"

"Is that so, Beth?" Jo said, whipping her head around to interrogate her mildest sister.

"I won't now," the girl said back, "now that Lorie might be waiting on the other side for me. But I'm sure they know I'd like to cross when I do it so often, and there's almost no one I haven't ridden with."

"But you could *say* something," Jo said.

"I'd feel so demanding, especially when I know they're seeking work, and I have nothing to pay them except whatever food is left over from a meal." Beth looked a bit self-conscious now that a behavior she'd thought perfectly normal had an audience discussing it as though it weren't.

"I speak up whenever I'm with her, so it's just lucky I don't go to school so I can come along," Amy declared, with the kind of sigh Mammy made when there'd been a lingering concern and now it was relieved.

"The worst that can happen is that I wait a little while, and I don't mind," Beth replied.

"Why, angelic Beth," Lorie said, reins in his hand and exaggeratedly bouncing as the horse pulled the somewhat rickety cart along. "That may be the closest I've ever heard you come to a self-defense."

"Sisters have no need to defend themselves against each other," Beth told him before Jo slapped his arm with the back of her hand.

"Around the two of you, she might," he replied without hesitation, nodding first at Joanna and then toward Amy.

"You won't endear yourself to us by playing devil's advocate, sir," Jo said. "I may have claimed you, but you would be wise to mind yourself where sisters are concerned."

"I'm advocating for Bethlehem, if anything, and *she's* no devil."

"Did I say something unkind, Beth?" Amy asked, her eyes wide and her lips downturned in the beginning of a very genuine pout.

"I don't think so at all," Beth replied, yanking her baby sister toward her. Amy was sometimes a mess of energy and self-conscious nerves when Lorie was around, Bethlehem had noticed, and she meant to give the girl a quick peck on the cheek, but just then one of the wheels sank into a small hole before bouncing back out, and the two collided foreheads instead.

"Lorie!" Jo cried. "For someone so concerned with the treatment of my darling sisters, you're a terribly reckless driver!"

"I'm sorry, girls," he said through a bellowing laugh. "I honestly didn't see the hole in the road until it was too late. We didn't lose anyone, did we?" He turned to survey his cargo, and threw his hand back as though to confirm all was still in order. Beth and Amy ducked out of his reach each time his arm swung from one side to the other. "Ah, there it is," he said, at the sight of Beth's dimple. "We're fine, then."

The four laughed and jostled over the road awhile longer, until they were at the front door of the big house, and Lorie leapt down to help Beth and then her bundles into the house.

"I'll come with you and Lorie today," Amy exclaimed to Jo

when Lorie had her under the arms because she'd waited for him to return rather than getting down on her own.

"No, Amy, you'll help Beth in the sewing room, as you're meant to."

"But I'm very little help at all, ask her! I tear too roughly and ruin the thread she'd prefer to keep, or I practice dance positions and turns, and I think the racket is horribly distracting for her!"

"Then be less distracting," Jo insisted, leaning in so that her forehead threatened to connect with Amy's the way Beth's had on the bumpy ride.

"Perhaps I'm a better writer's assistant than a seamstress," Amy pleaded. "She won't miss me, I swear—look, she's already gone up the stairs without me!"

"Amethyst," Jo said, in a serious tone that quieted her sister. "You need to keep an eye on Beth."

At the reminder, the young girl sank onto the soles of her feet, which was a very strange stance to find her in, and Jo knew it meant that she was listening.

"We don't want her to feel as though we're circling her at all times, or more so than before she fell ill," Jo said quietly, tugging lovingly on one of Amy's two curls. It had been positively awe-inspiring, the change she'd seen in her youngest sister. It wasn't just that she wanted to be near Lorie—it was what else she'd begun to tolerate. She'd let Meg moisturize and stretch her hair with a twisting twine method that for a night made her head look like a sea star, and then she'd allowed her near again with the curling iron so that the two halves of her perfectly parted hair now hung over her shoulders in spiral curls. It was a wonder what Lorie's coming had done. "Beth is accustomed to your company," Jo carried on, through a slight smile she couldn't help. "So it's best for you to be the one to keep close while she works. We can put our fun aside for family's sake once in a while. Can't we?"

Lorie tugged on Amy's other curl and then raised an innocent brow at her while he snuck both hands behind his back.

"Of course we can," Amy replied. "I'm a very good sister."

Lorie snorted, and then pretended to sneeze.

"You are," Jo said, nudging Lorie at the waist and then hugging Amy. She planted a kiss on the top of Amy's head, right on the impossibly perfect part Meg had drawn.

"The two of you will make insufferable parents, though," Amy went on as she danced up the few steps to the front door. Jo's head leapt back as though in astonishment, but before she could speak, Amy finished, "You're going to drive your children positively mad!" And she disappeared into the house, closing the door behind her.

When Jo still could not conjure up any words in reply, she simply turned with a gaping mouth and wide eyes to Lorie, whose own eyes drifted away. He began whistling, and he retrieved Jo's writing satchel and headed off toward a row of trees.

"*And if our able-bodied men are all enticed to war,*" Jo said her words aloud, her pen at the ready to continue when she was satisfied with the sentence's construction, "*we will be transformed into something the Freedpeople Colony never was: a contraband camp.* Or should I say instead . . ."

She trailed off, eyes fixed, though she saw none of the world around her. Not the beautiful loblolly pine Lorie had settled them beneath, with its long trunk and high canopy like a parasol made into a tree, and not Lorie, though he sat directly in front of her, hunched so that his back made a workable desk on which she could draft her next newsletter.

"Or should you say instead," Lorie repeated, hoping to coax her back to external conversation. When her mind began the work of composition, often she spoke in fragments or retired from speaking aloud at all. Lorie hadn't known Joanna in the old life, nor had he ever known an artist, to his knowledge. If he had, it hadn't been intimately enough to witness their creative process. "Or should you say . . ."

"Hold still," she said absently.

"You aren't even writing, Jo. I'd feel it, remember?"

"Shh."

"And I have no objection to playing desk for you, maestro, but it occurs to me that ink stains your fingers on a constant basis—"

"Shh."

"—in which case, it would likely do the same to my shirt, if that paper isn't thick enough, yes?"

"Lorie, would you *please* be quiet, for the sake of heaven!"

"I have but one shirt, Joanna, be reasonable!"

"Forget it." She snatched the paper from his back and laid it in the grass, using her pen and the ink she carried in a closeable jar to weigh it down. "You are dead set on disrupting my work, and I need to concentrate. Stop giggling."

"I'm sorry, Jo," Lorie said, still laughing when he turned and took her wrist to keep her from standing and storming away. She stood anyway and he was forced to as well, or else lose his hold. "But you don't need to concentrate at all. You'll be composing that newsletter in your mind until it's finished, whether I interrupt you with my charming wit or not. You couldn't help it."

"It's a different thing, to write something for unfamiliar eyes," she insisted, though it was clear she wasn't upset at him. She yanked her wrist away, and he waited with an open palm until she absently dropped her arm back into his grasp. "And to write something on behalf of so many people. They haven't asked me to, and perhaps they'll never read it themselves. But that's even more reason to take very seriously the freedpeople my words represent."

Lorie sobered at that. "I'm sorry, Jo. I don't mean to make light of your work. I take it seriously, too."

"Oh, Lorie," she said, pushing at his chest as though to shove him away, though she applied no pressure. "I know that. Of course you're fine. And you're right, I'll be composing it all day, whether I write it down this minute or not. That's how I wrote before Mammy and Meg supplied me with paper and ink."

"And your hands were unblemished then," Lorie imagined aloud, because he hadn't known her then and didn't like to think such a time existed. He held her writing hand in both of his now, inspecting each finger, though he knew which two wore the ink smudges.

"Yes. But only the March family knew my mind." Jo sighed, and Lorie glanced up from her fingers, though he didn't let them go.

"You sound as though you miss it," he said, and at first Jo only made a contemplative sound and looked beside him, at the shadow of the loblolly tree.

"It's not humility."

"Thank God."

"It's . . . I think I'll always prefer reciting my words aloud. Conjuring and arranging them, and meditating on them before they exist anywhere outside my mind. Spending time *with* my own mind." She took back her hands and let one drape around her waist before balancing the other on it so that she could rest her chin on a fist. "I know its value, but the writing is an exercise in itself. Yes, it allows me to commit my thoughts to history, but so does an oral telling. It's the way we shared our stories and histories before, isn't it? Not just me, in the old life, but all Black people. It never seemed flimsy or frail before. It wasn't the advent of ink or paper that gave our words their importance when the words existed first."

"But now ideas are judged by the precision with which they're recorded," Lorie continued when he knew just what she meant.

"Yes. Now there's a new way things must be spoken to be considered at all. A barrier that feels meant to rank and order those stories and histories and decide which deserve to be read and remembered."

"Yours will be, Jo. They already are."

"I know," she said. "It isn't just my exclusion that concerns me."

They stood quietly together for a while, and it was possible to hear people nearby, closer to the big house and off in the nearby woods. There was a children's chorus emanating from there, which likely meant Beth had enlisted the young ones staying at the big house for a mushroom foraging again. There were beautiful golden chanterelles to be found between the trees, easy for even the youngest child to identify. Beth wouldn't ask them if they didn't treat it like play, and they loved the fragrance when they found them, rewarded with a faint aroma like an apricot when they sniffed the cap to confirm what anyone could tell by the lavish color.

Beth used them to dye fabric, when she had enough of them, or a small enough piece of clothing, making something look extravagant that had once been dull or simply unremarkable. When Jo marveled at her younger sister's artistry, the whole family insisted that her own words likewise transformed naked and unremarkable paper. She tried to see it similarly, if only because her newsletters had a purpose she could not otherwise serve. She couldn't speak to Northern philanthropists otherwise, and she needed to, for the colony's sake.

"Where've you gone now?" Lorie said, tipping his head as though he might see more of her despite that she was right in front of him. "What are you thinking of?"

"My sisters, of course."

"Of course a sister," he replied knowingly. "I meant which one?"

"Bethlehem, just then. And now Amy, because she'd better not be in the woods foraging with the others. She needs to be at Beth's side, and she needs to know that without being reminded."

"Come on," he said, and Lorie offered Jo his hand.

"What?"

"Are we going to check that Beth is well, and that Amy is by her side, or aren't we?"

Jo snatched her paper from the grass, and the pen and ink jar, too, balancing them on Lorie's palm instead of her hand. He smirked and nodded.

"Of course we are," she said definitively, and led him back to the big house.

It seemed a silly question, but Meg wanted to ask Mammy whether at nineteen her mother considered her a woman or a child, and how she should know for herself.

It *was* a silly question, which is why she couldn't bring herself to ask it. She *must* be a woman. A young one, of course, but a woman all the same. She taught freedpeople their lessons, after all. All day, she worked at instructing and encouraging and correcting and explaining. There was much of it that overlapped the work of a mother, and she did try her best to be nurturing, especially with the children, as they could all do with more of that after the old life. Of course, only a young woman would be trusted to do the work she did.

When she came home, Meg cooked often so that Mammy wouldn't have to. It didn't seem fair in a home with so many capable people that all the cooking and cleaning should fall to one, and while the sentiment seemed shared at least with the two middle daughters, neither seemed to have Meg's imperative about it.

There was also the matter of her correspondence with Joseph Williams, which whether or not it was precisely romantic in nature must at least be prospective just by the fact that she received letters from a young man who had asked for the privilege. Her baby sister might think her dreadfully boring, and she might not have the gregarious appeal of Joanna, but at the reception Meg had danced with another young man altogether, and all day her thoughts threatened to gallop away from her lessons and students to one or the other of those young men, wondering which of them she was meant to court. Or whether either of them thought of her throughout their day, and when that mystery might be resolved.

All things considered, there seemed little question that she'd well and truly left childhood behind, but then Amy posited rather frequently that *she*'d done the same, and so

Meg resolved that the only way to know for certain was to ask Mammy, silly question or not.

In the girls' bedroom, while they changed out of their work dresses, Meg opened her mouth to begin several times before she was brave enough to follow through. Luckily her mother was unfastening the hoop frame that only she and Meg needed to wear, as their particular labor required a standard of presentability to which neither Jo nor Beth was held.

"I feel a persistent . . . tension," she told Mammy while they waited for Jo, Beth, and Amy to return from the mainland.

"What do you mean? About what?" her mother asked through a relieved sigh. "One day, the white folk will leave this colony, and I pray we shall all wear comfortable flat skirts, even outside the home. What a joy not to have every solitary aspect of our appearance used to judge and determine our civility, as though I could not keep a ledger without that hoop."

After a moment of simply enjoying the discarded weight, Mammy looked over at her daughter and smiled apologetically.

"I'm sorry, Meg, what were you telling me? A tension, you said?"

"That's right."

"Where do you feel it? In what regard?"

"I'm afraid it's corrupting everything," Meg answered, and her mother grew serious. "I know that's a terribly strong way to phrase it, but I don't know any other way. I wonder if I'm a proper adult yet, and then I wonder if I only wonder because I'm not engaged. You must be an adult once you're engaged, mustn't you?"

"I suppose so," Mammy answered, but she didn't look adequately contemplative and Meg worried she was only placating her.

"But engagement can't be the thing that *makes* someone an adult. I feel far from it, no matter how much I dream of being married, and that doesn't stop me feeling that same tension in other things."

"Meg," Mammy said, taking her daughter's hands and making her sit beside her on the bed. "Tell me what you mean."

"Now I've started talking before I'm sure I even know how," the young woman answered with a sigh. "Why don't my sisters ask me to go to the mainland with them?"

"They left before you were home from teaching, darling, that's all."

"But they always do. Is there too great a distance between us now? Is it just that they find me boring, and being too grown up has nothing to do with it? They adore Lorie, for one thing, and he's the same age as me. But he's so fun and funny . . ."

"I think I understand." Mammy took her by the arm now, and it made Meg look up into her eyes. "I know it feels like you're in a strange, in-between place, darling. I promise you, we all are, being free but with the war that made us so still ongoing."

"Is it just the war?" Meg interjected.

"I don't think war is a matter of 'just.' War splits the world in two, into a time before, and a time after, and then there's the time in between, when you're living through it. How can you separate yourself and your mind from that tension, to know whether you'd be feeling it otherwise? Of course, there's the bits that are just a part of growing up, but you're going through so much more, Meg. You must be gentle with yourself."

"Am I still a child if I want nothing more than for you to make it all make sense for me?" Meg said, letting a whimper escape her lips when she laid her head on her mother's shoulder.

"Oh, dear heart." Mammy laid her hand against Meg's soft hair. "I don't think anyone has ever gone through a moment such as this before, changing over while the world does the same. You're blossoming with freedom, and I am so envious of you. But I'm so sorry that it means I don't always know how to help."

"Mammy. *You* always help. Just you."

The two sat together that way for a little while, Mammy swaying very gently without realizing, because her arms remembered rocking beautiful baby girls many years before.

"I don't want to outgrow my sisters," Meg admitted quietly, and before Mammy could respond, a door opened elsewhere in the house and welcome voices spilled down the hall. Both women smiled as they righted themselves and went to greet them.

When a deeper voice bellowed along with her sisters', Meg hesitated. She was only happy her mother walked in front of her so that she didn't see. Meg was surprised then, when Mammy turned and gave her a gentle look. Her mother might not know how to help her traverse the transition before her, but she still knew so much.

"Will he always be around from now on?" Meg asked, in something more like confession.

"I think so, darling," Mammy said, and then pulled Meg into a hug so that she could whisper, "Lorie may be Jo's, but Jo is still yours."

As though in reply, Joanna barreled into the two women, throwing her arms around them to join their embrace. Meg smiled when her sister's hands clawed at her arms, as though with Mammy between them, Jo could not get close enough to her. Before long, Beth came, too, meeting them in the hall just outside the girls' bedroom and attaching herself to the side, where she could touch all three of the others.

"Me, too," Amy said, skipping away from Lorie and then dropping to her hands and knees. "But I'm the youngest," she almost shouted, while she pried the huddle of legs apart to make space for her to climb into the center of them. "So I should be in the middle!"

When she stood, she was at the heart of the hug, and Mammy and Meg laughed, kissing her cheek when she presented it.

"Who could have foreseen Amethyst needing to be at the

center of something?" Jo quipped, poking her baby sister's cheek with an outstretched tongue when offered it to kiss.

"Jo!" Amy shrieked. "Heathen." And then she extended her neck, forcing Mammy to strain out of the way without breaking the huddle so that she could collect a kiss from Beth as well.

IX

October 1863

"You've said very little of your correspondence with the Association," Beth told Constance Evergreen on the occasion of her latest visit. The young missionary teacher had returned periodically to the March home despite her lack of progress in finding answers about Beth's condition, and while Bethlehem didn't want to make the other young woman feel unwelcomed, she did wonder why.

"I'm sorry," Constance said as she bounced a gorgeous brown baby on her knee in the front room of the March home. "I know I haven't been as much help as either of us would have hoped."

Constance looked up at the third young woman in the room, a dark-skinned girl named Ella who wore colorful fabric over her hair. The baby was named Fanny, and she belonged to Ella, who Constance glanced toward in case at her admission the mother would reclaim her child.

As promised, Mammy had invited another family to come into the home. Ella was a mother, but she was only about Meg's age, and it was her father and not Fanny's who had accompanied them into the March home. The old man's name was Orange, and he spent much of his time taking long solitary constitutionals around the island and, according to passersby, looking out at the water as though he expected that a ship might come in. Old men were allowed an oddity or two, Ella said, especially those who'd only had the freedom to walk long distances after a lifetime of backbreaking labor that warped their legs.

Ella didn't demand her child back from Constance, likely because Beth had given the little girl one of her fingers so that she didn't fuss while Constance held her, and just now Bethlehem was smiling at the baby's great big dark eyes. Instead, Ella turned and opened the window shutter so that the little darling could feel the crispness of the air, now that the summer had burned away and fall was in full swing.

"It isn't that I don't appreciate your concern, Miss Evergreen," Beth said. "It's very apparent. And perhaps you're as engaged by the mystery as I am."

"It is mysterious. My letters about you probably seem too impassioned, but it is so difficult to understand when even the symptoms I myself have observed wane." Constance looked at Beth suddenly, her eyes wide with concern. "Don't misunderstand, I'm always pleased to see you return to your bright and upbeat self for weeks at a time, but I'm not when . . ." She trailed off.

"Please," Beth coaxed her. "You mustn't worry about discretion on Ella's behalf. She studies me as closely as anyone else does, and nothing you say will be news to me."

"I know your family must be devastated each time you succumb again to aches and pain and fatigue, and none of us know why," Constance acknowledged. "Sometimes, Beth, it seems we could forget you've ever fainted, or clutched your chest suddenly, or spent a day or more at a time in bed. Except . . ."

"Except that it happens again. And except, I suppose, for the bruises," Beth said softly, speaking of the marks she occasionally found while changing out of her clothes. She didn't mention the dark circles under her eyes, though she could always tell when Constance or one of her sisters were trying not to see them. "Had you worried that perhaps I was only pretending to be ill?"

Only Beth could ask such a question kindly, when if true, it meant Constance had accused her of something terrible, even if only in her mind.

"I can say, before God, Bethlehem, that I never have." And then her glance ticked away, first toward Ella, then as though she'd caught sight of some distraction on the other side of her chair, and Beth knew something she might otherwise never have been told.

"But the Association does."

Constance looked back at her immediately, and then she lowered her chin a bit as though in apology. When she remembered to bounce Baby Fanny again, she nodded.

"I'm sorry, Bethlehem, I'd no intention of ever telling you. I was certain if I kept a more detailed log of your symptoms and your ailments, we might stumble upon a pattern that the Association can make sense of."

"Are they God, that it must make sense to them or else be written off?"

"I'm embarrassed on their behalf, I must admit," Constance said, though it was obvious that Beth was not upset. "They've stopped offering any advice but that I consider the behavior attention seeking, and that if I am unconvinced of it, that I should fervently continue in prayer for discerning. Which, if I'm honest, has begun to feel like a judgment in itself.

"I'm sorry, Bethlehem," she continued, "if I've said too much. It does frustrate me, and I'm beginning to wonder whether it wouldn't just serve them right to have Joanna catch wind of their behavior and write about it in her monthly newsletter. It's reached some of the Association's own readership, I hear."

"Have you read Jo's writing?" Beth asked, enlivening at the mention of her sister's talent, because it mattered a great deal more to her than the very unsurprising machinations of any organization of white folk.

"Not personally," Constance admitted. "But I've heard that her pen is sharp."

Beth nodded, knowing the young woman would not carry on. She'd grown freer in Beth's company, confessing the hypocrisies and shortcomings of her organization. But perhaps because she was from the North, Constance would never divulge precisely how they spoke about Black people amongst themselves. Beth knew well enough anyway, and what she didn't know by hearing, she could guess at.

If they didn't think her mysterious illness wholly imaginary, they surely posited it was a side effect of the laziness many missionary teachers felt must be confronted before freedpeople were to benefit from liberty.

If they thought Jo's pen sharp, they likely thought it *too* sharp. They would rumor that her tone did not always reflect the gratitude expected of a freedperson—but perhaps that was also why the subscription list was growing so quickly. That, and the fact that little fault could be found with the newsletter being provided free of charge, allowing all donations to reflect the benevolence and genuine philanthropy of the benefactors.

"How have you felt this week?" Constance asked, to redirect the conversation and move away from what might be considered impolite chatter.

"Very well," Beth said, nodding, too, because she'd become accustomed to offering small confirming gestures in addition to her word.

"If she were seeking attention," Ella said, and because she had never interjected in Constance's presence before, the missionary teacher looked as cautiously at the new young woman as she had when she'd been allowed to hold her child. "Or rather, if your association thinks she is, wouldn't Bethlehem conflict her assurances somehow? I'm sure I've heard that even some Northerners think Black folk wily and mischievous. Instead of professing her good health on the days she's well, wouldn't they expect her to make her family probe and pry for information with slight insinuations that she's merely putting on a brave face?"

"That is a very reasonable point, Ella," Constance said. "I'll mention it in my next letter. And"—she turned to Beth again—"in the meantime, there's still no pattern you can see?"

"No. If nothing else, my new condition keeps me in a state of surprise."

"You must be joking," Constance said. "Not even you can be expected to find the good in something that's devastated your life in some ways."

"It's an interesting thing to have happen, though, isn't it?" Beth asked with a soft smile. "And if interesting things must happen, I'd like at least a few of them to happen to me."

"I wouldn't mind it being less interesting, in just this one regard. Do keep on taking the cod liver oil for now, Beth-lehem," Constance encouraged.

"It's a small improvement, if it is one," Beth confessed to both Constance and Ella without looking away from Baby Fanny. "But small improvements make for great impact, I suppose, if there are enough of them."

"Bless your grateful heart, Bethlehem," Constance said. "It isn't often one is as natural to exaltation as you are. I aspire to it, truly."

"Only focus on what's been done for you, and not *to* you, I think. I wish that I could do it more often, but Jo's writing has sometimes given me food for thought on the matter."

"What do you mean?" Constance asked.

Beth paused for a moment, wondering if her present company were appropriate for sharing these particular thoughts. Ella would more than understand, of course, so there was no concern there. It was Constance. The young woman was kind, but in a world where some could afford it without sacrifice, kindness was not enough. Beth had gotten to know the young woman a bit better than her sisters had, though, and while Meg and Jo were understandably standoffish with the missionary teacher, Beth had hope for her. Simply being in the colony was not proof of sacrifice or right motives, both her older sisters had pointed out after the unfortunate matter of Constance speculating on what might be best for Amy's education. Beth believed, though, that regardless who she'd been when she'd arrived, Constance Evergreen was changed by being here. That was a good sign.

There was a very good chance that Constance would not understand what Beth said next, but—if nothing else—she would at least hear it. Mammy often read the Bible to her and Amy, and it said that there are some who plant seeds, and others who water them. It gave Beth a peace in doing good. Whatever someone's immediate response, there was always a chance that later, they would be elsewhere nurtured, and though she would have no way of knowing, it meant that Beth's investment would not have been in vain.

"Do you think, then, that there is ever cause to focus on what one has suffered?" Constance asked.

"The *Christian Recorder* wrote of Jo's latest newsletter," Beth began thoughtfully.

"They even published an excerpt!" Ella said.

"They did, and in it, Jo wrote of the gratitude that's been stolen from those who must themselves keep the offenses against them in mind. That damage that is done when, because of the guilty party's refusal to acknowledge their crimes, the offended must keep a record and remind them." Beth paused a beat, and then concluded, "As Blacks in this country will, if all the nation does not repent of the great sin of slavery."

"And," Constance began timidly, "do you agree?"

"I do. When something is true, one has little choice."

Constance looked out the open window shutters, her knee settling and the quiet baby with it. Through it, she watched Amy March leap in front of her sister, Jo, and then whimsically glide across the avenue, her arms extended, one behind and one in front of her.

"Can something be true if it contradicts the scripture?" Constance remarked. "Love keeps no record of wrongs, and we are called to love our neighbors."

The missionary teacher was fortunate it was this March sister she spoke to. Beth was not indelibly good or impossibly pure the way some needed to think she was to excuse that they could be like her if they were willing to give up certain vices, but she *was* patient. She wasn't often taken aback by failures, in herself or others. It was perhaps not a character trait as often recognized as her others, but she did not expect perfection in others, and it meant she was able to conceive of people ending up far from where they'd begun. It was a gift no one deserved, and that made it easier for Bethlehem to offer to all.

"It's difficult to let those who held the scripture hostage and warped it to justify enslavement and treachery stand as authorities on its meaning. I don't mean to imply that there isn't a true and certain meaning, but it will rarely be championed by the same people who distorted it in their favor."

If Constance could fathom how to reply, she didn't share it with Beth and Ella, which was best.

"If we were loved by our neighbors, there'd be no record to keep, after all," Bethlehem said, in the graceful way that perhaps only she could. "Jo's talent has illumined many a simple phrasing that I once took for granted, and I'm glad to apply my storied gratitude to her for that."

She smiled and opened her arms to Fanny, who leaned forward into them, and Constance gave the child over. When the front door opened, the missionary teacher stood.

"Good day, Joanna. Hello, Amethyst."

"Constance," Jo said with a nod, and then opened her mouth wide toward Baby Fanny in an excited salutation.

"I've just been visiting with Bethlehem," Constance said while the three March sisters greeted Ella and then fawned over her child, taking turns kissing or nuzzling her neck without taking her from Beth's lap. Constance waited a moment, but no one seemed to notice that she hadn't taken her leave. "I'd hoped to visit with your mother, as well, and Amethyst."

The flurry of coos and peek-a-boos quieted, and the sisters turned their attention to the missionary teacher still standing in their front room.

"Why?" Jo asked. It hadn't been very long ago since Constance had spoken to Meg about Amy, in an attempt to add the youngest March to her classroom. Meg hadn't asked the missionary teacher to mind her own business, but she had made clear that a thoughtful decision had already been made, and that Amy was a capable enough student to perform her studies at home. Jo hadn't been there, but she wished she had seen Meg tell the woman no, even if pleasantly.

"It isn't about schooling." Constance made a stern wave of her hand, as though to ensure she'd not broach that subject again. "It's something else."

"Am I sick now as well?" Amy asked, her shoulders pinched high and her eyes wide.

"Of course not," Constance replied quickly, and at the sight of Joanna March's slight scowl, she clasped her hands together against her wide skirt and nearly curtseyed in apology. "I didn't mean to frighten you. In fact, it's something wonderful—at least I hope you all think so."

"Tell us, then!" Amy demanded, already happy, and already convinced that this wonderful something would change her life entirely.

Both doors of the March house opened before Constance

could begin, the front door as calmly as whenever Mammy returned home in the late afternoon, this time with Meg beside her, and the kitchen door as though blown open by a cyclone.

"Jo!" Lorie's voice erupted into the space before he could reach the great collection of women, and he was nearly tumbling when he made it into the room.

"What is it?" she asked, beside him before her eldest sister and Mammy were even properly welcomed.

"Come and see," he said between breaths, grabbing the hand she'd naturally extended to him.

"Have you run here from the shore?" she asked, laughing.

"Can't you tell?" he answered, and then he pulled her back through the house, and out the kitchen door, the two of them a hurrying, raucous whirlwind that left a startling stillness in their sudden absence.

"They are chaos itself," Amy said, shaking her head.

Meg said nothing, but she glanced discreetly between all who remained, to ensure they didn't all look at her. She couldn't say why she thought they would, or why the addition of two women who were not her sisters made her feel even more self-conscious over Jo's romantic fortune.

"Was there news, Miss Evergreen?" Mammy asked, when she realized the white girl was still there.

"None pertaining to Bethlehem's condition, as yet, Mrs. March. I only wish there were," she said, and then pressed on before some other event could distract the family again. "But there was something else I'd hoped to discuss with you.

Another way I might be of use to your girls. Amethyst, specifically."

The young girl beamed, nearly trembling with excitement now that the attention was on her and Constance was preparing to describe the wonderful something she could sense.

"I have a sister myself," Constance said, and she smiled warmly when she did. "Hortense."

It was an awful name, Amy thought, but she didn't let it distract her.

"She and I were given dance lessons from a very young age, though grace didn't take with me, I'm afraid. I had to go in search of my purpose, but Hortense was something of a prodigy. She was a natural, and it isn't just family who thinks so. She's done quite well for herself, not just in New England, but abroad. She's studied in Paris and further east, before returning to our home as a celebrated teacher and performer. I'm in awe of her, really. There are few who aren't. She shepherded her very first student to a placement in London!"

Constance took a breath.

"Do forgive me," she said self-consciously. "I don't mean to be so excitable, it's just that I've wanted to speak to you about Amy's love of dance from the first day I saw the girl move." Constance's brow furrowed then. "I daresay it hadn't occurred to me that negro children could be so naturally predisposed to something that I dedicated time and effort to." She stopped abruptly, realizing how quiet the family had fallen. Her eyes widened as though the last confession only seemed improper now that it'd been spoken in their company.

The March women did not rescue her. They did not speak or smile to ease Constance's palpable discomfort when their own had not been considered.

"I have learned a great many things since coming to the colony," she said after a moment. "Chief among which, I think, is that it is impossible to know what people are capable of until they are free. It will be hard work, of course. To truly succeed as a dancer, one requires diligence and sacrifice, of course, but more than that, Hortense has convinced me that there must be an irresistible tenaciousness. It's that tenacity and adventurous spirit that made me at first want to teach Amethyst myself, I now realize. It's why I'm convinced that she should go. That she must."

Mammy's arm curled around her youngest daughter before she felt herself move. "That Amy should go where?"

"To Massachusetts," Constance answered through an exhale. She felt a weight was lifted, having finally shared her conviction with the family. "To Boston."

Amy's mouth gaped, and her eyes sparkled back at Constance.

"Dear me," Beth said, hardly above a whisper.

"Why should Amy go to Boston?" Mammy asked.

"Why?" Constance echoed, the bridge of her nose wrinkling before she willed her face to ease. "To study under my sister, at her dance school. I think she must."

"I think so, too!" Amy exclaimed, and Mammy turned.

"Quiet, child," she said sharply before returning her attention to the missionary teacher. "Who are you to think what we must or mustn't do?"

Constance's brow curled again, the pale skin around her eyes already tight because of her taut hairstyle now looking pained.

"My husband built the house you're standing in, Miss Evergreen," Mammy continued, "and he means to find us here when he returns from war. And he will. The Marches don't mean to move north, not now and not when the fighting's done. Our place is in Roanoke, and Amy will dance here, if she must."

"I didn't mean to suggest the family move north, Mrs. March," Constance said quickly, seeing with some surprise that the idea was as offensive to the woman as it was to those back home. "I meant just Amy. And only to study."

"Yes!" Amy exclaimed again, this time with an involuntary bounce.

"Hush," Meg said this time. "Constance, my sister may be clever and tenacious, as you say, but she's also a child. Perhaps she wasn't in the old life, but we've decided that she will be for as long as we can sustain it. You can't think my mother would send her away at such a young age. To a strange city, no less."

"To Boston," Constance insisted, as though she could not see where she was going wrong. "It's one of the most accomplished cities in the nation, and perhaps the world. There's hardly cause to think it strange, in fact. It's perfectly safe in Boston—"

"For you." Meg silenced her at last. "It's perfectly safe *for you* in Boston. You've no idea what it would be for her. And having received a valuable education yourself since coming to Roanoke, I trust you'll forgive us that we could never take it on your authority that our fourteen-year-old Black child would be well cared for, as she's accustomed to being."

There was so much more that Meg wanted to say, so much more that she would say, if she had Beth's calm, or Amy's tenacity, or Jo's courage.

She would speak of the audacity it required and of the utter inconsideration on display when one stood before a Black mother and told her that her child must go anywhere without her. Brutal people had done it to the enslaved for centuries, and though Constance Evergreen did not look brutal, and though she was no enslaver or auctioneer, neither had that wealthy Southern girl been who'd stood before Meg and callously proclaimed her intention to steal her away from her family. Meg didn't want to be reminded of it, only here Constance was, conjuring up the same image and the same heart-stopping fear, all while seeming so elated and self-satisfied. All while expecting immediate gratitude, because she did not know what it felt like to be on the receiving end of those words, and she never would.

It seemed there was no age or gender among white folk that made them take care with Black people, or understand when they were causing them pain.

Meg said none of it, the way she knew she wouldn't.

Lorie had stolen Jo away, so *she* wouldn't say it, either, in far more impacting and impressive words, and Meg tried not to abuse herself for what would go unsaid, especially when Amy was already crying.

The youngest March girl had made up her mind to go, even if Boston were on the other side of hell, but as the beloved child in a family, she was acutely aware that very little was up to her. She felt on the verge of hysterics and only holding her breath kept it at bay. It wouldn't do. Mammy wouldn't be swayed, for one thing, and it would be a terrible display and reflection on her mother to do so in front of a white woman, familiar missionary teacher or not. Amethyst could only stay inside the arms Mammy had protectively clenched around her and silently weep while Beth and Ella looked on, Ella cuddling Baby Fanny close.

When Amy had daughters, if ever she did, she would let them do exactly as they wished, she promised herself.

"I fear I've said this all wrong. I would escort her myself," Constance pleaded on the girl's behalf. "I've already written to Hortense about her, and my sister has agreed to waive the entirety of the fee, if Amy lives in the dormitory, and helps with the wash from time to time—"

"My child will not be a washerwoman," Mammy interjected, sternly and with finality. "She will be a child."

"But she wishes to be a dancer," Beth said at last. "She can be a child and a dancer, can't she?"

"She can dance in Roanoke." Mammy didn't look away

from Constance in answering her daughter, but one of her shoulders slipped low.

"Or," Beth said, in her gentle way, "she could be taught, in Boston. Where none of us has ever been able to go."

"We don't all wish to move away," Meg said.

"But perhaps, given the opportunity, we won't all wish to stay." Beth looked from Meg to Mammy, her face bearing an open expression that no one could think combative or unsympathetic. She did not mistake her mother's justified concern for ignorance or anger, as Constance seemed to. If anything, she thought the teacher very slow to learn. She repeatedly made requests concerning Amy, whether to teach her personally or to whisk her away where someone else in her family could. She might not have seen the organized institution of slavery, but being from the North did not mean that Constance Evergreen was a different kind of white woman. Beth—and indeed all Black people—had seen the kind of benevolent attentiveness that made them projects or pets, and either way they were less than autonomous people, and as ever expected to perform.

To Constance's good fortune, Beth was capable of overlooking the familiar motive in favor of considering the wishes of her little sister, and so she said to her mother and eldest sister, "Wouldn't this new life be glorious if we were each allowed a wish of our own?"

Amy lifted her chin and looked through a curtain of tears at Beth's face.

"I'll escort her," Bethlehem said. "I'll make sure she's looked after, and I will be the washerwoman, if it means Amy can learn new ways to dance."

The room was still for a moment, Constance and Amy holding their breath while Beth's suggestion calmed her mother.

"You're good to her, Bethlehem," Meg said. "No one could ever question that. But you must know having both her youngest gone would break Mammy's heart. I think suggesting it has done enough to convince us both that perhaps it must be considered, for Amy's sake."

Meg looked at her mother to confirm her suspicion, and Mammy laid her fingers across her own lips.

"I can't take you," Meg told Amy. "I have students of my own, and work to do here. And besides being young, Beth isn't always well."

"But Jo . . ." Amy followed her eldest sister's thinking, interjecting in a voice that squeaked as though it had been previously trapped. She spun in her mother's arms, her eyes pleading with Mammy. Meg looked, too, though she could feel Beth's thoughtful gaze on her.

"Jo's pen might've taken her north anyway," Meg said. "Her writing is a credit to the colony, but perhaps there are possibilities for her work beyond our community's needs." She drew in a steadying breath so that she did not glance at Bethlehem. "And you wouldn't need to worry over them, if her Lorie went as well."

"They aren't married, Meg," Mammy said, but her voice was too soft to be chiding.

"I only meant he could escort them both," she clarified.

152

"And perhaps there is work he might do there, too?" Meg raised a brow at Constance, and the woman reanimated.

"I'm sure there is. I'll see to it at once, if it means you'll consider letting Amethyst go," she said, inclining her head toward Mrs. March and tightening her clasped hands as though in fervent prayer.

Mammy looked from Meg to Beth and, finally, to her youngest daughter, Amy.

"I suppose there's no harm asking if the boy could do some work. If he'd even agree to go."

"He belongs to Jo," Meg said, and she tried to lace some measure of sweetness around the words. "And Jo adores her baby sister. She'll want to go," she promised Amy, "and he is sure to follow."

She smiled then, though her heart pinched. The smile wasn't broad or bright, but it held until Constance Evergreen had said her goodbyes, and Meg could slip into the kitchen to see to supper.

Jo and Lorie had not gone a day outside each other's company since the reception. He'd taken to working some portion of the week with Jo, building houses in the village. Whatever his tasks had been before their meeting, they must have fallen to someone else. He didn't abandon his mother, and when he came to Roanoke he was sometimes later reaching the island than he'd hoped or left sooner than he would've liked so that he could be of use to her. Though he lent himself to work on their behalf, he was gracious in refusing things from the colony when they were offered, since rations and clothing were only supplied to those who lived on the freedpeople's site. Those living at the big house or other confiscated and otherwise unofficially inhabited places had to fend for themselves, and Lorie insisted he was capable of doing so.

"There isn't any need for that. Why not bring your mother and live here now?" Jo had asked days ago.

"Because I don't have a mind to," Lorie'd answered, and Jo had to stop her work so that she didn't smash her thumb with the mallet.

"She'll swear she misheard him," Honor Carter quipped from his seat on the frame above their heads, guffawing so as to get his brother's attention. Wisdom had taken to self-conscious quiet around Jo since dancing with her sister, and he gave his brother a half smile, but otherwise pretended not to overhear. "I never thought I'd see such a look on your face. You honest-to-God didn't think he could refuse you, Joanna. I'll be. Maybe you should have kept to Yann after all."

"Careful," Yannick said, making an offending gesture at the young man whose long legs dangled overhead. When it wasn't enough to quell Honor's laughter, Yannick lifted his mallet as though reminding the young man that he had one.

"Careful, says the French boy with the broken heart," Honor shot back, through a laugh. "Don't feel bad, Yann, until this fellow came along, we thought she despised all men, not just you."

"You can't help but disparage the name your mother gave you, Honor," Jo said, putting a snide emphasis on it. "What an embarrassment it'll be if my sister is fool enough to love your dog, let alone your kin. I pray God send Joseph Williams back to Roanoke and spare my family the shame. He could lose three limbs and still be more a man than any Carter. Or did you think one dance was all it took to woo a March?"

It hadn't been what Jo intended to say. She'd meant to defend her friend's reputation by explaining that Yannick had never wanted more from her than friendship, and that he suffered no broken heart on her account. She'd meant then to ignore Honor Carter completely and finish the conversation he'd interrupted with his dim wit, but there were only so many times she could hear the same ridicule or suffer the same insults just because she was not more like her eldest sister. It hadn't occurred to her to dispute the insinuation around her and Lorie, as Lorie was the only person on earth who needed to understand their bond, and, happily, he did.

It didn't matter what she'd intended, though, because Wisdom Carter heard what she said instead. He didn't lift his head, he just made a kind of stutter step, as though unsure how to walk away. When he did manage to leave, it was with an awkward gait, and under the watchful gaze of young men he'd have to see the next day and the next. His brother swung his leg over a beam and leapt down from the frame, scowling at Jo before following.

Yannick shook his head without saying at what or whom, but went back to his work, and Jo was left with a certainty that she hadn't overreacted, but that the precision of her counter would always overshadow an impotent attack.

Now, days later, Lorie half led and half pulled her to the shore, and Jo recalled the way the conversation had begun that day at the build.

"Just tell me your news!" she exclaimed when they finally slowed, Lorie collapsing forward so that his chin nearly met his chest, his hands on his knees. "Have you changed your mind? Will you bring your mother to the island?"

"What? Of course not," he said, shaking his head while his breath escaped him in quick bursts.

She looked at him quizzically, raising her hands as if to question either why not or what else it could be.

He gestured wildly in reply, and it might have been comical if it made any sense at all.

"What?"

"This!" Lorie finally collapsed into a small boat that had been pulled ashore without being properly moored or stowed. "I wanted to show you this! It's ours!"

"Ours?"

It wasn't long enough to accommodate his size in recline, and Lorie threw his legs back over the side of the vessel and sat up, slapping his hands against the wood.

"For Beth to come and go as she pleases, without bartering with fishermen or ferries, and without waiting on soldiers who'll only take her across if they need her sewing machine. And so that I can travel freely as well. Or take new work, on the water, I don't know!"

Lorie watched a series of expressions travel across Jo's face.

"Isn't this wonderful?" he almost demanded.

"Yes. Yes, Lorie, it's . . . Beth won't know how to thank you. And Mammy. It'll mean so much, and that you thought of her at all."

"But?" Lorie's shoulders sank, but his mouth curved as though to smirk.

"But nothing!"

"Except?"

"I don't know," she hesitated, drawing out the words. "It means you've spent valuable coin or something else on a boat to cross the sound when you could very well cross the sound for good."

"Or you could."

"What?"

"You see, it's that confusion that confuses me. You think nothing of asking me to come to the colony, but you've never considered coming back with me."

Jo's forehead was a landscape of wrinkles and folds, and she could not keep her head from shaking.

"Why would I go backward?" she asked, though it was more a statement than a question.

"Why would returning to the big house be going backward, if I'm there? Is this colony the only way forward, then?"

Jo shook her head intentionally now. There were too many paths and diversions for one conversation. The life she was crafting in the colony and through her pen was evidence

157

enough that progress was always a precarious and temperamental thing. Lately, in trying to communicate with her Lorie, at least about this, it seemed impossible.

"I'm not used to feeling like you and I are at cross purposes, Lorie," she said, looking earnestly enough at him that the young man rose to his feet. "I can't figure out why we suddenly are. And only since I asked if you'd come to Roanoke for good."

Lorie pulled Jo into his arms. They were almost always in contact, arms brushing or lying against each other, one of them leaning their full weight on the other, but their fingers only ever laced together when one was dragging the other somewhere in a hurry. There was no discomfort in proximity or touch, but rarely was it as intentional as an embrace. Still, Jo was relieved. Her face against Lorie's thin shirt, his vest grazing her nose before she pressed it against his chest and kept her hand there.

"We're never at cross purposes, Jo. And I don't think I could ever be cross at you, at all."

"Then what is it?" she said, not wanting to draw away but needing to see his face.

"We think differently of this place, and I haven't wanted to say so." His hand moved slowly up and down her back, as though to console her before he'd said the offending words.

"Of what place? Of Roanoke?"

"Of the Freedpeople Colony," he said, and there was a criticizing emphasis on the word much like the one she'd used for Honor's name.

Now she drew back more completely, the arm that had curved around his back falling limp, her eyes narrowed.

Lorie noticed all of it and let his arms loosen as well, so that she could disconnect entirely if need be.

"I knew you wouldn't want to hear it," he said, "when you yourself write eloquent missives about the necessity and the gravity of this place, when by your own talent it thrives."

"There were others at the colony before my family arrived," Jo replied. "It thrived by their work before mine. I only want to do my part to keep us free."

At the word, Lorie all but grimaced. He rolled his head high so as to keep Jo from seeing it, but the gesture came too late.

"Whatever you have to say, Loren, say it," Jo demanded.

He hesitated.

"Am I Loren now?"

"Am I fragile?" she retorted. "Am I unfamiliar with opposition? Am I not a Black woman in this country, every day? Don't treat me as though I've ever been accustomed to coddling, and I won't treat you like a stranger."

"Pardon me if I don't want to be the thing opposing you, Joanna."

They were both quiet then, and the water lapped at the shore and at the tail of the boat still within its reach.

Finally, Jo took a deep, acknowledging breath and nodded for Lorie to proceed.

"If you insist that I speak my mind, then I'll do it plainly," he said, but then seesawed his shoulders so that his discomfort was obvious. "I'm sorry, Jo. But life in the Union's shadow does not feel free. Congregating around their encampments feels too much like cowering to be that. Being despised by them, or at the very most tolerated, is more than I am willing to endure. And why would I? To be picked off and set to their tasks or to their front lines? It feels like slavery, and I know that life too well to say so lightly. I didn't steal away with my mother, and with dogs at my heels, to settle for half measures, and that's how your colony feels to me. I am sorry, Jo," he repeated. "If it's up to me, I'll never spend a night there, in the barracks, or the village. I'll never accept anything for which white men can demand my gratitude, when they owe me more than can ever be repaid."

She took it all in without speaking. Though he tried, Lorie couldn't divine her reaction by counting the space between or the length of her breaths, nor by watching the course her eyes traveled when they drifted away from him and meandered before coming back.

When she did speak, as on the day at the build, she couldn't seem to say what she meant to. She could only make matters worse.

"I don't know what's more upsetting . . . That you believe that, or that you kept it from me."

"Come now, Joanna," he said, more gently than carefully, though it was both. "Is my position so difficult to understand? I'd think it just radical enough to be yours, if I'm telling the truth."

"I suppose I can't argue with that," she said, but she still stepped away and turned toward the water, and toward Manns Harbor on the other side. "I'm the last person to feel indebted to the Union, or prone to its defense. I live alongside them, for heaven's sake. I know what they're like, and why they're here."

"And yet?" Lorie tried to peek around her shoulder, but he didn't reach for her, to turn her or embrace her again.

"And yet," she said, turning back to face him. "I'm angry to hear you say it. I feel something in me rile up that you would speak that way, about a place my sisters call home."

His eyes fell. "That's the real offense, then," he said knowingly. "Isn't it?"

"I could carve a path of wrath and fire across this entire country, and know that it was just and deserved, believe me. But where would Meg raise her children? Where would Amy dance? Where would we wear Beth's masterpieces, if we refuse freedom except on the purest terms? If I believe the way you do, Lorie, there is no place for us, and no hope. Nothing can be salvaged. No reparations could satisfy the debt we're owed. And after everything you've said, that must sound like grace to you. Mercy, for them. It isn't. It's for my sisters."

"I know that."

"I can be demanding, Lorie—anyone who's read my newsletters knows that. I can be relentless in pursuing what we deserve, and I will be. But I've come to decide that nothing is slavery, except slavery. Otherwise we will never be free."

"That's fair enough, Jo."

"Don't patronize me," she said, smirking so as to lighten the exchange. "It's worse than coddling. You don't have to agree with me, but you must know that what's a half measure to you is a first step to me. It is only failure if you stop there."

The sun was already low, and now it rested on the water. Though it was red and orange, it didn't burn—it glowed. It cast a soft pink across Jo's face, and Lorie admired it, content as much with the words they'd finally exchanged as with the silence that followed it. The tension was released. He knew by the way his breath came easily again. They'd disagreed, but they hadn't detached, and now things were as they were before. Better still, the two of them might find the courage to leap from the cusp on which they'd been teetering.

"The world is bigger than North Carolina," Lorie said, stepping close to Jo again. "We have more to choose from than the big house and the colony, someday."

"Someday," Jo replied, through a relieved breath of her own, and turned her face toward the setting sun.

"For today," Lorie said, turning her chin back toward him, his own dropping low. "It's enough that my whole world is you."

His lips fell gently toward hers, and Jo only turned away in time for them to kiss her cheek.

She didn't close her eyes. If anything, they widened. While Lorie's mouth pressed into her skin, Jo's mind raced, and she needed the distraction of the Croatan Sound, otherwise all her thoughts and questions might have tumbled out. She might have vacillated between disappointment and anger, and said something that she'd regret by the end of the night. She felt the warring reactions swelling up inside her, competing for a chance to be expressed and heard, but each time, she told herself, *Wait.*

Please wait, she thought, her heart pounding, the hand that Lorie rubbed against her back as heavy as stone, applying a pressure she hadn't felt til now.

Wait, she pleaded with her tempestuous self, when she felt him retract that hand.

When finally he pulled back, Jo's eyes flicked up to find his. Perhaps Lorie would speak first, explain what he'd done and what he'd tried to do, and what it meant. Whether he'd wanted to all along, and whether or not he thought she wanted it, too. Whether there was only one way for a young woman and a young man to be connected, when they weren't born as kin, and what she'd thought they mutually understood, they hadn't.

She could cry.

Everything would be different now. It had to be. If he meant what he'd done, then he'd never forgive her not wanting it back. If he was only just realizing that she hadn't meant to claim him that way, then he'd have to revisit all the things they'd said and done, and decide if they were still enough. Perhaps he hadn't known her the way he claimed to, and perhaps he wouldn't want to know her anymore.

She was trembling, and there was a breeze coming low across the water. It might be mist soon, and even though it

was a very short trip to the other side, it might make it difficult to see.

"Jo," Lorie said, and if there were lines in his dark skin, she
couldn't make them out now.

"Yes, Lorie?"

"I am lucky to have you for a friend."

She did cry now. She hoped he couldn't see it, though
she'd never thought to keep something like that from him
before, but there was no masking the way her shoulders
relaxed and her head fell forward.

"I'm in awe of you, Jo, that's all," he said, and though she
couldn't understand it, she could hear that he smiled.

She wanted to lay her hands against him, but didn't.
Where she'd been totally free with Lorie before, now she was
aware. She would worry from here on, over what she did,
and how he might take it. It was her objective now, never to
hurt him.

"I adore you, Lorie," she said quietly, and he lifted his chin
so she could see the boyish smirk on his lips. He couldn't
help the melancholy that stained it, and she couldn't take it
away.

"I adore you, too."

Lorie crossed the sound and Jo did not return immediately
home. She meant to, but she left the shore to the melody
of his boat parting the water and walked back toward the

barracks, which she should have passed to get to the colony's village on the other side.

She didn't.

She hadn't intentionally decided to reflect on what Lorie had said before the kiss, nor did she intentionally look upon the overflowing barracks and the various other buildings closed for the night, but when she caught sight of them, she couldn't help it. It was a safer harbor for her thoughts than recalling Lorie's lips against her cheek, or speculating on what it meant—or what it might require of her to keep the boy she'd claimed.

Jo went where she felt safest and strongest: into her thoughts and among her words.

She was standing just outside two posts that perhaps had been intended as a frame, only there was nothing at the top to connect them. A Union flag had been affixed to one, and it was limp and unenergetic without an evening breeze to set it waving.

The Union's banner should be an unequivocal comfort, many a Northerner will say. Freed Blacks, or those of us still confined who pray freedom stretches far enough to meet us—we should swell with gratitude and bend our knees as though before the cross from whence comes our salvation.

When she recalled the words she'd written in her latest newsletter, Jo still felt as strong a disdain as when she'd woven them together. It took an academic's concentration—a committed study of the world in which she found herself—and a poet's fantasy to put such things to words. She was certain the only reason anyone read them was because they were at first completely incredulous that she could. She hadn't obscured her identity by taking on a man's name before sending her work out, as she might've done were she seeking to be published in some existing journal. Instead, she'd asked that her own letter be included in a single edition of a few progressive papers, and the inquiries had trickled in on their own, each reader aware that she was not just a woman, but a Black woman.

Perhaps it was a kind of sideshow to some, or a screed, but those who held that opinion were not her concern. Others had read and responded, and others after them, so her piercing prose found its audience.

Only the white in America can believe that those of us who've lived terrible injustices can or do make a distinction between the kind of white American who would put us in chains and the kind who would only stand idly by. It is too great a request that Blacks, emancipated or otherwise, look upon the Union flag and feel anything more than skeptical relief. Yes, it is a welcome symbol, but that is because there is an alternative, and that is a truth they would do well to remember before asking one who has spent a single day enslaved to offer gratitude or trust.

A woman wandered out of the dark entry of the barracks and into the evening, a sleeping child in her arms. The little boy was older than Baby Fanny, but still young enough that his arms and legs were soft and round, and he was only heavy because of how deeply he slept. The mother was tired, Jo could tell, but the woman's head fell back a bit while she drank in a full, deep breath, and Jo knew she'd needed the air and the space more than slumber. It was likely pitch black and impossibly cramped inside, and it might have been painstaking and slow just to escape it without stepping on another person, especially while carrying a child she hadn't felt comfortable leaving there, even just for a moment, so that she could breathe.

Jo felt the pressure in her expression, her written words still playing in her mind, and though the woman hadn't seemed to notice her, Jo forced her features to relax, lest the woman think her grimace due to the odor.

There was one, and it could be detected even from where she stood outside the posts. There always was, when many people were kept in close proximity. There had been one at the big house, too, in the library where she and Lorie had passed most of their first night together. She might've told him if he'd stayed with her tonight, and were at her side. Besides that, she'd tell him, the smell wasn't as bad here as it was said to be in so many other places. In contraband camps, and makeshift towns fashioned in a hurry and just as quickly disassembled if the Confederates returned. Here, it had never been unpleasant to Jo, and in any case, it was usually masked by the smell of cooked or cooking food, or of animals, horses owned or confiscated by the officers, though some had come with the freedpeople. Animals were expected to have a smell, Lorie, she might say, and you couldn't mind it. Most importantly, the smell of food meant there was something to eat and safety in lighting a cooking fire.

If there were only barracks, if people poured in by the hundreds and mothers had nothing to look forward to but nights spent traversing wayward bodies just to steal a few breaths of untainted air, Lorie might've been right. If there was nowhere to go in this colony but the barracks, before overflowing into the woods that the soldiers had already cut down, Jo, too, might only have seen the colony's faults. But there were homes. They were building more every day, and there were dozens more now than there'd been a matter of months ago. Each home was not exactly like the one her father'd built for their family, Jo didn't deny that. How could she, when she put her own hands to the building? The swift progress of the village was accomplished by forgoing the luxury of room divisions, so that each new home was a single spacious square with a roof, but it didn't change the fact that Black folk had supposedly belonged to people not long ago, and now there were things that belonged to them.

Jo clucked her tongue, crossing her arms over her chest as though Lorie were right beside her and might see her consternation.

They were only in the shadow of the Union right *now*, but the war would end. When the fighting was over, the soldiers and the officers and the missionary teachers, praise God, would go home. The white folks would return from whence they came, and the barracks and the buildings at the front of the camp could be repurposed. It wouldn't be so cramped, and the odor, faint as it nearly was, would dissipate. The Black schoolteachers like Meg could move their lessons from the tents into these buildings, and then . . . who knew what else.

The mother had retired back inside the barracks while Jo's attention was elsewhere, and Jo began to walk, finally passing between the posts and into the colony.

"These buildings could be storefronts, easily," she told her phantom Lorie, with an exasperated shake of her head. "Instead of walking to the fisheries or all the way to shore, the freedpeople can have our own shops, on land we own."

And she was right. Corinth in Mississippi already turned a profit, and Roanoke could do the same.

Lorie just wasn't looking far enough ahead. He looked at the colony and saw the present. The white presence.

Jo sighed and wished he really were there beside her. She'd lace her arm around his and push her forehead into his shoulder while they walked.

It made sense that he was still too hurt by the recent past to imagine life after it—but white folks didn't define Roanoke. It was called the Freedpeople Colony because that was who it was for.

"How do you not see that?"

They were too alike for him not to, she thought, and then her phantom Lorie said something back.

Then we're too alike for you not to have known the way I love you.

She spun to find that, of course, he wasn't there. She could pretend he hadn't said it, because he hadn't. So Jo turned and walked past the building where her mother worked, and then she picked up the pace.

The village was up ahead, and thin, docile smoke curled in the evening air. Signs of life and community, like the glow of candlelight that created a warm halo over the three avenues and their grid of streets.

There was a warm glow inside Jo to match, and she would see it last. The light and the colony. They would all see it evolve, as living things were wont to do. Instead of fleeing north, the colonies, like Corinth and Roanoke, would see Black people from up north migrating south. Why wouldn't they? If they could live among their people, in safety and certainty, in their own homes, to harvest their own fields, and profit by their own work, and have time away from even the friendliest white citizen so that perhaps in time even the wounds of slavery could heal?

Then he would, too.

"All right, Lorie," Jo said to her phantom friend when she realized she'd already begun composing her next newsletter. She could hear the words coming together, like water after the oar departed. They were meant for a different audience than she had spoken to before. Many of the donors and patrons she'd attracted were white Northerners with complicated motives behind their support.

If nothing else, Lorie's words inspired her to turn her attention away from them. To enlist more than financial support from afar, but rather to encourage citizenship. To invite those who wanted to live in freedom together, as a community. It would show more than Lorie that Roanoke was not a Union camp. It wasn't a wartime sanctuary. It was a new way of life. A new world.

My whole world is you.

Jo stopped before she stumbled.

A conversation from a nearby home swelled up around her, the voices replacing Lorie's. A man and woman were laughing on the other side of an open window shutter, and she didn't have to look to know that they were probably man and wife. Men and women of a certain age always seemed to be.

"Maybe I *am* the odd one," Jo said, but softly since now she really and truly spoke to herself.

She didn't feel odd. She never had. In fact, up until the end of their conversation at the shore, Jo had felt wonderful. She'd begun to feel wonderful again, as soon as she'd put something else at the front of her mind, and she hadn't needed to push Lorie out to do it.

She took a careful step forward, as though testing that there was still ground before her, and then tried to return to walking without having to take care.

"You aren't odd, either," she said of Lorie, and she was sure of that. If she told Meg or Mammy what had transpired between them, she was certain they'd pity him. They'd likely think his attempt perfectly understandable—and in that case, would they think her reaction wrong?

Jo stopped again, at the corner of Lincoln and 4th, as though concerned her mother and sister might see her from there.

She didn't know why, but she felt convinced they could not both be right, and at this very moment, the man and woman she'd heard laughing seemed to blame. The way she loved Lorie and the way he apparently loved her could not both be normal, or else she'd be able to recall a single relationship between a man and a woman that looked like theirs without becoming something else.

If it was Jo's reaction her mother and sister would find odd, then what must they have thought was between her and Lorie all this time? What must they have made of her calling him hers?

"All this time," she whispered aloud. All this time, she'd thought it made perfect sense to everyone, or at least to Lorie and those who knew her best. If it didn't . . .

She didn't know what to do, and that was foreign in itself. She wanted to rush to the shore and find an abandoned skiff to cross the sound, and run all the way to the big house, to find Lorie and ask him for his help.

That the problem had to do with him was what finally weighed Jo down as she walked the final steps back home. No thoughts of the colony, and a new objective, and the fervor that always accompanied one could distract her again.

Something had to be done about Lorie, and Lorie could not help her decide what.

X

THE WEATHER WAS MILD NOW, AND BETH OFTEN SPENT time in the yard, holding one of Baby Fanny's hands while Ella held the other so that the child thought herself a prodigy. She was too young to walk on her own, but it amused the two young women endlessly to watch her dimpled thighs and chunky legs lurching forward, one puffy foot stomping the soft earth after the other, a look of concentration and hubris on the little girl's face.

"She thinks she's doing it all on her own," Beth said, smiling as she and Ella kept their backs bowed so that they could reach the infant, whose tight grip on their fingers did not dissuade her self-satisfaction.

"I'm glad she does," Ella replied, laughing. "I want my help to be so natural to her that she credits it to herself. She thinks she's strong, look at her! Imagine thinking that from birth, Bethlehem. Imagine what she'll do."

Ella released Baby Fanny's hand so that Beth could take them both, watching with a palpable adoration as her friend and her little one twirled around. After a moment, she scooped Fanny up, the baby tumbling over in her mother's arms until her naked belly reached the young woman's lips. When Ella blew against it, Fanny squealed her long, loud baby giggle, and Beth laughed along.

"There's my littlest favorite girl." Wisdom Carter stood just outside the lawn, on the dusty avenue, as though he couldn't cross the property line before being invited.

Ella and Beth straightened, happily, and once acknowledged, Wisdom stepped forward, lowering his head in greeting.

"Who's your favorite of the big girls then?" Ella asked him, bouncing Baby Fanny in the air until Wisdom caught her with an openmouthed smile. "Didn't you hear me, Wisdom?" she goaded.

"I'm saying hello to Fanny if you don't mind, Ella."

He'd let go of the mower he'd brought to hold the baby, and Beth righted it, holding the handles as though she might put it to use herself. She wouldn't. It was the reason Wisdom had come. Or, it was his excuse anyway.

True, the grass was just shy of an unruly length, and in danger of becoming unsightly, but it was also patchy at best. The village had once been forest, and when the trees were felled to make lots, a local sounder of pigs had been employed to turn the earth, rooting around in the soil to find their food. After that, some goats made quick work of the bramble and the harsher stuff. When grass finally began to grow, and before Jo's newsletter sped up the building process and the homes began to sprout up, the occasional grazing of a cow or horse had been enough to keep things trim and in order. Once families began to move in, every animal occasionally set free in the village to graze was tromping down personal gardens, when they didn't devour them first, and becoming a nuisance among clotheslines.

Among the treasures at the big house, there'd been a British mower, though it'd taken awhile before anyone knew what it was. They were accustomed to scythes, which, despite being a long blade completely unencumbered by rollers—and despite that they were swung from side to side—were considered perfectly safe tools. The imported contraption reduced the laboriousness of mowing—which was enough to make folk suspect its effectiveness—but Wisdom had become quite good with the machine. The day that Jo mentioned her eldest sister's concern over how the village would keep itself tidy now that it was being properly inhabited, Wisdom became the colony's lawn man.

He'd showed up first to the March house, with his short coily hair parted neatly on the left side as a symbol of his new professional station. He'd begun working before anyone knew he was there, having not announced himself and requesting no pay for the service. Meg only spied the tall young man once he'd started on the lot across the avenue, and when she stepped outside the front door, she saw his handiwork.

Now Beth held his machine upright while he tossed Baby Fanny over his head like she was his own. Wisdom didn't have any children yet, and he wasn't courting the child's mother, but he couldn't help entertaining the young ones whenever he came upon one. He had a mild enough manner that the sight delighted people, and so long as the child didn't shy away from his company, he was looked upon like any other young person obviously looking forward to starting a family of his own.

"Meg's in the house," Beth told him when Ella had received her baby back, and Wisdom reached for his mower to begin work.

"Is she?" Wisdom's eyes darted to the front door as though Meg might be standing there. Almost immediately, he dropped his gaze, watching his hands twist around the handle.

She hadn't meant to make him self-conscious, but Beth couldn't help but smile.

"Well," he said. "I hope she's had a lovely day. Teaching and reading, like she does."

He stopped speaking, but his mouth remained slightly agape, and then he glanced up at Beth. She offered him the faintest smile, as encouraging as she could make it without causing discomfort.

"I'll be at my task," he said at last.

"All right, Wisdom," Beth replied before following Ella into the house, where she immediately opened the window shutters.

Meg was in the kitchen, removing a cast iron skillet from the stove with thick pot holders she'd embroidered herself.

"Don't you just adore that smell?" she asked at the sound of her sister's entry.

"It's lovely, Meg. Nothing's as fragrant as your sweet bread."

"Well, it'll need time to cool, Beth," she said amusedly when the girl remained. "And you're free from working today, remember? That includes this kitchen. So do not bother asking whether I need any help."

"I haven't forgotten." She laced her fingers behind her back as though to assuage her sister's suspicions.

"Then what may I help *you* with?"

"Well, since I apparently am not permitted to get Wisdom Carter a glass of water, would you please take him one?"

Meg tensed and then tried to recover, though her eyes danced around the room for a moment.

"He never takes long to mow."

When Meg didn't take her hint, Beth made a rushing motion at her older sister until she snapped to action and rushed to prepare the young man something to drink.

She'd gotten all the way to the front step before Meg slowed again, collecting herself while Wisdom applied all of his strength to pushing the mower over the ground, sometimes pulling it backward over the same swatch of earth and mowing forward again if the blade didn't seem to have made an impact.

The young man stopped and used the bottom of his shirt

to wipe his face. He'd only been at the task a few minutes, but it was more strenuous than it seemed a task should be when one had the benefit of an imported invention, and his exposed skin was already gleaming with a light cover of sweat.

"Have something to drink?" Meg asked, leaning forward instead of approaching. When Wisdom saw her and quickly tucked his shirt back down the front of his trousers, she held the glass of water high and then cringed at the entire exchange. "If you can spare a moment."

"Of course I can," he said, releasing the handles, which remained upright because the machine was caught up in some unruly earth. For a moment he tried to lower them, his chin ticking back toward the porch, so that Meg knew he was painfully aware of her gaze, and then finally, he abandoned the thing and made his way toward her, wiping his hands on his pants.

He received the glass with a gratitude too quiet for Meg to hear anything but his breath escaping, and then held it without drinking.

"You're very good with the mower," Meg said, moving around him to look at the work he'd hardly begun.

"It'll be a great convenience, I'm told. If I can learn it."

"I think you're learning quite well."

"I appreciate that, Miss March. A compliment being paid by a teacher." He smiled and looked down at the glass in his hands, though he could just as easily have looked at Meg. "I intend to take your lessons someday soon. If I can ever get my brother to agree to it."

"And if he doesn't?" she asked. "I'm sure Honor can make up his own mind, and you make up yours."

Wisdom gave a soft sniff and raised one side of his mouth. When he finally met her gaze, Meg was smiling, her face too gentle to mean whatever he was accustomed to hearing.

"Although," Meg continued, as though to prove it, "I know what it's like to enjoy a sibling's company. I'm sure you'd enjoy it more if he were there."

"I guess I'll have to grow out of that anyway," he said, and then he looked at her directly for what felt like the first time since she'd come outside. Meg felt her breath catch, but she didn't look away. She'd never let her eyes roam a young man's face before, especially not when he was aware of her gaze, but Wisdom didn't seem to mind. And he was such a handsome boy.

"I suppose," Meg answered, but it was so belated, and it came out so breathy, that even she wondered what she'd meant by it.

Wisdom was still watching her, in that same mild manner that made his love of children something delightful rather than suspicious. His eyes were moving slowly back and forth between hers, as though he was daydreaming, and whatever he'd conjured in his imagination was something serene.

"I made sweet bread," Meg told him.

"I bet no one cooks like you, Miss March," Wisdom said,

and it was so gentle and earnest that she had to stifle a laugh, lest he think she was making fun of him. She wouldn't, ever. In fact, she wanted nothing more at the moment than to share what she'd prepared with Wisdom Carter, and she'd very nearly worked up the nerve to invite him inside.

"Why, Wisdom Carter, I'd no idea those new mowers operated unmanned." Jo's voice broke the space between them. "The things the British think up, my heavens."

As though jolted from a dream, Wisdom pressed the glass of untouched water into Meg's hands and half stumbled back to his machine.

"Hello, Jo," he said, dipping his chin. "Lorie."

"How's the work, Wisdom?" Lorie slapped his back.

"I'll just get back to it."

"Anything I can do to help?" Lorie asked while Jo sidled up to her sister.

"Poor boy," she said to Meg without taking her eyes off of Wisdom. "Oh." And she turned her nose high in the air as though she'd caught a scent. "You made sweet bread, didn't you? Oh, bless you, Meg."

Jo took her sister's face in her hands and kissed her cheek, until Meg could wrestle away.

"What's the matter?" Jo asked, squinting.

"You'll make me spill my water, that's all."

"Oh." Jo smirked at her. "I thought it was Wisdom's."

"Can I ever have a moment's peace from you, Joanna?"

Jo's neck recoiled as though she'd been slapped. "What does that mean?" she asked, but Meg's brow had already broken, and she'd begun shifting her weight from one side to the other while her eyes welled. "Meg—"

"I'll see to the rest of supper." And she whirled around without saying goodbye to Wisdom, and left Lorie and Jo looking between each other and the quickly closed front door.

If she went after her sister, Jo felt certain the embarrassment she felt would become tangible, and the others would see it, too. She couldn't explain the feeling herself, but that didn't stop it existing, and being as accustomed to Meg's encouragement as she was, it was almost unbearable.

It would've felt awful to be out of step with any of her sisters, but Meg especially—and especially now, when she so needed someone of Meg's maturity and familiarity with courtship and expectation to help her determine if there really was anything wrong with her. While Lorie watched Wisdom work the mower, stepping back and dropping into a squat when asked whether the blade appeared to be turning, Jo swallowed hard. She tucked her thumb into her fist and squeezed, to feel the pressure and then the release.

Amy's voice carried down the avenue, and when Jo looked up the street, she saw her youngest sister coming. She'd been running, and then suddenly threw her full weight into a leaping twirl, nearly crashing when she landed and catching herself on the toe of her brown boots and all ten fingertips as though she'd decided to do calisthenics right out in the open road.

Jo smiled because Amy laughed at herself. From her safe but unplanned landing, the youngest March girl's mouth broke into joviality, and Jo could just hear the trill of it from where she stood. It was why she had told Mammy she'd take Amethyst to Boston. That joy. Even if Jo had no interest in the North, or Constance Evergreen's benevolence, she had an interest in her sister's joy.

Lorie had been there when the subject was broached with her, and he'd agreed, too, on the spot. He said nothing after, about the kiss Jo had spurned. He hadn't asked what it meant if they took Amy north together, and she hadn't offered an explanation. She'd only decided on something she hoped might ensure it never came up again—which she'd planned to ask Meg's opinion on, before whatever had just passed between them.

"Did you see me, Jo?" Amy asked when she reached her sister.

"I did." Jo swept the girl's wayward wisps of hair back from her face, but it was no use. Amy had improved in habits pertaining to her hair, but despite that and despite that the weather was mild now, the amount of exertion she performed each day ensured that she sweat out the hot iron's effect—especially now that she was meeting with Constance several times a week to practice techniques none of them had ever heard of. It was wild in a way Jo would always find more lovely than the neatest flat braid, some hair straight and some reverted back to its natural curl, and tendrils of it framing a face vibrant with enthusiasm.

In Boston, Jo would have to be the voice of Mammy and Meg, though. She couldn't be her tempestuous self, or encourage wildness, not where Amy was concerned.

The distance she would soon travel made Jo glance over her shoulder, though she didn't quite look at the house, or the sister hidden inside.

"Am I quarrelsome?" she asked aloud, and only Amy was there to answer.

"What a question, Joanna." The younger girl took both her hands. "You're angelic. You exceed every wish I've had in a sister."

"That's what I get for asking the sister I'm escorting on a life-changing adventure, I suppose." Joanna brought their laced fingers up between them and then leaned a bit into the sturdiness the hold provided.

"Is my opinion less valuable because I cherish you?"

"Am I less angelic if I've changed my mind about Boston?"

"Jo, I'll die!"

"And there's my answer."

"All right, Joanna, you're quarrelsome indeed."

"Don't pout, Amy," she said with a laugh, and kissed her sister's forehead. "It's not becoming."

"You'd better not become tame and mundane just because you're my chaperone."

"I've promised Mammy I would, and that's a condition of our agreement. Am I quarrelsome or angelic now?" She gave Amy's hands a squeeze.

"You're impossible! Lorie's the one escorting us both."

At the sound of his name, he looked over, and Jo briefly held his gaze before turning back to her little sister. Behind her, Mammy approached, traveling the same path Amy had taken, with a much more reasonable pace and cadence, and no leaps or twirls. Jo wished sometimes that her mother would.

She turned Amy around by the shoulders, and, as expected, the girl sprang to life, waving both hands above her head as though instead of welcoming her mother, she was bidding bon voyage to a ship and its seafaring passengers.

Mammy tucked two envelopes into the waist of her skirt and threw her arms out wide to catch Amy. When she had her youngest in an embrace, Mammy kissed the air at Jo, who blew one back before heading in the house to make peace with Meg before the whole family was together inside.

"May I help with anything?" she asked when she met her sister in the front room. Meg was already placing the sweet bread next to a large serving dish of chicken salad.

"No, thank you," Meg answered, wiping her hands on the apron tied around her waist.

Afterward the two stood without speaking. Beth and Ella could be heard in the room that used to belong to Papa and Mammy, and the tenor of Lorie's and Wisdom's voices wafted in from outside.

"Perhaps Wisdom would like to eat with us," Jo said, with an uncharacteristically awkward cadence.

Meg bit the inside of her lip, but her brow seemed to perk up at the idea.

"He's done such fine work in the yard on our behalf, and the Union doesn't pay him for the upkeep. He should at least have a good meal," Jo finished, to compliment her sister's cooking without seeming too effusive.

"He does, doesn't he?" A small smile tugged at Meg's lips. "Perhaps I'll invite him for supper then," she said, and immediately took steps toward the front door, which opened just before she arrived.

"Hello, my dears," Mammy said as she and Amy entered.

"Hello, Mammy." Meg meant to kiss her mother on the cheek and then slip around her before Wisdom could finish his work and his conversation and be on to the next yard.

"There's a letter for you," Mammy said, and Meg stopped just as abruptly as if her skirt had gotten caught on a wayward nail. "Look, darling! Joseph Williams has written again!"

Meg didn't look out the open front door, but when Wisdom walked past the March house with his mower in his hands, she saw the way he dipped his chin toward her in place of goodbye. She didn't go after him. She didn't turn and look at Jo, either—she only took the letter her mother offered and noticed that on the outside of the envelope, there was a landscape. It didn't cover more than half the paper, but Joseph had drawn what she knew must be Roanoke's shore.

"He's decorated it this time," Mammy said, smiling. "Isn't it lovely, Meg? And despite that you hadn't written back."

"Or perhaps be*cause* I hadn't," Meg said, and her wonderment could not be hidden. She was genuinely pleased while she turned the envelope over in her hands. She'd taken a strong stance, after all, not replying to the sterility of Joseph's last correspondence, and that he'd written again must mean he'd understood.

She had nothing to apologize for, because her excitement

185

returned and fluttered about in her chest despite that she'd been on her way to invite Wisdom Carter to supper. Hoping to one day marry and *being* married were very different things, and she hadn't made a promise to anyone, nor had she been asked to. She'd done nothing wrong, she was certain. She only wished someone else would say so.

For her part, Jo wanted to say that Meg had done well to withhold her attention from a man who hadn't even taken the trouble to woo her, but she didn't. She didn't want it to come out wrong, as so many things seemed to when she was speaking to those she uniquely loved.

Newsletters were simple matters, it turned out, requiring only that she stand firm in her convictions and in what was observably going on—and going wrong—in the world. These days, Jo had much less confidence in her ability to communicate when the matter was her own heart, and when the feelings of her favorite people were involved. It made her nervous to go so far away, even in service of another sister, in case distance compounded such strains.

Meg did not quite turn toward her sister. She only looked back over her shoulder because she knew that Jo was there, and when Meg had tucked the letter at her waist as Mammy had done, she went back to the kitchen alone.

When the women and Lorie were already sitting at the table or nearby in the front room enjoying their supper and animated conversations, Orange hobbled into the home. He was a stout older man with a bald head and bowed legs, and he rocked as he went, though he refused a cane or walking stick. Ella found a way to wrap her arms around her father's arm when they walked side by side and she leaned into him so that she always appeared to do the work of a tent pole, but honestly he managed fine on his own.

Orange came behind Ella's chair and reached around to kiss Baby Fanny, who was sat on her mother's lap as though it were a throne. When first his daughter and then several others asked him to join them for supper, the man waved them off. He rarely ate at the table, preferring to take his portion and return to the bed Mammy had given up so that he and his family could move in. He liked having his legs drawn up, though the time that Amy had asked for her breakfast to be brought into the bedroom so that she needn't fully wake in order to eat it, Mammy had chastised her laziness. Rules were of course different for adults, especially those advanced in years, and allowances were made for Beth, too, when she was weak.

Orange came up alongside Beth's chair next and unwrapped the kerchief he'd been holding, gingerly taking cooked crawfish from inside and arranging them on her plate.

"Oh," Beth said, smiling up and down the table, and then at the old man himself. "Mr. Orange, thank you."

"Why does he only bring enough for Beth?" Amy asked Jo in a whisper, but her older sister wore a look of quizzical amusement just like all the others, and she only shrugged in reply.

Orange didn't speak, or at least no one in the March family had heard him do so. He must, since Ella often told them her father's thoughts. Sometimes they would overhear a man's gruff timbre when he played with Baby Fanny, but though the sounds he made matched the melody and intonations of a conversation, when they listened closely, the family found they could make out no words.

He was doing it now, making his low and rumbly noises as he transferred the crawfish from his hand to Beth's supper plate, and the young woman inclined her head toward him as though he were merely speaking softly. Whatever Orange meant, she couldn't know without waiting for the old man to finish his task and turning to his daughter. When he was shuffling back to his room, shaking out the handkerchief before tucking it into his pocket, Ella spoke not just to Beth, but to the entire family.

"It's for her condition," she explained. "That's why he brings them just to Bethlehem."

"Crawfish?" Mammy asked, and everyone exchanged glances before returning their attention to the old man's daughter. "For Beth's illness?"

"Daddy's seen it before."

Their eyes or mouths grew wide at the news, though Amy might've been the only one distracted by wondering how exactly Orange had relayed this to Ella. Perhaps he spoke to her through hand signs or by scribbling on a small slate chalkboard like Meg said some of the missionary teachers had brought south with them, despite that Amy had never seen one. She wasn't permitted in the family's bedroom to check, of course, though it had belonged to her parents. And perhaps there was such a thing as transferring thoughts without speech at all. It had happened more than once that she'd meant to say something, and another of her sisters said that precise thing in her place. Though a father and daughter were different, perhaps without a larger family something like that magic had developed between Orange and Ella.

"Go on, darling," Mammy pressed Ella, nearly perched at the edge of her seat and helpless to keep her eyes from darting to her dear Bethlehem. The girl had winced when leaning over the kitchen fire or the watering pump out back for two days before finally confessing a strange pain that seemed to live on one side of her lower back. When told, Constance Evergreen had been confounded, by her own admission, as embarrassed as she was absolutely clueless. Beth seemed to have myriad ailments, she'd said, and none of them connected in any discernible way.

And now an old man who'd never seen the inside of a medical book—or a schoolroom for that matter—was said to have seen it before.

"How much of what Beth suffers has he seen in others?" Mammy asked, not wanting to sound skeptical enough to offend. "We've lived in the house together for a little while now, I know, and certainly your father must've noticed at least a selection of Beth's symptoms. It's just that our nurse has been at a loss because there seem so many, and so inconsistently."

"I've sat with her and Miss Evergreen a time or two," Ella agreed. "And I know it seems to defy a pattern or diagnosis."

It didn't bother Beth to be spoken of in her own presence, something which always frustrated Amy and Jo.

"If not a pattern," she said, her voice lilting with what she hoped might be encouragement, "I've begun to think of it as something like a round. Someone sings, and then after a moment, someone else takes up the melody, but from the beginning, so that even one melody begins to sound like many."

"What a whimsical way to describe chronic illness, Beth," Meg said in a soft voice that was at once adoring and melancholy, and perhaps afraid.

Ella had noticed the way the March women brightened their faces or intentionally lifted their brows and lips whenever discussions turned to the mystery that had befallen their Beth. They didn't seem able to lament or even properly express their worry, when there were so many of them. One never knew who among them would be devastated by the hearing, and so all five lifted their chins when they might have let them fall. They smiled at each other as though they knew when it was needed, and though auctions meant that Ella had not seen her own siblings in years, she felt certain that the March women did know, always, when a heart among them was heavy and in need of care.

"Daddy has kept watch," Ella told them, and then grinned at her child, to lighten the mood for her kin as the Marches had taught her by example. "And so have I. I've seen the fainting, and fatigue, and weakness—"

"Bruises, sometimes," Beth offered, with a pout that didn't linger long. She turned her forearm one way and then the other, though the latest discoloration was finally beginning to fade.

"Aching," Amy said. "Sometimes I try to sleep very still, so that I don't hurt her legs." She lowered her head when she was done, and a quiet fell over the room for a moment. If her sisters had reached for her, the youngest March girl wouldn't have been able to help but cry, so it was a relief that it was Lorie who pulled her off of her chair and onto his lap. She stayed just long enough to lay her head on his shoulder before leaping back to her own seat, her forlorn expression replaced with a wide grin.

"And the trouble in your back." Mammy resumed the listing of ailments. She locked eyes with Beth, as though she'd be able to see into her and find any hidden things. There was a special kind of fear that a mother experienced when she couldn't be certain she knew all of what her child suffered. "You said it felt tight, like a stone had been put there."

"Constance says it's common enough in older patients," Beth said. "And those who are already very ill."

A hush fell again.

"I must drink water regularly, she said, and I do try, but . . . ." Her voice tapered off.

"Beth," Meg urged her. "What is it?"

Beth glanced toward Lorie a time or two and, understanding, he placed his fingers in his ears and began to hum.

When Beth leaned forward, all the women at the table did as well.

"I hate having to get out of bed so often to relieve myself."

At first no one said anything, each holding their breath and the gazes of another. It was Mammy who finally broke, an unladylike snort escaping her before transforming quickly into a laugh. The boisterous sound was met with incredulity from her daughters, Ella, and Lorie, but Baby Fanny—who was unaccustomed to such an outburst from the matriarch—fell into frightened tears.

"Oh, my dear," Ella cooed to her daughter amusedly, turning the child around so that the girl's chubby arms could wrap around her neck.

"Mammy," Meg said, covering her mouth to hide a smile and shaking her head.

For her part, Mrs. March was happy to be so overwhelmed with something other than fear or sadness where her Bethlehem was concerned, and she pushed back from the table as laughter made tight balls of her cheeks, sore already. She came around the table, arms outstretched.

"My funny angel," she said when her daughter stood and with a smile of her own curled into her mother's embrace. Beth laid her head on Mammy's collarbone, so she was the only one who didn't see when the sadness returned, and her mother's face, which had been rouged with her delight, crumpled into tears. "You're my angel, Bethlehem."

"I love you, Mammy," Beth whispered.

Lorie took Amy back into his arms, while Ella hugged her own child close, and beneath the table, Meg took Jo's hand.

Lorie said goodnight when the front room had been returned to order and all the chaos of supper calmed, with Jo and Meg helping Mammy clean the dishes.

Ella put Baby Fanny down with Orange and then relaxed on the bed Beth shared with her younger sister.

Amy hummed to herself while she swayed in the small space still unoccupied. Mammy had taken to sleeping on the floor, and because there was very little room to move about, Amy eventually drifted back out to the front room, or else to the kitchen where her dancing could be admired. Only then did Ella furnish Beth with a tattered pamphlet.

"*About Going To Liberia*," Beth read aloud before turning to her friend. "What's this?"

"Have you heard of it?" Ella asked, and there was excitement in her eyes.

"Have I heard of Liberia? Of course I have. I think everyone must've by now."

"And have you read about it for yourself?" Ella pressed, and Beth's brow crinkled.

"No. I suppose I never had reason enough to, since I'd never have been sent there by an enslaver."

"That isn't the only way Black folk have gone, though,"

Ella interjected, and Beth, seeing that her friend had many thoughts on the matter—enough at least to bring the subject to conversation unsolicited—let her lips rest together in invitation. "I'm sorry, I don't mean to be forceful. I'm overexcited."

Beth gave her an encouraging smile.

"I've been waiting to share this with you. Daddy said the condition you have comes from the continent. Africa."

"What does that mean?"

"It's a condition that white folks don't understand because it doesn't afflict them. Their medicine hasn't yet developed beyond what they experience for themselves."

"I see," Beth said, temperate in her replies until she understood all that Ella had been preparing to tell her.

"It isn't a mystery simply because they have no name for it, Bethlehem. It's proof that you're descended from African peoples, and it's almost like a birthright, inviting you home."

At that, Beth's lips fell. She didn't grimace or give an unpleasant expression, but she no longer smiled.

"Roanoke is home, Ella. The Freedpeople Colony, with my sisters."

"May I confess something to you?" she asked, and waited for her friend to gesture permission. "I don't think home can be found on these shores. Not after what's been done. Not this island, and not the mainland, either. It seems to me that it'd require an inhuman and unfair gift of forgiveness to those still certain that we're inferior, and I cannot offer that any more than I can raise my daughter to do so." Ella glanced up as though surprised at herself. "I'm sorry, Bethlehem. I don't mean to upset you."

"You haven't upset me at all. If anything, perhaps I'm confused. I thought this Liberia place was the hope of former enslavers and Yankees who wish the predicament of Black folk to disappear. I didn't know there were any of us who wished to go there, of our own accord. But I admit I've had very little education on the matter." Beth laid her hand across her friend's and lifted the pamphlet with her other. "I'm happy to have my ignorance cured, if this writing will do it."

"Thank you, Beth. It would mean a great deal to me."

Whatever the two might've said beyond that was interrupted by a frustrated Amy stomping back into the bedroom and closing the door.

"I am quite old enough to be included in delicate conversations, I think," she said before hurling herself onto her sisters' bed. She'd immediately let her face fall into the blanket and then brought it back up with a start to say, "I'll be studying dance in Boston, for heaven's sake, and I should like to be treated with some amount of trust and concern, which isn't too much to ask, at all."

She received only blinking stares in return for all her exasperation, and the girl threw her face back into the blanket and huffed.

Mammy had followed Amy as far as the hall outside the bedroom door to ensure the child had gone out of earshot, and now she returned to Meg and Joanna waiting in the kitchen.

"Please tell us if something's happened to Papa," Jo said when she could wait no longer.

"Your Papa's well, darling. I didn't mean to make you worry over him," Mammy assured her, touching her second daughter's arm and speaking in hushed tones to them both.

Meg held her mother's gaze with an urgent look. "But you've heard from him, haven't you? And you sent Amy away so that she wouldn't hear what he said in his letter. What has Papa said, Mammy?" she asked.

"It's what I told your father, girls, not what he's written back."

"Please, Mammy, my stomach is a tangled mess." Jo crossed her arms against her abdomen as though that might alleviate the anxious discomfort.

"I'm sorry, girls, I haven't meant to drag this out, or make you worry. I just don't know quite how to say it. And I don't know what to believe."

At the sight of their mother's despondent expression, both Meg and Jo quieted their insisting. Whatever Mammy had gathered them to say, and whyever she'd not read aloud their father's latest letter, there was something she'd been worrying over in secret well before tonight. That on its own warranted attention, though she wouldn't ask for it. She was a mother of four daughters, and wife to a man gone to war; Margaret March deserved attending, too.

"Are *you* all right, Mammy?" Meg asked, and touched her mother's face the way the woman had comforted her so many times before. "Is there some way Jo or I can help?"

"I don't know. I feel my worry can't be real, it couldn't possibly be, and I'm not sure I want to pass it on to you. Even if it turns out to be." The woman gasped a little then and covered her mouth with her hand, her eyes closing for a moment so that both her daughters understood just how troubled their mother had become.

"We're the oldest," Jo told Mammy. "Meg and I aren't children anymore, not really. Childhood may be something we can insist upon for Amethyst, but I would rather share your burdens than be spared it while you carry them alone, Mammy. And Meg feels the same."

When Mammy looked between the two, her eyes welled with tears, and then she finally confessed what she'd written to their father weeks ago.

"I've heard the officers discussing Corinth," she began, and Meg felt as though her heart went cold.

Inside her chest, it was just like the bitter night when the southern wind had carried a chill few had ever experienced. It was strange and unexpected, especially for autumn, as it had been then. Meg had been a young child, or else she would have hated herself for the way she longed to be inside. Not inside the shack where her family slept that night, huddled together under a dilapidated roof with too few boards to keep the cold away. When her two younger sisters were already asleep, Meg had squeezed her eyes shut while her teeth chattered and wished that the terrible little rich girl who lived inside the house would wake up in tears, and someone would be sent to retrieve Meg. She would have to get up and walk down the hard gravel of the driveways between the shack and the big house, and then cross dew-soaked grass, which would make her small feet even colder—but at least after that, someone would use thick, plush towels to dry her and then they'd put one of those nightdresses on her and make her climb into a bed so large it could've fit the wealthy Southern girl's whole family, too.

No one had come for her until morning, and Meg had passed the entire night awake and aware of how little the rich girl cared for her, despite what the family would say. When the family began to hastily pack a carriage with as many of their prized possessions as they could, and no one rode a horse up and down the length of the field to ensure the work was done, it was years after that cold night. Meg had stood a safe distance away while the father oversaw his wife and daughter's hurried departure, the only pause when the wealthy girl caught sight of Meg and reached for her. She'd expected Meg to run into her arms. To leave her family and choose the wealthy girl's, or else to weep at the abrupt end to their lifelong pairing.

There were men in gray uniforms there that day, as the wealthy girl and her mother were swept away for safekeeping, though only a few. They did nothing to stop the Marches or anyone else from slipping through the fields and away from the place. The soldiers were readying themselves, though they proved ill-prepared for the Union's arrival.

The Confederates had returned.

That was what Mammy would say.

Their hideous gray had overtaken the Mississippi colony, and the Union had been beaten, and the tide of the war had turned, and freedom was at an end.

In the moments between Mammy's words, Meg saw everything she'd escaped, and worse, spilling into their colony and claiming them back. She saw the wealthy girl reaching for her, and though Meg had already lived it once before, she had not thought to live in fear of the old life returning. Now Mammy must be preparing to tell her that it had.

She was a silly girl, indeed. There'd been no need to worry over Joseph Williams, or Wisdom Carter, or whether it was indiscreet to dance with one man while corresponding with another. The worries that had dominated her thinking vanished, made too small to matter by recalling that but for the one of them who'd been permitted—forced—to take lessons with a terror of a wealthy Southern child, it had been prohibited not so long ago to write letters at all.

"Mammy," Jo said breathlessly, and she seemed to fall back a step, steadying herself on the stove behind her.

Meg looked at her sister, who turned her incredulous gaze away from the nothingness of the middle distance to meet her. Meg had been swallowed up in her terrible thoughts. She hadn't heard a word of what her mother disclosed to them. She only knew by Jo's reaction that it was terrible enough to match her fears.

"What is it?" she asked her sister.

"Haven't you heard her?"

Mammy's hand was in front of her mouth again, tears already on her face. She could not repeat the words.

"Jo, what did she say!"

"They're going to undo Corinth." Joanna's voice was gravelly at the end, as though it was suddenly difficult for her to speak, or as though the tears that did not well in her eyes must have lodged in her throat.

"The Confederates," Meg whispered when she lacked the breath to give the words volume.

"No, Meg. The Union." Jo took their mother in her arms so that the stove could support both their weight. "The Union is going to evacuate the colony when the troops there are called away."

For a moment Jo studied her sister, trying to find something in Meg's unresponsive eyes, before she gave up and watched her own arms tighten around their mother, pressing her face against Mammy's hair.

"That's what the officers say, at least. It's what Mammy's been overhearing while she works."

"But"—Meg turned her chin as though she might shake her head, but didn't—"Corinth makes a profit."

That was the pride of the Union and freedpeople alike. Corinth had become a proper town, cultivating hundreds of acres of farmland, earning thousands of dollars each month. It was nothing if not a remarkable success. And it was home to so many freedpeople, to wives and families of Black men who now served in the Union army.

"But why? If it's true at all," Meg insisted. The cold in her chest seemed at last to shrink, smothered by a heat she was unaccustomed to, and it allowed her voice to lift, and for her limbs to reanimate, though she couldn't think what to do with them. When she gestured, they were jerking movements that betrayed the depth of her frustration. "Then *why*? Why would they dismantle such a labor, simply because the army is deploying somewhere else? Why? When so many have made it their home?"

Jo couldn't help but think of Lorie, and everything he'd said the night he'd kissed her. As always, she was almost sure he was with her, even when he wasn't, and when she spoke next, it was in agreement with him.

"Because they have no more respect for our labor than the Confederacy does," she whispered bitterly.

"It can't be true," Mammy said, almost too softly to hear. "It can't be. Where would we go?"

At the question, the cold that had threatened Meg's heart returned, infesting Joanna as well. Because that was the great terror, if the news was true. If Corinth was profitable and had been written of and lauded by Northerners and abolitionists as a wonder and a prime example of what freed Blacks could build once their citizenship in this nation was instated properly . . .

If Corinth could be remarkable and then callously disassembled . . . evacuated . . .

Then so could Roanoke Island's Freedpeople Colony.

"*If* it's true," Jo said, grounding her older sister with the declarative tone she used. "A rumor—even one passed around among soldiers—is only a rumor. Right? It isn't gospel truth simply because it's conveyed by men."

"If it's true at all," Meg replied, and she nodded, her voice working toward steadying.

"If it's true," Jo continued, "it isn't true tonight, at least. Corinth is still an example. It is still an operating and profitable farm, and town, and home to freedpeople who've carved pride out of their new freedom."

Despite the way Meg had envied her confidence and conviction lately, Jo's clarity anchored her now. She nodded again, and kept her sister's gaze as though everything depended upon it, even if it only seemed to. That Jo was here beside her when she heard what might be terrifying news did make all the difference.

Jo stopped speaking before the more difficult words could scuttle free. Because at news of Corinth's potential fate, she had to wonder whether their success wasn't part of the problem, even for the Union. If there wasn't something undesirable about how quickly Blacks could accomplish the unexpected, once the chains were removed. She hadn't thought to worry what impression their triumphs would make, their happiness and productivity, until now.

She could not help but meditate on it while her older sister went into the backyard to fetch their mother some water.

"What did Papa say?" Meg asked their mother upon returning. Mammy had regained her composure enough to stand on her own, though once she'd had something to drink, she held one of her daughters' hands in each of her own.

"He sends his prayers, and a promise. That he'll come home at the first possibility, and see that our home is not disturbed, regardless of how the Union effort moves on and away. And he says to send you and Amy on to Boston."

"Mammy, how could we leave now?" Jo argued, dropping her voice when it threatened to raise too much.

"Bethlehem was right. We must all pursue each new opportunity," Mammy said, and then she drew in a shaking breath. "Especially now, when we aren't sure anything is certain. I want nothing more than to have all my children close to me, all the time. But if the war does not end as we've all hoped, I think I would be more at peace to know you were north. I only wish Beth were well enough to go, or that you all could." She looked at her eldest.

"I couldn't leave my students," Meg said. "My teaching seems more important than ever now. And I wouldn't go north to depend on the charity of a white family, even Constance Evergreen's."

Mammy nodded. Meg was right, and her hope in sending all her daughters to safety was unreasonable. "I'm only terrified what it will mean if any of this is true," she said. "If it can happen to Corinth . . ."

"Even if what the officers say comes to pass," Jo told her mother, "Corinth is not our colony's only inspiration. Our fates aren't aligned. *We* will decide what becomes of Roanoke

Island, those of us who've lent our service and our love to *this* colony. Please trust in that, Mammy, and I will, too. I'll take Amethyst to Boston, and I'll write, pleadingly if I must, and be mild and kind, the way only Meg and Beth are, if it means I can make the least difference."

"Joanna," Mammy said, smiling despite the heaviness on their hearts. "I have a Meg and a Beth. I need my Jo, too. The whole world does. I hope you won't change too much, ever. I hope you'll pass through life's gauntlet of trials with all your passion and fire intact. 'We are all members of one body,'" Mammy quoted the Bible, "'but with different purposes and gifts.' Only you can accomplish yours."

She was tired, and after her exhorting words, which Jo accepted with a grateful squeeze of her hand, Mammy slouched as though only just realizing how much. She bade her eldest daughters goodnight, kissing them each before retiring to their bedroom.

Jo hoped that Meg would linger when their mother was gone, though she didn't know how to begin. She was entirely unprepared when Meg did.

"The world is constantly changing, it seems," Meg said, looking at nothing at all. She at least breathed evenly so that Jo knew she was only in concentrated thought, and not over-whelmed the way Mammy had been.

"It is," Jo answered.

"Are you ever terrified?" Meg looked at her now, suddenly.

"Of course I am. How could I not be sometimes?"

"I suppose it just looks different on you. On everyone. We're different, as Mammy said."

Jo could sense that there was something more that her sister wanted to say, and she waited.

"I would never forgive myself if I let the world change in ways I cannot foresee, and our relationship with it, without offering an apology to you, Jo."

"An apology for what? I know I'm quarrelsome—"

"You aren't."

Now Jo tilted her head at her sister.

"All right," Meg said, through a soft laugh. "Sometimes you are. Or tempestuous, as you say. But there's nothing wrong with that. And it isn't to blame for the hurt between us."

Meg took a deep breath.

"I suggested that you escort Amy north," she said, so ashamed that she lowered her chin until it was nestled against her chest. "You and Lorie, both."

"Is that so wrong?" Jo asked carefully. Her sister's confession seemed a burdened one, and it meant that there was some offense. She felt a strange unease to have agreed to the task when there had been an unknown motive, but she could not for the life of her determine what it could be. "I've no qualm with taking Amy, and it makes the most sense. How else would she have gone otherwise?"

"Mammy wouldn't have let her," Meg blurted, her eyes closing for a moment before she forced herself to look her sister in the eye. "She wasn't going to go, and it wouldn't have been the end of the world. I suggested you escort her . . . so that *you* would go."

When Jo's heart shrank, Meg saw it. She saw the hurt in the eyes looking back at her. She saw the crease between Jo's brow, as though she'd been pricked by the doctor's needle. She wouldn't cry; Jo rarely did. But that didn't mean she didn't suffer.

"I'm so sorry, Jo."

"What have I done?" she asked quietly. "Whatever it was, I didn't mean to. I try to take care with people, especially with you, Meg," she carried on, speaking quickly when Meg shook her head as though she might interrupt. "And I know I'm not very good at it, but I do try. I don't ever want to hurt one of my sisters. Who else will love me the way my sisters do?"

"Lorie," Meg answered, and that quieted them both. Finally Meg's shoulders sank and she leaned all of her weight against the wall beside the back door. "I'm sorry, Jo. You've done nothing wrong. You've only fallen in love, when I wanted it so badly, and you came by it so easily."

Jo went rigid, but kept her tongue.

"I had no right to take personally your fortune, Joanna, and I'm ashamed that it's taken me this long to apologize. There are no excuses . . . but I do believe it's that I think so much more highly of you than I do of myself."

Whatever stamina had kept Meg from exhaustion seeped out of her, and she slid down the wall to sit on the kitchen floor. Tonight, her mother had cried over the terror of Beth's illness, they'd been advised that white nurses would never help them unravel it, and then Mammy had told her and Jo in confidence that life in freedpeople colonies was not as certain as they'd dreamt. It was news that made her want to be close with Jo again, but it was all so taxing, when taken together.

"We're never given the privilege of facing one difficulty at a time, are we?" she said when Jo joined her on the floor. Her sister gave no reply but to take her hand. "I am sorry, Jo. Truly."

"I think I'm just glad to know what the matter's been," Joanna answered. "But I'm so confused. You have not one but two attentive young men—"

"Oh, Jo. I think we all know that Joseph Williams never had such an interest in me."

"Did he say so in his letter?" Jo asked, her voice tinged with a budding anger.

"Not in so many words. But he apologized if he hasn't made clear his dedicated interest in my friendship. And he isn't a villain because we all decided something must be between us before he ever arrived for supper that night." She looked down at their joined hands, and then at Jo. "And I only wanted to impress him because he so impressed you."

Joanna tried to subdue it, but a smile tugged at her lips.

"But we're not the same person, Jo. You charm everyone, and I can only charm a select few." She looked back into her own lap. "You despise the Carter boys as dullards, and I . . ."

Jo smiled completely now and let her forehead rest against her sister's hair.

"And you like the dullard Wisdom," she said, nudging Meg with her head until the older girl smiled, too, but shyly. "Who is not nearly as smart as you, but who could be. He's handsome, and helpful, and looks adoringly at you, as he ought to."

"He looks so adoringly," Meg said, almost whispering it, when she leaned into her sister's head. "But how can I adore someone who does not live up to my brilliant sister's standards?"

"You must allow me to be wrong sometimes, Meg. Especially when it's your own heart's concern." She bit her lip before saying, "And especially when something may be wrong with mine."

Meg pulled back so that both girls had to sit straighter, and when they had, she searched her sister's eyes.

"What do you mean?"

"I mean," Jo said, dragging out the words. "That I haven't fallen in love with Lorie. At least not the way everyone thinks. Not the way the world expects."

"How do you know?" Meg asked, because she didn't know what else to say.

"Because he tried to kiss me, and I turned away." Jo tried not to take offense at the way her sister gasped. "And the fact that it had never occurred to me to kiss him must mean . . . something."

Perhaps the greatest sign that Meg was no longer a child was the good sense she had to let her lips rest together at unexpected news. She and Jo both fell quiet the way they had several times that night, thinking instead of speaking, because they understood the gravity of what they'd heard.

"Are you not in love with Lorie, or do you simply love differently than some of us?" Meg asked at last. "Or have you only thought of love as it's been presented to you? It would be no fault of your own, if you haven't known how."

"I know that I love Lorie," Jo said, her brow furrowed in earnestness. "Because I cannot do without him. I speak to him when he isn't there. But I wouldn't ever have thought to kiss him. Or . . . anything else I suppose follows love. But I want him with me, anywhere I go. I'm excited to go to Boston because he's coming, too."

"Has Lorie changed at all, since you declined his kiss?"

"No. He's taken no leave of me, though I worried he would. He is himself, even when I can't think how to be. Even when I worry it's upsetting to stay so close."

"You must let him decide, Jo."

"But I could make it easier for him, I thought."

"How?"

"The Union pays for hair . . ."

Meg squinted at her sister. "What?"

"I thought," Jo said, rolling her eyes because it sounded as silly as she'd imagined it would. She'd wanted to ask Meg's opinion in case it was a completely daft idea, and clearly it was. "I thought it'd help if I sold it. Not all of my hair," she said, touching her neck because her hair was neatly braided and pinned away. "Just the length of it. I've heard short hair is unbecoming to men."

"And you think Lorie would be so easily discouraged?" Meg asked with a laugh. "He's yours, Joanna. No matter how you maim yourself. But he won't impose on you, will he?"

"No," Jo said. "He wouldn't."

"Then maybe that's enough for now?" Meg asked, stroking Jo's arm with her free hand.

"I hope so," Jo answered, and the sisters rested their heads together again, and passed most of the night there, in relieved silence.

XI

The white men credited with Corinth, and indeed my own Freedpeople Colony at Roanoke, are said to have been driven to do so by grander hopes. They are soldiers and reverends, and sometimes they are both. They are spoken of in their absence, and cast noble shadows even when they are never seen. They may never materialize beyond names on a ledger or in a report, yet I am certain they are promised space in the annals of history. They will be legends no matter how these colonies turn out, because it is not difficult to imagine heroes who look like all the ones christened before.

I must be plain: I am not puzzled by Americans' persistent lionizing of those they've been taught to lionize. What I find curious is the persistent omission of those who by our identity, and because of our heinous oppression, have far grander hopes.

Who hopes more for Blacks than we ourselves?

Whose homes were in Corinth, and still are in the Freedpeople Colony?

Ours.

We have no other homes to return to, if the grand hope of a colony comes to nothing. We have no citizenship that permits us even to move freely throughout the Union to seek a new homestead. Permission must be asked, emancipated or not, and transportation papers supplied. It is not too much to say that, in fact, we are kept—by the grand hope of the white men whose names will be etched in stone at the base of statues crafted in their likeness—in a state of dependency. We are forced to align ourselves and our hopes with those who can see their passion atrophy or transfer and still be merry.

And now Corinth has fallen. Despite hopes and victories, its people have been relocated to other camps and colonies in which they will never find rest, knowing as they now do that such places are impermanent. That such grand hopes are replaceable, when they are held by those whose lives do not depend on them.

To save Roanoke, I must leave it. I must try my hand at buttressing it from the outside. I must *appeal to yet another population of Americans that, though Black, might feel no stake or compulsion toward my colony.*

And yet, from Corinth I have learned that I must consider the impermanence of Roanoke, despite myself. I must, at the back of my mind and to the depth of my spirit, be prepared to have grander hopes than these.

–Joanna March

PART II

XII

February 1866

AMETHYST MARCH HAD AT FIRST BEEN OVERWHELMED AT the prospect of ever navigating the city on her own, and now she was racing through a network of pedestrian alleys to make her lesson on time. It was a remarkable turn of events for two reasons, the first being that she'd worried over the shadows buildings cast when they were fitted so close together, and her imagination had been helped along by the newspapers and the cautions she received from her fellow dancers, and from Hortense Evergreen herself.

Three years ago, she couldn't have imagined rushing up and down alleys without a concern, when she'd lived all of her life before in what turned out to be wide open spaces. Dangers didn't lurk where Amy was from. They were right out in the open, all the time, and one knew just what they looked like. In the North, one was warned that danger lingered in shadows and waited for perfect opportunities, of which there

were many more in the city, because there were so many people everywhere.

The second reason her hasty travel was remarkable was
that, until a few years ago, she'd never seen snow, or at least
not what they considered snow in New England. And if she
had been unaccustomed to the rapid accumulation and hard-
ening of the stuff—which on major avenues was piled knee-
high, and by April would be higher still—she certainly could
not have foreseen becoming so familiar with the harsh winter
weather that she could half run, half skate to reach her destination.

If she fell and broke her neck, it'd be her own fault, given
her particular talents. It was those talents she was being paid
to pass on, and regardless of the neighborhood or race, folks
in Boston were very unforgiving over punctuality compared
to North Carolina. She had no desire to lose her clients, which,
thank heavens, was rather unlikely since she was one of very
few Black dancers with her training. Still, Meg would think
her a grave disappointment to find out that Amy was being
paid to teach—as her eldest sister had only rarely been while
the Union was stationed on Roanoke Island—and that Amy
could not be bothered to arrive on time.

"Careful!"

Amy skidded around a corner and directly into Lorie's
arms.

"You know, if you managed your time better, you might
not have to run on ice-covered paths, Amy," he said.

"I'm hardly ever behind schedule, Lorie, and you know it.

Now let me go before the girls come down to find me!" she said, yanking away, though he was only trying to keep her upright. "And what's Jo still doing here? She'll be late, too!"

"I'm not permitted inside when Mr. Babcock, Esq., is out of the house, or I'd be telling her the very same thing!"

Just as Amy reached the flat face of the Babcocks' brick home, Joanna opened the door and hustled out.

"Amy, you should've been here by now," she said, as they kissed each other roughly because there wasn't time to be delicate or to linger.

"And you should've left," Amy clucked back as they traded places.

"Don't worry, Mrs. Babcock is out, but"—she turned and jutted out her gloved finger, her other hand closing her scarf around her neck while Lorie struggled to keep a second March sister from falling—"do not make this a habit, young lady. You'll only get lucky with Mrs. Babcock's errands so many times."

"I'm not a child anymore, Joanna, I don't require your rearing."

"You're not even seventeen, Amy," Jo threw back as she was pulled away.

"Which is still almost as old as you were when we left the island, so old enough, I'd say!"

"Ladies, please!" Lorie finally interjected. "Can we stop yelling down the walkway at each other and go our separate ways at last?"

Amy stuck out her tongue at him before closing the

Babcocks' door, and Joanna poked him playfully, though she very nearly lost her balance.

"She'll still be not even seventeen and in need of your rearing when your salon is finished and we meet at the skating rink," he said.

"Writing salons can wait while I discipline my hardheaded sister, Lorie."

"Is that what you were doing? Disciplining?"

"Someone has to. She's a disaster!"

"Joanna March."

"Well, it's gone to her head anyway."

"What has?" he asked as he directed her around a corner and nodded hello to a passing couple.

Jo should have known by now how to get from her rented room on the first floor of the Babcocks' home to her salon, which gathered in an equally lovely home on Pinckney Street, but as it happened, Jo was awful with directions. It isn't something they could have known when the only places they ever traveled back home were the colony, the big house, and the space between—most of which was water—but Lorie had no idea how Jo would have managed in a city on her own. She needed someone to mind the road while she went on her tangents or mentally composed new work, or read aloud from a newspaper as though she needn't watch where she was going or into whom she nearly collided.

"Is it the dancing school that's spoiled Amy," he continued, "or the fact that she's better at it than even we imagined? Or maybe it's the way she can support herself in just three short years by her talent, whether in private recitals, or in teaching the daughters of wealthy Boston professionals?"

"I am not being unreasonable, Lorie."

"Of course you aren't. Why would you be? When have you ever?"

"All right, that's enough."

"Why, I can't think of a single occasion on which I thought—" And they stopped abruptly to avoid being trampled by a carriage before proceeding across the street. "On which I thought, 'Joanna March is being unreasonable.'"

"If you think for a moment that I'm skating with you now, you're sorely mistaken," she said as he deposited her outside her destination.

"Should I be punished because I think you entirely reasonable?"

Jo did as her youngest sister had done and stuck out her tongue at Lorie, though any of the women sitting in the drawing room could see them through the window, and then she went inside to attend her salon.

"We must forgive her her lackadaisical Southern ways, ladies," Madeleine Plender crooned in an obvious attempt to sound as though it were part of an ongoing conversation about Jo's tardiness. "I'm sure she means no disrespect."

"I'm perfectly capable of voicing any slights I intend, as you well know," Joanna said, rounding the corner from the entryway into the finely decorated drawing room. It was well into winter and still the heavy, velvety drapes that reached floor to ceiling were bound back to show off several layers of sheer lace before the window. What heat was lost for the aesthetic was made up for by the fire crackling in the hearth.

It was the greatest revelation uncovered in Boston, that such things belonged to Black people. More than the houses lined up against each other, or the fact that there were entire neighborhoods of them without porches or personal space or acreage. More than the fact that there were such things as neighborhoods. Funnily, the close quarters in Boston's Beacon Hill weren't so unlike back home, if one meant the rows of cabin shacks where folks lived when they were enslaved, and not the grand plantation houses, or the small but spread-out homes of the white Southerners without much more than Blacks.

But here, she rented a room from a Black family whose patriarch studied and represented the law, if she understood correctly, and even after almost three years among them, she sometimes felt sure that she didn't. She'd been certain the North was not some other world of equality and "good white folks," but sometimes the difference in the way Black people moved through the world was undeniably awe-inspiring.

Even this salon was more than her imagination could have devised. It was Madeleine Plender's home, and she was wife to a dentist and a doctor. They were the same man, but that was no less fantastic than if she'd really taken two husbands. Madeleine did no work of her own, not with her hands, the way Mammy and Meg and every other woman Jo knew back home had. Madeleine was an advocate, as everyone seemed to call Jo as well, and she had the fortunate position of being a mentor, and a sponsor, and a host of other words that meant that she gave her name and her financial support to those she wanted to see succeed. She'd begun this writing salon in her home and, despite that she did not personally write, she'd been able to attract the bright minds of women who did. It was only for Black women, and by invitation only, though, once invited, each member was allowed to invite one woman of her choosing, if she was thought to have something to contribute.

Jo had received an invitation because despite not attending, Mrs. Babcock, her landlord, was well respected among the group, and she was very pleased to have a Southern writer and freedpeople advocate staying with her.

"It is in fact your Southern heritage we'd like to discuss today, Joanna," Madeleine proceeded, as women finished their milling and tea making, and sat on her dimpled sofa or in plush armchairs.

"Oh?" Jo received a cup of tea from someone who smiled too excessively for her taste. It made her suspicious that perhaps she *had* been the topic of the conversation before her arrival. "Shall I regale you with yet more stories of the colony? I assure you, I did in fact wield a hammer myself in building homes for my community."

"Yes, we know all about that," Madeleine said with a nod. "You're not at all what we imagined of Southern women and their delicate natures."

"I think because you can't imagine what it is to have been enslaved," Jo replied. She'd meant it to be just another sharp but playful retort traded between the two, but she could tell by the way the room hushed that it had seemed like more than that. She couldn't think how to remedy it without going on, speaking of how the image of the delicate Southern woman was reserved for white women. One had to have the luxury of leisure, and the stomach for tradition, of which Jo had neither.

Madeleine pressed her lips together and looked into her teacup. Just as Jo worried she might be asked to leave, the woman lifted her chin and smiled softly.

"You're right, of course," Madeleine said. "Which is why we hoped you'd consider writing about it."

"Oh," Jo said, relieved enough to sigh and sip her honeyed tea. "I sometimes feel it's all I write about. First in my newsletter, and now in the journal you publish."

"You've written wonderfully about your love of the Freedpeople Colony at Roanoke, Joanna, and brilliantly on the predicament that faces the Black Southerner, and the miseducation of the white Northerner on not only the institution of slavery, but their role in it."

"Except that . . . ?"

"It's not an exception," Madeleine said, sitting up a bit to politely insist. "Never that." She looked around the room, and the other women quickly agreed, lending their own assurances to Jo. "It's just that there is so much more you have to say, and to give. Insights that few but you could, as your talent is a rarity."

There was no way to reply without agreeing with her own

praise, so Jo waited for Madeleine Plender to reach her conclusion.

"I know it seems an indelicate time, with the colony you
so love and have worked so faithfully to improve facing so
uncertain a future, in addition to all its other trials," she said,
and Joanna steadied herself against the way she might bris-
tle. She knew from her family's letters that Roanoke had its
share of concerns, but her natural response to such talk—
particularly from someone who, Black or not, had never set a
foot inside or a finger to its care—was not at all mild or polite
enough for present company. And besides, she'd heard that
just a few months ago, Roanoke's colony had seen a signifi-
cant influx of freedpeople. Its fate was not at all decided. It
would not go the way of Corinth.

"What is certain," Madeleine continued, "is that the war
was fought and won. All across the country, the enslaved are
free."

"Did you read of Freedom Day in Galveston, Texas?" one
of the women interjected, and a chorus of excited conversation followed.

"Did you read that it came two years late?" Joanna couldn't
stop herself from responding. She regretted it immediately,
when all their eyes found her, and their chorus quieted. "I'm
sorry. You'll know by now that I do not possess a mild or
accepting manner," she told them. "And I certainly don't
mean to dissuade you from celebrating, as the enslaved in
Galveston did for days after. But having been enslaved myself,
it's impossible for my happiness over the matter not to be

tinged with the bitter understanding that they were meant to be free long before."

"No, Joanna." Madeleine put her teacup on the table before her and turned fully to face Jo. "Don't apologize. You know something about this that we don't. We are all a part of the same race, but I think you've probably come to see how different our struggles are from each other. Especially those of us born to freedom. You know intimately how to mourn those two lost years of freedom, because you were born into slavery. That's why we want to publish you."

"But"—Jo's eyes bounced from one smiling woman to the next—"you already do."

"Not in the journal, and not about the freedpeople," Madeleine said with a shake of her head. "We want you to write about the time before. About what life was like before you went to Roanoke. We want to publish your slave narrative."

Jo looked again at the many faces of the Black women surrounding her. Her eyes drifted from one to the next, from high-necked lace collars to pearl drop earrings, from precisely draped hair to perfectly placed cameos. She had never seen Black women dressed so finely before coming to Boston, or considered that they might have any interest in telling a story like hers. Not her thoughts on the war or the Union, or her convictions about what the Freedpeople Colony could be, but Jo's story.

"That is, if you'd like to tell it."

"It had honestly never occurred to me," Jo said. "To make my writing about me."

"I believe, Joanna," Madeleine said, and Jo turned back to hold her gaze, "that when you write about you, and if you do it from the same impassioned, honest place that you've written about everything else—you'll be writing about us all. I hope you'll consider it."

"I will," Jo said, and smiled. "I absolutely will."

The park was bustling with what seemed to be hundreds of people, despite the cold, clear sky and the brisk wind. The ice rink held only a portion of them, but it was busier than Jo could manage, being untalented on skates.

"If it were snowing, it'd be warmer," she huffed.

"Speak up, no one can hear you beneath that warm blanket," Lorie replied, and he leaned over the sleigh's handle as he pushed and skated behind it.

"Honestly, Joanna," Amy said, carving an elegant figure into the ice to slow her speed and draw near to them. "You look like an old curmudgeon, bundled on a sleigh and being pushed around the rink as though you don't have two working legs."

"We are not all as graceful as you," Lorie said, with an intentional grunt.

"Don't let him fool you," Jo threw back over her shoulder. "He prefers this. He needs the sleigh as much as I do, or he'd never make it all the way around the rink."

"It's embarrassing," Amy said, and skated a wide circle

around them, her skirts billowing beautifully as she leaned toward the two without losing her balance.

"And that's sorcery," Lorie told her, but he smiled, and made her do the same. "What would your family say, to see you dance just as well on ice as you did back home?"

At the thought, Amy's shoulders settled with a whimsical sigh, and her smile softened into something nearly melancholy. The three of them were quiet but for the sound of skates and sleigh, each imagining the ones they'd left in North Carolina, and what they'd make of a great many things that had become routine.

"I wonder if they miss us as much as we miss them," Amy said, still skating alongside them, but with fewer flourishes now, her gloved hands staying closer to her sides. "Or if they speak of us this way, too."

"Of course they do," Jo said, and reached for her baby sister's hand, pulling her down onto the sleigh.

Lorie grunted, to no one's concern, and continued pushing the sisters along the ice.

"Mammy misses you most, of course," Jo told Amy as the younger girl straightened her legs and adjusted the blanket to cover them both, and then she snaked her arm through Jo's and let her head fall on her sister's shoulder despite that they were the same height now.

"I don't feel like the baby anymore," the girl said. "Not without a Mammy to care for me. Or a Meg."

Jo laid against her sister's head.

"I miss Meg so much," Amy continued. "I wish she could

see the way I am with my students, so she could tell me if I've got a gift for teaching the way she does."

"I'm lonely for her at night," Jo said softly, though not so softly that Lorie couldn't hear. "It's lovely to have a bed just for myself, but it's lovelier to have a sister close by."

"Would they be upset at us, for not living under the same roof? Have we become too citified?"

"We came so you could study dance. We were always going to sleep in separate beds, with you in the dorms, even if I had stayed nearer to the Evergreen family. I'm more afraid they'd think me selfish, wanting to live in Beacon Hill, but look at this place."

Laughter and conversation swelled as though by Jo's invitation, and the merriment of the rink and the surrounding park put smiles back on the sisters' faces.

"We've always lived among our people," Jo said. "But when have we seen them live so well? Or at least, have so much. I'm more than happy to pay a boarding fee to a Black family, given the choice."

"It's easy to consider it all meaningless earthly possessions when you may have them," Amy agreed. She had become accustomed to so many things in so short a time, and she didn't want to think that it made her a bad person, because she could tell the difference between having a little and having a little more. "I'm pleased to have things I didn't have before, and I'm proud that I can afford myself them. Although I suppose it was a blessing to live in the colony for free, too."

"For free?" Joanna asked, her head snapping toward her sister's.

"Well, being given the land and the lumber for Papa to build our house by the Union."

"Amethyst," Jo said with a shake of her head. "No one lives in the Freedpeople Colony for free. Why do you think Mammy worked every day, and Meg, and me?"

Amy's brow crashed down in confoundment.

"But that isn't fair," the young girl said, at which her sister's eyes roamed either as though an explanation might reveal itself in their surroundings or as though Jo was equally confused by her sister's confusion. "How could anyone be expected to go from captivity, wherein they benefited from our unpaid labor, to being required immediately to give our first wages directly back? Perhaps you misunderstood, Jo."

"Amy, really. We paid a rent to the Union, always. And if we hadn't worked all that time, when Papa joined the war effort they would have taken the cost of our upkeep from his earnings."

"The villains!" Amy huffed.

"And the land isn't properly the Union's to give, as it turns out," Lorie said, managing to move the sleigh to the outside of the rink so he could rest, and so that the sisters could watch the other skaters glide by.

"What does that mean?" Amy asked when he pushed her farther center so he could sit down.

"Mind your skates," he said absently, lifting her crossed ankles and replacing them on his longer legs anyway.

"What do you mean it isn't theirs? Of course it is now, if not before. We won!" Amy insisted.

"*They* won," Jo muttered distractedly, her eyes watching the lively park.

"My mother's settled in New Bern," Lorie said to Jo as though her sister weren't sitting between them.

"Are you pleased?" Joanna asked, her brows tented so that he knew she was concerned most with how he fared with the news.

"Why has she left the big house?" Amy looked from one to the other of them, annoyed that in their presence, she still felt very much like a child, despite being seventeen. They did it intentionally, she could tell. "I'll see myself home if no one plans to answer any of my questions. Honestly, it's terribly rude, and not at all as mature as you seem to think. Hortense Evergreen could teach the two of you something about common courtesy, and its place in a civilized society."

"I doubt she'd tell me the same, given the opportunity," Jo said with a snort. "Constance must have warned her to be a bit more courteous with *me* before she returned to the colony, and rightly so."

"I'm glad no one has to fear my temper," Amy declared.

"Only your spoiled disposition."

Lorie sometimes thought Jo and Amy bickered back and forth not because they were a budding young talent and a sharp-witted advocate-writer who could not see eye to eye. He smiled at their sparring because he knew it was how they managed being too homesick. They fell into the routine regularly, despite it leaving no lasting discontent or upset, and he'd decided some time ago that it was because they were all they had. Everything else had been new for so long, and Northerners had such a complicated way of speaking, even in pleasant company, that their tiffs had been the only familiar thing for a while.

"My mother left the big house because the home was unconfiscated," Lorie replied to Amy, leaning toward her to win her attention back. "When the Union presence dwindled on the island, white folks came back for their property, and any that wasn't in military use, they reclaimed." He sighed, and settled back against the sleigh. "I guess now I wish the Union *had* made that place part of their shadow. At least then there would have been someone to contest the deed, and those enslaving heathens would have had to fight for it."

Amy pouted and took one of Lorie's hands in both of hers, her eyes wide with heartfelt sympathy. Her brushed gloves were the same royal blue as the tailored coat she wore over her dress, and they were much nicer than Lorie's fingerless ones.

"Whatever did this cost, Amethyst, I swear?" he asked, losing in his attempt to keep from laughing when she'd been so genuine.

"What a crass question!" she shot back, and tossed his hand away. "My finances are my own business."

But then she held up a gloved hand so all would see, and traced the stitching on the lovely tapered fingers, before joining Lorie's laughter.

"Oh, Jo!" Amethyst turned to her sister with a start. "Do Papa and Mammy still pay to live in the colony?"

"Of course," Jo answered.

"Then perhaps I can help."

"What do you mean?"

"I mean, I could pay some of it, what do you think?"

"I think you could pay it all," she said. "You're paid more for a single private recital than any of us received for a month's work on the island. And Boston is a much more expensive place than North Carolina, to be sure."

Amy's face brightened with excitement.

"Oh, but dear heart, they'd never let you," Jo told her quickly, and then watched her sister's face fall. "I'm almost sure they wouldn't."

"But we can ask them, at least," Amy almost pleaded.

"Of course we can. I'll put it in the letter I was going to send tomorrow," Jo promised, and pulled Amy closer. She meant to relax then, and let the skaters floating past carry her thoughts with them—until she saw someone she thought she recognized.

"It couldn't be," she said, leaning forward and pulling the blanket away from Amy and Lorie in the process.

"Courtesy, Jo!" Amy tried to wrangle the thing from her sister, who easily discarded it as she stood from the sleigh in a wobbling trance before beginning to skate directly across the rink, despite the flow of the crowd.

Joanna could hear her sister and Lorie's quizzical exchange over her behavior, and could imagine them craning their necks to see her intended destination, while both refusing the effort it would take to stand and follow her.

She wasn't sure she'd seen correctly, as it was. She couldn't have, unless all the nation intended to descend on Boston, now that the war was over. And maybe that was the way of the future. She couldn't pretend to be entirely surprised, knowing the difference in standards of living from personal experience. She loved her home, the way even people who had every reason not to often did. She'd known a brutality she could not wish on anyone, and still, every joy she'd known—every memory of laughter, and love, and family—had happened in the same place. It should be easy, outsiders must have thought, to despise the South, but even now it wasn't the land's fault that Black people newly free could not expect to be treated much better than grudgingly. It was not the land's fault that emancipation had been contentious and a matter of war. She could not despise the loblolly pine or the creeks, or the smell of wide-open fields and forests before the summer rain.

Jo finally crossed the rink, only very nearly falling and bringing down an innocent patron a handful of times, and when she had to catch herself on the arm of the man she'd been studying, she was relieved to find that it was, in fact, Joseph Williams.

"I had heard the March sisters were Northerners now," he said in greeting, steadying her, while the group he'd been conversing with looked on. "It's lovely to see you again, Joanna."

"And you, Mr. Williams." She smiled because he smiled so broadly down at her.

"Joanna March, this is Leonard Carson, and Timothy Miller, and this is Mrs. Timothy Miller," he said, gesturing to each in turn.

"Francine," the only woman in their company introduced herself properly, with a roll of her eyes. "How do you know our Joseph?"

"The Marches gave me a proper Southern greeting and homecooked meal when I was touring the region with General Wild during the war," he answered before Jo had the chance. "I'll admit I was delighted when I heard you'd come to Boston."

"And *did* you hear it?" Jo raised an eyebrow.

"I like this girl," Timothy Miller interjected, slapping Joseph on the back, who was still holding Jo upright on her skates while the group of friends stood on the snow just outside the rink.

Francine Miller tried discreetly to hush her husband's boisterousness to no avail, and then smiled again at Jo, who was quite sure by now that they all had the wrong impression of her acquaintance with their friend.

"This is the kind of firebrand you ought to marry," Timothy continued, as though to confirm her thoughts.

"Miller, really," was all Joseph replied, though he smirked and squared his still-broad shoulders. Clearly the friends had a jovial rapport, and the subject of Joseph's singlehood was recurring, if it could come up so immediately with a stranger.

"Firebrands don't tend to like being spoken of as though they're hard of hearing," Jo told the man, smiling graciously.

"Forgive my good man, Joanna," Joseph said, putting hand over heart. "The stability of marriage can make some men far too comfortable, I think."

"Is that how you've kept your head, Joseph?" Timothy quipped. "By failing to attract a bride?"

"That's why we've invited him to Boston," Francine joined in, if only to make her husband's behavior seem less obnoxious. "It would be impossible to remain a bachelor with a city so rich in beautiful, brilliant women." She gestured toward Joanna. "Even from as far as . . ."

"Roanoke Island," Jo answered.

At that, the group became even livelier, if such a thing were possible.

"You've come from the Freedpeople Colony?"

"Well, now!"

"We've read so much about it!"

"It's Joanna's work you've read," Joseph informed them with a laugh, and his three friends' heads swiveled to find her. Joanna froze, just as she had upon first seeing a group of rodents catch sight of a meal in the middle of the street, who then descended upon it to gorge. It was a very particular spectacle, and one she'd witnessed more than once since moving to the city. When Joseph turned back to her, it was with a much less ravenous expression. "I've kept up with your newsletter, and was pleased to see you published in the *League of Negro Women Writers' Journal*."

"Which," Jo conceded, "is how you heard of my coming to Boston, I presume."

"Yes," he said, smiling. "So you see, I spoke true. I've come to live and work in Boston, and I was hoping to repay my debt of hospitality to the March family. I just didn't expect to find you so soon, and skating!"

At the reminder, Jo immediately wobbled on her blades.

"Nor shall you again," she said, and shook her head. "I'll just take these ridiculous things off and bring you to reacquaint with Amy."

"And how is Beth? And Mrs. March? And Meg?" Joseph's gaze was interrupted by a quick series of blinks that perhaps only Joanna noticed. "I so enjoyed your eldest sister's friendly correspondence during the war, but I'm ashamed to say I let it taper off when I heard you'd come North."

Jo nodded, her mouth slightly parted in recognition. It turned out Meg had been quite right in her discerning, then. Whyever else Joseph Williams had asked to write her, his primary interest was in continued news of the colony, and perhaps more specifically the village. He'd thought the young woman lovely, anyone who'd seen him in her presence could not deny. It must have been, then, that he had no marital imperative, as he so clearly seemed to now.

Jo had to decide quickly whether or not to hold it against him, as he and his rapacious friends were awaiting news. In the end, she could find no intentional fault. It was true, Meg had been heartsore a time or two on his account, but Jo supposed he hadn't done much more than be a few years behind her sister's ambitions. Perhaps it was because of her own experience of disappointing someone she adored, but she decided Joseph Williams should not be villainized for that.

"Beth and Meg are still on Roanoke," she told him gently. "Only Amethyst and I came, for her to study dance."

Despite the presence of his friends, Joseph and Joanna held each other's gaze for a moment longer, and she watched his recognition settle. It must really have been years since he'd written her sister, and all the while on the assumption that she'd left the colony.

"I suppose a better friend would've known that," he said after a deep breath, and Jo's only response was to dip her chin. "Perhaps I should write—"

"I'll send along your greetings," Jo interrupted before he could say any more, and Joseph closed his mouth in understanding, nodding once and resuming his smile. "Come and see Amy. Or help me back to the sleigh, anyway." She laughed, and Joseph and his friends did as well.

XIII

Winters in Boston looked absolutely otherworldly to Beth, and she wondered if perhaps the picture painted on what Amy informed her was a postcard was the result of artistic license.

It wasn't that North Carolina didn't have mountains, on top of which Papa said there was snow—it was just that Beth had never seen them herself. She lived in the Outer Banks, and despite that she knew she'd lived somewhere farther inland before that, it seemed she uniquely could not recall the old life. Uniquely because, despite that it was not often the subject of conversation, Beth knew her family recalled it. She could sometimes sense when they did, or see it in a faraway look. The memories seemed sometimes to transport her family members, such that they were unaware they were being watched, as though they'd somehow forgotten they were visible at all. It was not very unlike the look Papa took on whenever he spoke of the war, since his return home. That was how she came to understand that what they'd lived through was as terrible and devastating as battle. And it had lasted so much longer.

She didn't remember deciding not to, but before the big house, where she'd lived just before coming to their home in the Freedpeople Colony, she remembered most things in still pictures. Like the postcards Amy sent.

She remembered Papa and Mammy, though she'd seen them so infrequently during the day, and she remembered her sisters, though mostly she remembered asking Jo where Meg had gone, and why their eldest sister often wore such grand-looking clothes. She couldn't remember when Amy had come to join their family, and so she'd had to be reminded years later that such a thing had taken place. They said of course Mammy hadn't borne Amy in her belly, but Beth wasn't sure she would have known one way or the other.

There had been a very old woman, or at least a woman who to Beth's young eye seemed quite old. She didn't remember the elder's name, but she knew that any work the woman did had to be brought to the stool outside her shack, and that Beth had been in her care during the workday when she was very young. She remembered turning, beneath the heat of a morning sun, and she couldn't remember the year or the season, but she recalled the way the old woman's eyes softened when they lifted from her sorting something between two wicker baskets and found young Bethlehem.

Beth didn't lament what she couldn't recall. She wouldn't have even if it were her way. There must have been a reason memories from the old life faded as easily as they did, and it didn't upset her. It *had* worried her when Jo and Amy left for Boston that it might happen again, in their absence. She'd worried that the memories of their new life would fade and now that she had so many, and had spent so much time in the unbroken company of her mother and her sisters, she thought this time, forgetting would be torture. She was overwhelmed with gratitude when the forgetting did not happen again, though it meant that she ached so often for them.

"It feels as though we exchanged Jo and Amy when we got Papa back," Beth told Ella. She'd let her hands collapse into her lap, and the garment she darned with it. "The old life is over, they say, but it's still impossible to keep a family whole when our opportunities are always far away."

"I know how you miss them," her friend answered, watching her daughter play near the water. Fanny was no longer a baby, and she had no need of their hands in order to walk or climb. They'd carried her down the incline, into the shade of the creek bed, canopied on both banks by treetops. It was too cold to play in the water, but the earth nearby was soft and pliable, and the little girl enjoyed patting it between her hands. "I'd never had the privilege of missing anyone until Daddy passed. It makes the heartache a little easier, knowing it means I got to know someone in my family that well." Ella looked up at Beth, whose brow creased gently at the memory of Orange. "Only a little easier, though."

"I miss him, too," Beth said. "I'm so glad I got to know him, Ella. Your father was so kind, and I don't think I would ever have known what to make of my condition, or where it comes from, without him."

"I only wish he'd gotten to die where he hoped. I wish he were buried in Liberian soil, the way we planned."

"You tried your best to see him sponsored, Ella." She did not say what both young women already intimately knew, that their previous status as enslaved Blacks meant that even organizations supporting the American Colonization Society and its campaign to send Black people to the new nation often refused sponsorship to the emancipated. They did not want to be seen as taking a side, which was a terribly strange privilege the nation retained. Having fought a war supposedly toward the goal of abolition, and then being more concerned with mending relations between themselves than with those who'd suffered slavery in the first place.

"You have been my witness," Ella told Beth. "But he still went to his rest here."

Beth only nodded, because there was nothing to say. There was no way to express the grief of burying the dead in earth they'd been forced to toil, on land that did not belong to them, and might never.

"When the enslavers win back their land, and the colony is gone, I won't even be able to visit his bones," Ella went on, watching her daughter play.

If Beth were either of her parents, or Meg, or even Jo so far away in Boston, she might have resisted Ella's conclusion. She might have felt it imperative to defend the permanence of the colony—but part of having a memory that faded was accepting that things passed. She felt that must be part of why she'd come to accept what so few wanted to consider, both about the colony and about Liberia.

"I want no ties to this country, Beth," Ella told her. "I have none by blood, since they rended me from kin, and I have none in my heart. I'm ready to go home."

Bethlehem nodded, her eyes studying the creek and the incline on the opposite side, and the way the wind moved the trees and their shadows.

"Nothing is forever," she said, and when she did, it was about a great many things.

To Freedomsville we soon shall go,
And there still let the people know
That we have minds that do expand
Beyond the scope of "Contraband."

Meg was glad for Lorie's boat, now that work was so much farther away. She had her students in the colony, but with the end of the war, rations and pay had dwindled from the Union, and she, like so many others, needed to travel to the mainland to make ends meet.

Lorie's mother had taken the cart when she left the big house for New Bern, but when Meg could not accompany someone else heading to a nearby town, she was willing to walk. It was better her than Mammy or Papa.

As she crossed the sound, Meg hummed the song her mainland students had sung for days now. It had made its way all the way from Arlington, Virginia, and Freedmen's Village, which had been established on the abandoned estate of Confederate general Robert E. Lee. She didn't know why her students should take up singing it now, except that there had been no anthem composed for Roanoke. Now as their own colony was rumored to be in decline and folks had to pin their hopes to somewhere new, perhaps they reasoned that Freedmen's Village's song meant it would last.

"We have minds that do expand," Meg sang, as she passed between the flag posts that marked the entrance home. "Beyond the scope of 'Contraband.'"

She stopped amongst a scattered crowd outside her mother's office. There were no officers there anymore, except in passing, or when they came to survey the colony's status, and Mammy had become the administrator. She would be the one the freedpeople asked questions, and voiced laments and concerns and criticisms. She would be the one to answer for the coffins.

Leaning against the building, or stacked in twos side by side, they were impossible to ignore.

The coffins had drawn this smattering of people and accounted for the vacant look in some of their eyes, the soft crying Meg could hear, though she couldn't see who made the sound. There was the ever-present undercurrent of coughing behind all of the hushed conversation, as there had been in the colony for some time, and the sight before them made it all very despairing.

Mammy emerged from the building, opening her arms as though to embrace them all, and then addressed them, turning one way and then the other while she spoke.

"Don't mind them," she said of the coffins, and despite the hitch in her voice, she stepped to one small cluster of colonists and touched an arm gently before moving on to another. "A doctor is coming, too, and a hospital steward. Soon. Hold on a little while longer. We'll see this season pass."

Slowly the gathering dispersed, and only then did Mammy see her daughter standing farther behind. Meg let her shoulders settle so that her mother would do the same, and then she went to her, took the woman's hand, and led her back inside the office.

Mammy slumped in what had been an officer's seat.

"What happened?" Meg asked.

"I asked for a surgeon, and medical assistance." She laid her forehead against the desk. "There are so many ill already, and the sickly season has only just begun."

It was not that Meg wasn't aware of the number of deaths in the colony, and that the overflowing barracks and the village were beginning to look ramshackle because of the way the population had outgrown the land. She knew also that family crops were not enough to make up for the lack of rations since the war's end.

"I hadn't let myself accept the reality of it all," she said aloud.

"I have had little choice," Mammy said into the desk. "But this . . . How are people meant to survive when their deaths are presupposed by those given authority to maintain us from afar?" She sat upright, as though her will and strength had returned. "I asked to hire some of our own back from the mainland, if burying and managing the dead were necessary, and they send us coffins instead. No matter what Horace James says, more and more it is clear that the reverend is the only white man who desires that the colony continue."

Mammy let her head fall back this time, and looked up as though communing directly with her Heavenly Father.

"Coffins before the doctor. How much can our beleaguered hearts stand?"

"Look, Mammy," Meg said, picking up an envelope from the desk. "A letter from Jo and Amy."

Of course her mother would have received the mail delivery and set the letter aside herself. She hadn't opened it. She never read them without Meg and Beth, and Meg supposed it was like having all four of her girls together for a time.

"Come on," she said, taking her mother beneath one of her arms and hoisting her to her feet. There was nothing they could do to conceal the coffins or repair the wounds caused by the sight of them, and Meg knew little would give her mother a peaceful reprieve, except perhaps hearing how well the two in Boston were faring. "The sooner we find Bethlehem, the sooner we can hear their voices."

It did wonders, just getting Mammy home. Papa was standing with Wisdom out front, and the two were guarding

Fanny while she wandered about, Beth and Ella visible inside the open window shutters, setting the table.

"Good day, wife," Alcott March said, reaching for her when Mammy was still more than an arm's length away. It made her smile that he was still impatient after all this time, and it made Meg blush under Wisdom's waiting gaze.

Both pairs embraced before Wisdom scooped Fanny into his arms, and they came inside for supper.

After their meal, the family read Jo's letter together as though it were a dessert, and it did serve to sweeten the evening.

"Can you imagine?" Beth said, sitting on the floor with Meg, Wisdom in a chair beside her. "Joanna will be published, with a book of her own, telling the world a story of our enslavement from our words."

"I should like to teach from my own sister's work," Meg said, as though to Wisdom, who had taken to smoking after supper as Alcott did. "I've taught so many how to read with *Uncle Tom's Cabin* over the past few years, but soon Jo's narrative will take its place."

"I'm just in awe that there can be so much brilliance in one family," Wisdom said, arranging his pipe on the other side of his mouth as though he hoped it might distract the Marches from appraising his intelligence in comparison.

"Five ravens, my five girls," Alcott said, resting back in his chair, holding his pipe with one hand and his wife's hand with the other.

"Ravens?" Wisdom asked, looking to Meg as he often did when he was unsure of something.

"Black birds are the most intelligent," she answered, her cheeks glowing from her father's familiar praise.

"Intelligent and lovely, like all of you," Mammy added. "And Amy, look how she's grown. I'm afraid we'll scarcely recognize her when we see her next. Offering to send us money, the dear girl."

"If she ever did send something, we'd only set it aside and then give it back," Alcott said, and Mammy nodded in confirmation.

"Have you heard from Honor lately?" Meg asked Wisdom when the matter with Amy had been settled. "How does he like Beaufort?"

"I'm not sure," he answered, his eyes flitting across the faces of her family, knowing they were aware of his troubles. His eyes fell into his lap, and he pulled the pipe from his mouth. In a moment, Fanny was standing at his knee, staring up at Wisdom, and he couldn't help but smile and clip her chin between finger and thumb.

"I don't like to see brothers draw away from each other," Alcott said. "Especially not in the strange state this world is in."

"I think he still thinks I betrayed him by choosing to stay."

"Did the colony not deserve to keep *any* able-bodied men?" Mammy asked, though she did not expect an answer.

"But I didn't stay for the colony's sake," Wisdom said, as though in confession, and Alcott and Margaret, and Meg and Beth, and even Ella met him with broad and genuine smiles.

"We know that, son," Alcott answered, and clicked his teeth back into place on his pipe. "We know."

It was another day or so before new mail came, and by then Mammy had received the doctor and the hospital steward from New Bern and directed them to a working space, where they would keep their belongings and provisions when they weren't visiting people at home in the village. It was one thing off her mind, and it must have been why she paid more than a glance's attention to the letters addressed to Bethlehem, and from where.

"What am I to make of Beth receiving correspondences from Liberia now?" she asked Alcott in a hushed tone. They'd reclaimed their bedroom after Orange's passing, having slept in the front room together when Alcott returned home from war. Now Ella and her daughter shared Amy and Beth's old bed, and Beth joined Meg in hers, or some variation of that, depending on the day. The point was that Papa and Mammy had privacy again, but she was still unaccustomed to it, and so when she snuck Beth's letter into their room without delivering it to her daughter, she spoke in a whisper.

"Margaret," her husband said through a sigh. "You'll only work yourself up. Ask the girl, and let her tell you. I'm sure writing to settlers in Liberia is perfectly normal these days."

"What about these days would make that normal?" Mammy asked, crossing her arms over her chest and turning away.

"What is normal these days at all?"

"No, Alcott. None of your playfulness or charm. Our

daughter is eyeing a dangerous path, and I would like some support on the matter."

"And you have it. But I can't make up my mind about what she's doing without asking her."

"Perhaps I should read the letter first."

"Margaret!" He very nearly stumbled back now. "What have you done with my measured and reasonable wife? I've never heard you suggest such a thing. Bethlehem is nineteen now, darling. You couldn't do that to her. What's gotten into you to even consider it?"

At that, Mammy sat on the chest at the foot of their bed and tossed her hands in the air.

"What's gotten into me? I'm a wife and mother and administrator who has known enslavement and emancipation, and who is still waiting on freedom, and who has had to love and release those dearest to me in turn these past several years!"

Her husband crouched down in front of her, though she knew his knees were not fully recovered from the buckshot he'd taken that had not been entirely removed. He hadn't lost the use of his legs, and that was blessing enough for both of them, but she would always mind his comfort closely now.

"Sometimes I fear you have endured more than a man can fathom," he said softly. "And I fear there's nothing I can do to ease your worries."

"She was ill for so long before we understood. I thought I would lose her, Alcott, with you away. And even when I didn't, it was only because we came to accept that this illness, it will never pass. Not completely. Not for long. It returns like the tide. Always."

"And now you fear she'll go away anyway." He laid his hands over hers.

"At first it was Ella receiving the letters, and I know she and her father had hoped to join the American Colonization Society, only he got too ill. And I know it's been decades now, but so many died who first went over there to stake some claim," she said, though she knew her husband was equally aware of those Black Virginians who'd gone so many years before. "Eighty percent of them, Alcott. Dead from disease."

"It would be difficult to imagine, wife," he said. "If I hadn't been to war, and if we didn't see our fellow freedpeople falling ill and dying in this very colony."

Mammy could not bear to mention the delivered coffins, news of which had spread quickly anyway.

"Can we promise our daughters long life anywhere?" he asked, and it was not meant to be answered, but he kissed her forehead when her chin fell low, and then he helped her stand before handing her the envelope with Beth's name across the front.

Together they crossed the hall, Papa remaining in the open doorframe of his daughters' room when Mammy went inside.

"Bethlehem," she said, drawing the attention of all the young women and the little girl in the room as though they shared a name. "A letter came for you today. From Liberia."

Beth rose from where she'd crouched beside an open

trunk, and behind little Fanny, whom she was dressing up in the lovely pieces she'd sewn.

"Thank you, Mammy," Beth said, accepting it, and then kept her mother's gaze a moment before opening the letter, despite that everyone's attention was on her. She peeled the envelope open, calm and mild as she always was, and then she read the contents to herself, a smile blooming on her lips.

"Well?" Mammy asked, trying in vain to quiet the shudder trembling through her neck and shoulders. "What news from so far away?"

Beth took a deep breath in and looked at her eldest sister, Meg, and then at Papa still in the doorframe, before offering Mammy a gentle expression.

"There's work for me. In a dress shop, with a sewing machine, and dress forms, and virgin fabric." Her eyes sparkled and began to well. It struck Mammy to see it, and her shoulders, which had been tight and coiled, relaxed. "There is a place on the continent for me. And I feel that I belong to it, though the cost is being separated from you."

Now tears welled and fell throughout the room, and where Papa stood, just outside it. It was quiet, the way it was when Beth herself cried. Though her sister and her mother felt that their hearts were breaking, they did not mourn loudly, when it was in her honor.

"I have a birthright, Mammy," she said, and behind her, Ella hugged Fanny to herself, grateful to hear her friend say so but wiping tears of her own. "But I know that I'll be homesick for you. Even if it's heaven."

XIV

April 1866

It had become custom to find Wisdom standing in the yard with her father when Meg returned from the mainland at the end of the day. The young man worked odds and ends around the colony, at her mother's direction. He kept at the lawn mowing, if only because little else could improve the disarray of having too many people on too little land, and he chopped wood, and helped at the fishery, where there were more fish than coin to purchase it.

Wisdom Carter was a man who appreciated direction, because he knew his talent was in assisting. It was nothing more specific than that, and so he went where he was needed, and was pleased to find anything of particular importance to the people important to him so that he could accomplish it.

Meg had learned to discern when he had an accomplishment to share with her, by the way his lips snagged up on one side, and the way he rose up on the balls of his feet before settling down again. The sight reminded her of her baby sister, Amethyst, and the way she used to bounce up onto her toes. She could not express how much she adored that something of Wisdom reminded her of someone else she loved so completely.

Wisdom only grew more excited the closer Meg got to the house, and when she was very nearly to him, she noticed the way her father clapped the younger man on his back before retreating toward the front door. He didn't go inside, though, only gave the pair some space.

Her breath was coming faster now, and she didn't wish to become light-headed, so she parted her lips and exhaled a long breath.

Wisdom's hand shot up into the air, and clutched inside was a slip of paper.

"What's that?" Meg asked in greeting.

"It's a transportation order, Miss March." His lips moved and shifted after he'd spoken, as though too excitable to rest.

"Where to?" she inquired, careful not to get ahead of him.

"To Mississippi. A man's been sent to the colony to recruit workers, and the Union's encouraging, as there isn't enough work to go around, and not many close by to work for, which I know you know, Miss March, being Mrs. March's daughter, and taking care of the colony the way you do—" He was rattling on, speaking in long, winding sentences because he had too much energy to stop.

Meg took a deep breath so that he would.

"And," he began again, speaking at a more reasonable pace now, "I hadn't wanted to impose such a question on you before I could offer a life worthy of a teacher."

His eyes locked with hers.

"Such a question?" Meg asked when it seemed Wisdom could look down into her face for the rest of the evening.

"Oh," he said quietly, and then Wisdom Carter went down on both knees in front of Meg, and her hands began to shake. "Meg March, I know you're too brilliant and lovely and good for me to suppose you'd have reason to say you would. But I couldn't live with myself if I didn't ask, now that I have something to give, too."

"You've gotta ask, son," Alcott March feigned to whisper, from his place near the front door.

"Meg March," Wisdom began, while Meg held a laugh behind her lips and nodded emphatically.

"I will marry you," she said, and when he lifted her off her feet, and her father whooped so that the whole colony could hear, it was like the night they'd danced in the big house, years ago.

Dearest Jo,

Meg will be wed! In June! I don't have to tell you that her marriage will be to Wisdom Carter, who is such a doting, lovely young man for our sister. I think the way he admires her, she feels very much like you, and I am so glad for her.

Please write and tell us that you're coming, as I know you will, and bring your writing so that I may see it before the rest of the world descends upon your narrative and swallows you whole. You will be carried so far by your gift, the way Amy has been. You both have always been the extravagant ones, and it made sense for Meg and me to stay behind.

You will be surprised, then, to learn my news. It seems I will go farthest of all, Joanna, and even when I long to be together, I can't explain the tug in me to go to Liberia. It feels like it will be like returning, like a place I've never been is somehow already part of me. I might not have known that, without my illness, so Constance Evergreen will be pleased to know that I've not been dissuaded from crediting it with a great purpose in my life.

When you do return, Joanna, I am sorry to tell you that you will find the colony greatly changed. It will not seem as idyllic and spacious in the village as it did when you were here. Yannick and your boys have all gone, drawn away by promises of work and independence, while here we are still dependent on the benevolence of white people, which we never desired, but which it seems was engineered into the colony's design. As it happened in so many places before Roanoke, the men are first to leave, encouraged and rewarded for it, by keeping what wages they make, rather than having them taxed to feebly support a wife or family in the colony, whose rations have been reduced almost to nothing. And fewer of the colonists qualify at all.

It has been so difficult watching Roanoke's decline whilst reading your words on our behalf, and perhaps it has been even more painful, worrying that we have not lived up to your talent. I am so pleased to know that you will go on, despite the colonies that rise and then are sabotaged to spoil. You will still be Joanna March, and your audience will follow your passion wherever you lead them, as long as they know it's you.

I don't exhort you to keep true to your voice because you need such encouragement, but because I think it is your integrity that has given me some of my passion. I am so excited to craft dresses from something new, to not have to reclaim material from a wardrobe worn by an oppressor. And I am so pleased that this excitement tells me something of myself, and who I am.

If I have seemed too quiet over these years, I hope my sisters will come to see that I have listened to you. I have learned from you. There could be no Liberia for me, if there had been no Meg, or Jo, or

Amy. I think you will understand this best, Joanna. If ever our sisters doubt it while I'm away, I entrust the truth to you to share.

Bethlehem March

Though he intended to repay the entire March family's kindness, Joseph Williams had insisted that Jo and Amy let him entertain them in the meantime. He'd invited the sisters to supper with the knowledge that Lorie would come along, and scheduled the occasion for an evening when his hosts, Timothy and Francine Miller, would be unavailable.

"I only met them briefly," Amy said as she, Lorie, and Jo walked toward the Miller residence. "But I quite liked Mr. and Mrs. Miller."

"That's precisely *because* you met them briefly," Jo said breathlessly. She had to walk at a faster clip to keep pace with her youngest sister's long, graceful strides, a fact which she was certain Amy observed without adjustment.

"You weren't with them any longer, Jo. You just dislike society types."

"I won't argue that," Jo huffed, hooking her arm through Lorie's so that he'd pull her up the inclining street.

"But it's insufferably contrarian to *like* to dislike society types," Amy chastised her.

"How's this," Lorie interjected. "Amethyst, you may like them enough for the both of you, all right?"

"I'll argue with my sister if I like, Lorie."

"I'm very well aware, but hopefully not in front of Joseph, when he's invited us to supper," he answered. "You're a society type now, too, aren't you? I wouldn't want you to make an ill impression."

Amy lifted her chin as though to elongate her elegant neck, and laid her gloved palm to the smooth side of her coifed hair. She didn't notice when Jo rolled her eyes at Lorie's knowing smile.

"You do make a fair point, Lorie," Amy said, dipping her chin cordially before recommencing her dancer's stride.

When the trio arrived at the Millers' door, it was opened before any of them could knock, and their jackets and gloves were taken by a uniformed maid who curtseyed before gesturing for them to proceed deeper into the house.

"I won't pretend to approve of that," Jo muttered.

"Be reasonable, Joanna," Amy whispered as they followed the maid. "Service is not the same as enslavement. I'm sure the Millers pay their staff a fair wage, and I'm sure maids and butlers are free to leave if they so desire."

"Make whatever justification you like, Amy," Jo said quickly, as though aware they'd soon be in their host's company. "Only remember that the people who fought to keep us enslaved had theirs, too. And I'm not so certain of what anyone who *must* do someone else's bidding is free to do. The self-importance of hiring folks to wait on you hand and foot, and the hypocrisy of free Blacks to immediately replicate such—"

"Good evening," Joseph bid them from in front of the hearth. He didn't know he'd interrupted Joanna's increasingly passionate rebuttal, and when he'd turned fully to face his guests, he saw Amy first. Whatever else he'd meant to say seemed trapped then, despite that his mouth gaped slightly.

"Good evening, Mr. Williams." Amy returned his greeting. "What a beautiful home the Millers have. You must give them our regards and thanks when they return."

His eyebrows lifted as though he would reply, and Amy lifted hers, too, as though in invitation.

"It is a feat, furnishing a house so splendidly and yet still retaining the welcoming qualities of a home. You must tell Mrs. Miller I think so," Amy finished. If she were Beth or Meg, she might've become coy beneath Joseph Williams's unbroken but unsteady gaze, but she was Amethyst, so instead she turned away gracefully and continued admiring the room.

"Evening, Joseph," Lorie said, stepping between the two and shaking the man's hand. When he clapped the man's shoulder, it was perhaps a bit more roughly than was customary, though not enough to provoke confrontation. "A pleasure to see you again."

"And you as well," Joseph answered, apparently grateful to be jostled back to his senses.

"You'd think our coming surprised you," Joanna said, taking her sister's hand and then crossing the dark wood floor of what appeared to be a gentleman's study to sit with her.

"Have we changed so much since you saw us last, Joseph? It's only been a couple of weeks."

"True," Joseph said, fully composed now, one hand in his suit pocket. "But then our reunion was too brief to take it all in." He looked equally between the two sisters, as though he'd never faltered. "I'm so pleased you've all come, so that we can get reacquainted at our leisure."

He was the gentleman he'd been on Roanoke, if more polished in his city attire, and more relaxed outside the subject of war. His shoulders were exactly as broad as Amy remembered, despite that she'd been so young when he visited. She remembered him well, though she hadn't thought of him since—except that he was much younger than she'd assumed the night he'd come to dinner. Perhaps it'd been the talk of war and recruitment that made her think he was a very mature man at the time. Now she was sitting beside her sister, her hands lying neatly one over the other on her lap, and she could see that he was barely older than Lorie.

Jo nudged her waist.

"What was that for?" Amy whispered roughly when Joseph had led Lorie to a handsome dark wood sideboard on whose buffet sat a host of liquor bottles and drinking glasses.

"I can see you," Jo whispered back.

"You have eyes, haven't you?"

"Amethyst."

"I think you're more bothered because you can see *him* seeing me."

"Fine," Jo confessed, and nodded sharply once.

"Well, what's the matter?" Amy continued discreetly, a delicate smile on her lips when the young men glanced back at the sisters. "Should young men be unaffected by me because I'm your baby sister? Am I not something to behold?"

"Of course you are."

"And I have no desire to sound conceited, but I'm rather used to causing men devastation, Joanna. It can hardly be avoided."

"Heaven save me," Jo answered under her breath, before cutting her eyes at her sister. "Who on earth would say such a thing *except* to sound conceited, Amy, really."

Amethyst waited until Joseph Williams and Lorie had turned their backs again, and then shielded her face with one hand before sticking out her tongue at her sister.

"Will you never outgrow that habit?" Jo snorted in an unladylike fashion, and only one of the young men nearby turned, quizzically, to find the source of the sound.

"Not while it still amuses you," Amy answered, matching Joseph's gaze from across the room until the uniformed maid returned and beckoned the four to supper.

The next night, life returned to its normal routine and Lorie sat reading on the Babcocks' sofa, in the sitting room off the staircase landing. He was twisted at the waist, one knee drawn up onto the cushion, so that he seemed despondent or troubled, hunched as he was. Behind him, Joanna held a fountain pen at the ready, her other hand pressing the paper against Lorie's back, while her gaze fixed upon her thoughts and not the world around her.

Sometimes she mouthed a word, to feel its shape, and determine whether it was the one she meant to use, and occasionally she cocked her head to the side when she was still unsure.

It was a completely silent practice, this writing trance the two had been performing since the days they sat beneath the loblolly trees together. The silence was why occasionally Mrs. Babcock drifted past, her skirts sweeping the floor and her finger absently tapping the tie at her throat. When not Mrs. Babcock, it was her husband, needlessly passing the sitting room to witness the strange spectacle, until finally Mr. Babcock stepped into the room properly, pocket watch in hand, and announced, "Until tomorrow, young sir."

It pulled the two from their collective meditations, and Jo replaced the cap on the lovely pen Madeleine Plender had furnished her with upon her first publication in the journal. Immediately, she uncapped it again.

Tonight she had a sentence or two left to transcribe, so between mutterings and writing, Jo gave a hurried, "Good night, Lorie."

He patted her on the top of her head, which she swatted away still without looking up, and then Lorie followed Mr. Babcock down the staircase to the door.

"Loren," Mr. Babcock said after pausing with his hand around the doorknob. He retracted his hand completely and turned to the younger man, who was never made to feel unwelcome in the home, despite that he still wore the vest he'd brought from Roanoke, and had never adopted any finer a wardrobe. Now when the lawyer looked him over, Lorie didn't have to consider that the appraisal had anything to do with the fact that he did not seem to have ever assimilated to city fashion.

"Mr. Babcock?"

Whatever had seemed to require delicacy or caution before, now the older man smiled, knowingly. Lorie was, after all, a very self-possessed young man, in the best possible way. He retained his country appearance because he meant to, and because he was not bothered to change according to the opinions or customs of others.

"You've been friends with Joanna for some time now, haven't you?"

"I have. She's my best friend."

"I'm not surprised. I could tell even by the quiet between you two. And by the way she's more prone to write against your back than any number of the desks available in this house."

"Yes, she prefers my company when she's working, and making me a desk means I can't wander off," Lorie said with an amused snort.

"Well. I do feel intrusive, interrupting the two of you every night. You behave perfectly respectably together, of course, but one must be mindful of appearances," Mr. Babcock said, even as he remembered that neither Lorie nor Jo behaved out of such an adherence. "Let not your good be ill-spoken of, and all that."

"Yes, sir. We understand."

"Have you considered simply proposing marriage to her?"

"Not at all," Lorie answered easily, and without shock or reservation, which made Mr. Babcock feel that perhaps the suggestion needed clarifying.

"You mean to remain this close, don't you?"

"Of course."

"And you aren't interested in courting someone else?"

"No, sir," he said with a chuckle.

"I didn't think so, Loren—there are only so many nights in the week." And Mr. Babcock had a chuckle himself. "But then, what is it? I hope you're not one of those young men resistant to the institution of marriage, as I couldn't in good conscience permit your company, I'm afraid."

"No, sir, it's nothing like that."

"Well, then?"

Lorie thought for a moment, of what he might say that didn't betray his friend's confidence, while respecting the man who provided her a home, and them a place to enjoy each other's company.

"We're happy as we are," he said, settling on disappointing Mr. Babcock's curiosity rather than speaking too freely. "I'm happy where she is. I'm happy to matter so much to the process of her work."

"And you're sure she's happy with this arrangement, too?" Mr. Babcock pressed. "You don't want to awake one day and find she's accepted another proposal because you misunderstood."

"We have this arrangement because it makes her happy, and that is enough for me."

Mr. Babcock's forehead was desperately creased, and he seemed simultaneously at a loss for words and very certainly unsatisfied that the conversation had run its course, so it was Lorie who reached for the doorknob with a smile.

"Good evening, Mr. Babcock." He let himself out, and from the dark street outside the home gave a kind of salute. "I'll be back tomorrow."

It was a moment before Mr. Babcock gathered himself enough to leave the entry and head back up the stairs. When he did, he found Jo standing just inside the sitting room, her pen and papers held close, and a faraway smile on her face so that he knew she'd heard everything.

"Miss March? A gentleman is waiting for you outside the stage door."

Amy spun around at the young girl's voice, and not a hair slipped out of place, nor did the gilded laurel crown she still wore. Everything was fastened tight, from her straightened hair in the high spiral bun all the dancers wore, to her corseted waist, from which the dance skirt billowed. When she was a girl, she recalled despising the feeling of being pulled too tightly, or at least the practice of sitting long enough for the preening to take place. She could not be more different now. Many girls kept clothing to change into, escaping their costumes at the earliest convenience. Amy could live in hers. She never arrived to a hall or a home, or wherever she was performing, in common clothing. She always came stage ready, and she always left the same way. The performance was far longer than some imagined, and she delighted in its entirety. She could not imagine receiving her audience in anything less than the spectacular attire they'd watched her dance in, whether she'd been a soloist or not.

"Shall I send the flowers to the dormitory, Miss March?" the young white girl asked now, as she helped Amy into her cloak.

"Yes, Anna, thank you. And you'd better be getting back, hadn't you? First years have an early curfew, as I recall."

"Not if we're assisting a performer, Miss March. I thought we could walk back together? There are so many things I'd like to ask you, and Miss Evergreen told us you won't have time to tutor this spring, with your recital schedule."

Amy softened, delighted by the young girl's enthusiasm.

"Is that why you've volunteered as stagehand tonight?"

Anna nodded, and held her hands together before her, her feet naturally resting in first position.

"How's this, then. I'd better go and say hello to whoever's

waiting for me, but come to the barre room tomorrow at six A.M. Is that too early?" Amy asked, already knowing the girl's answer.

"I've already done my calisthenics by then," Anna said excitedly, and she almost bounced away, leaving Amy to glance once more in the vanity backstage before heading for the door.

"Something told me it was you," she said as she entered the early spring night to find Joseph Williams there.

"I told you I'd like to attend one of your performances," he said, a bright bouquet in hand, which he didn't offer because Amy hadn't yet taken an interest.

"And I told you I'd suggest one that might be to your liking," she said, beginning to walk.

"I found that this one was. It's just lucky I looked into the matter myself." He stepped into her wake, but idled until she turned back. "I thought it best to come to an ensemble production, so as not to distract you during a solo revue."

"Mr. Williams, whatever makes you think I'd find you a distraction?" she asked. It was an innocent enough question, intentionally made to sound complimentary despite that both parties knew better.

"Perhaps I'd hoped to be," Joseph said, lifting the bouquet as though to entice Amy.

"You have very lovely taste in flowers, Mr. Williams."

"Amethyst," he said through an amorous sigh, his hand and the bouquet sinking.

"I find it quite improper, Mr. Williams, that I refer to you so formally, and you say my name so freely."

"What would you like to be called? Miss March? I called you Amy when I made your acquaintance, didn't I?"

"I was a child then, wasn't I? And we all thought you had an interest in my eldest sister."

Joseph sobered, adjusting his once-playful expression at the shift in conversation. Amy made no such adjustment, but waited for his reply.

"I was worried my poor handling of your sister's affection might complicate my very genuine interest in you, Miss March. Although I'd foolishly hoped it wouldn't."

"No need for such dramatics, Mr. Williams. My sister is an engaged woman, and I assure you her childhood and momentary infatuation with you is not what complicates your interest," Amy said.

She adored standing beneath the moon, with a nearby gaslight as a spotlight, a gentle breeze moving her costume skirt, and the edges of her cape. She had no intention of saying so to her company, lest he attribute some of her enjoyment to himself. Joseph Williams had proved to be a man accustomed to being desired, and she would not suffer any expression of arrogance.

"May I ask what does, then?" he asked, a sparkle returning to his eye. They might as well have been playing a game of strategy. After all, Amy could admit to herself, she enjoyed complication.

She took a deep breath before responding, turning her chin so that the light above them caught the glisten of makeup on her cheek.

"I'm afraid I find myself in much the position you were in when you met my sister."

"How do you mean?"

"You seem as lovestruck as she was thought to be at the time, and I unfortunately . . . ," she said, and then she sighed.

"Yes?"

"As you were, Mr. Williams, I am devout in my ambitions. I cannot be parted with them on your behalf, as you could not part with the war effort for her."

When Amy curtseyed in goodbye, and turned again to walk home, Joseph Williams followed.

"I would not think of parting you from your ambitions, Miss March," he said, and she stopped again. "Though I would appreciate the occasional invitation to be an admiring spectator, and perhaps furnish you with a carriage afterward to safely transport you home."

Amethyst turned back to face him.

"I have no objection to that courtesy," she said, stepping back and glancing down at the bouquet of flowers until Joseph understood that he should offer them now. "But you will be the one to wait this time, if it's me you want, and not just a March bride. I'll not be engaged before eighteen, not for any man in Boston."

"A very clearheaded and well-communicated stipulation, Miss March. Now," he said, gesturing toward the street where a carriage was waiting. "May I see you home?"

Jo was late again, though at least this wasn't a proper salon meeting, so only Madeleine Plender waited. She rounded the corner onto Pinckney Street and wove around a couple as they strolled, hurrying as best she could without losing the pages she'd bound with twine and stuffed under her arm. She'd given Madeleine at least thirty pages at the last salon for her and the other members to peruse, and had promised to deliver more soon, which was what she was running to do.

When she reached the home, she tried to collect herself on the stoop before using the knocker, and then posing with as much calm as she could muster.

"Joanna, I'm so glad you were able to come!" Madeleine said, and reached in to kiss the young woman on the cheek.

Jo hesitated and then quickly pecked Madeleine's cheek before she pulled away. It was not a greeting they'd ever shared, though it was common among the salon members. She entered when invited and led Madeleine into her own drawing room.

"I did not intend to be tardy to see you again, I must apologize. I lost time writing these last few pages, and wanted to include them." She offered them to the woman, almost shoving them in her excitement, and then patted the twine as though it were more difficult than she expected to part with the work. "I was worried, at first, that writing a book would prove outside my talents," Jo said, her eyes on the pages.

"And yet, the more I write, the freer it comes. It is something entirely new, the experience of writing of my life. I don't think I would ever have thought to do it, had you not suggested it."

Jo finally met Madeleine's eyes, and the woman was smiling softly.

"I'm so glad you've taken up the challenge and are finding it rewarding. That's more than we could have hoped for."

"And the words themselves?" Jo asked, and she took a seat to demonstrate her readiness. "I'm eager to hear your feedback, and that of the other women."

"I've had the chance to read it, and one or two others, and Joanna, we are beside ourselves with excitement," Madeleine said, joining her. "Your narrative has all of the elements of successful books of this kind, and you are so skilled at juxtaposing the beauty of your family and your home against the heinous nature of enslavement."

When Madeleine spoke, she had a way of adding delicate flourishes with her hands and creating a kind of melody with her words that let the hearer know when she was drawing to a close. It surprised Jo to find that Madeleine Plender did not write herself, because she had clearly been instructed on the proper way for a woman to hold an audience's attention, and she excelled at it. It was how Joanna knew that she was not finished with her assessment. Madeleine's voice had ended on a higher register than it did when she had come to the end of speaking, and now she watched Joanna, politely, as though awaiting permission to say something that—without invitation—might seem indelicate or upsetting.

"Thank you so much, Madeleine, for your kind words and attention. I would welcome any criticism you might have as well."

"That's very gracious, Joanna," Madeleine said, and she nodded approvingly. "And I find very little to criticize in your work, as you well know. We want in no way to interrupt your unique voice and heritage. In fact, it's something the women and I have agreed we would like to see more of."

"I'm afraid I don't know what you mean," Jo said, and it was evident in the way her brow creased.

"We expect the audience for this slave narrative to be much broader than any you've had before. It won't just be likeminded Northerners and Southern abolitionists taking an interest in this book. Not if we have anything to say about it," she said, leaning forward, as though sharing a scandalous secret. "Literature has such a power to unite this country, even if only in readership. And any feedback we offer is merely in service of that."

Jo wished the woman would cease with her long and winding and horribly polite preamble, and tell her what changes she had to suggest, but she only returned Madeleine's smile and nodded.

"We've found that even among the educated Northerner, there persists an affinity for the slave dialect, in writing. Especially when it's authored by a woman."

Jo blinked. "Pardon me?"

"It's what I meant when I spoke of your Southern heritage, Joanna. There's some authenticity lacking, in the way you present your enslaved past. In the crisp and intellectual wording you choose. We'd hoped you'd consider rewriting it in a more familiar, more rudimentary voice. Which I think would see this book sell well, after which there is so much good work you'd be able to do!"

Jo blinked at Madeleine again, aware of the way it unsettled the woman. She was attempting to maintain a certain kind of friendly candor, and Joanna's facial expression, or the lack of one, seemed to make that difficult.

"Do you suppose that I spoke in broken English until the moment I was freed?"

"Well, I'm sure it took some time to master the language as you use it now!"

"I have always spoken this way, as does my entire family, and a great many other Black people I knew back home."

"Of course there may be exceptions, Joanna, but I think it's reasonable, given their circumstances, that readers would find it hard to believe slaves speak the way you do."

The room fell quiet then, except for the almost indiscernible sound of Jo's quick breathing.

"I hardly think you should blame anonymous white people for the way you particularly feel about those of us born into slavery, Madeleine."

"Joanna, mind your temper—I am only trying to help you succeed at your craft."

"No, you are trying to help me recognize my place, and stay there. Which is not something I have a mind to do." She stood abruptly, and forced Madeleine to stand as well.

"Joanna—"

"I would like my pages back, please, Madeleine."

"I wish you would reconsider your behavior, Joanna. I am not the villain here. I'm the one offering to publish you!"

"So long as I diminish myself. So long as I don't threaten to take your place, in which I have no interest, though I can see the ways you make up to remind the others not to admire me too much, being from the South and formerly enslaved as I am."

"How can you speak so impolitely to me, in my own home?" Madeleine said, her hand at her chest.

"I will take my leave of it, if you would please give me my pages."

Madeleine stood a moment longer, staring at Joanna and clearly beside herself at the way the visit had gone. Then she assembled the early pages Joanna had furnished her with and the ones still bound with twine before leading the young woman back to the front door.

"I do hope you will reconsider your behavior, Miss March," Madeleine said when she'd let Jo out and handed her her work. "It has been boorish and indecent, if I am honest."

"I have come to regard Northern society politeness as being just as deceiving as the etiquette that lived alongside enslavement back home, Mrs. Plender. And so I hope that you will reconsider yours. You have done many great services to this community, and I would hate to think you would so overshadow them."

Madeleine Plender closed her door without saying

goodnight, and once the exchange was over, Jo felt herself shiver with the immediacy of regret.

Jo couldn't go home, not when she would only toss and turn for the rest of the night. Not when she needed to know whether she'd proved herself impossible. There was a worry and it would not be relegated to the back of her mind: *What if I am the problem?*

She stopped on the street, which glistened wet under the gaslights, arrested by the question. There wasn't enough water to have been from the uncapping of a hydrant, nor was it hot enough to warrant it, and there hadn't been any rain for at least a week. Its presence shouldn't bother her—water on the cobblestone streets was not a cause for hesitation or concern to city dwellers, and they never seemed to wonder over its origin.

"Perhaps I think too much," she told a phantom Lorie, who of course was not beside her that night. He was at his boardinghouse, either rabble-rousing with the other young men who lived there, and who like him worked as daily hires throughout Beacon Hill, or sleeping.

"I shouldn't go," Jo said, still standing in the street, and then turned around because the boardinghouse was actually back the way she'd come. "I've already been called indecent today."

She arrived at the brownstone in no time, as the streets were almost entirely deserted, and she'd stalked down them in a particularly unladylike fashion. At the door, she'd rung the bell, and had been met by the woman who oversaw the house and lived in a room directly off the entry. Probably she was situated there to enforce a curfew, if men's boarding-houses had them.

It wasn't until the woman had opened the inside door to the foyer, pulling a robe around her, hair hidden beneath a white sleeping bonnet, that Jo realized she'd have to give good reason for the woman to wake Lorie.

"Oh," Jo whispered to herself, or to her phantom Lorie, who'd suggested that it was always upsetting to see a young woman cry. She blinked a dozen times and then tried squeezing her eyes shut, but no tears came.

"This is a gentleman's boardinghouse, miss," the woman said immediately upon opening the front door.

"I know," Jo replied, still batting her eyes in hopes of becoming teary eyed.

The woman squinted at her. "Well, it's too late for visi-tors, and unless you have family here, I don't suggest visiting young men in the dead of night."

"It's nothing like that." Joanna stopped her fruitless attempts and looked at the woman before her. "I only need to talk to Lorie for a moment."

"And I'm sure you'll find him in the morning, or, if he's as fond of you, he'll come calling on his own."

"Please," Jo said, reaching toward the door when it began to close, though she made certain not to touch it. The tears were welling now. She couldn't go home without seeing him.

She couldn't take her encounter with Madeleine Plender to bed with her without the comfort that at least Lorie knew. "I promise," she said, self-conscious now that the tears might actually fall when she was so unaccustomed to crying, let alone with an audience. "It will only be a moment."

The woman pulled her robe tighter despite that it hadn't loosened, but her stern expression relaxed.

"You must be Joanna," she said, to Jo's surprise. "One moment. I'll wake him."

"Thank you," Jo managed to the closed door, and then she could not be still. She turned and faced the street, eyebrows lacing in thought. The den mother at Lorie's boardinghouse knew who she was, without introduction, simply because she was there. It was only strange until Jo recalled all of the ways Lorie came up in her conversations with people he'd never met. How if he showed up at the salon, all of the women would know exactly who he was. It wasn't because she'd told them any distinguishing features, or because she spoke of him any particular way. It was just that she spoke of him. Often.

She thought of him often.

Always.

"Jo, what's the matter?" Lorie exclaimed before she heard the door reopen, and he had his hands on her shoulders, turning her to face him before she had the chance. He only looked into her damp eyes for a split second before pulling her into an embrace and laying his head atop hers. "What's happened? Are you all right?"

He sucked his teeth, which must have been his male

equivalent of shushing or cooing, because he began to gently rock, too.

"I'm all right," Jo said, pushing back against his night-clothes and barely holding back a laugh. She'd forgotten her worry entirely at his dramatic response. "Are *you*?"

"Miss Esther said you were crying, and that you needed to see me right away," he told her, letting her pull out of his arms but taking one of her hands before she could go too far.

"I only cried so she'd fetch you." Jo wicked at her eye-lashes with her thumb, and Lorie cocked an eyebrow at her.

"It's convincing, to say the least." And then he tipped his head to the side, and held her gaze. "You aren't all right, Jo."

She tucked her lips into her mouth when the tears swelled again, and this time, she let them fall.

Lorie's shoulders sank, and he gently tugged at her hand so that she'd come back into his arms.

"There isn't a chance that Miss Esther isn't hiding in the dark, watching us," he said when his head was laid against Jo's again. They were pressed against each other so that he felt the laughter ripple through her. "I'll be evicted come the morning, so thank you."

"I'm sorry."

"There are many beds for rent in this city, worry not." He released her again and led her to sit at the top of the stoop. "But do tell me what's happened."

Joanna sank onto the step, crumpling even farther until she rested her head on her knees, her arms wrapped around her skirt.

"I'm too proud," she said.

"Are you?"

"And too boorish."

"Boorish," he echoed, as though it was news to him.

"And I've thrown away an opportunity that will not be presented me again, because I have more conviction than I deserve, or than is decent."

"If you've thrown it away, then it wasn't an opportunity. How can something be that inspires such a response from you?"

"People waste opportunities all the time, Lorie."

"People do, but not you," he said, and she cast her eyes up to see his streetlamp-illuminated face. "People don't know what they want or who they are, and so when opportunities arise, they don't recognize them. That isn't you. If you've declined Madeleine Plender's offer, it's because there is fault in the offer, not in you."

She sat up with a start. "Who said it had anything to do with Madeleine Plender?"

"Are there other recent opportunities I'm unaware of?"

"No," she muttered, sinking back down into a slump. "But now I'll never be published."

"By her. Maybe."

"Why are you so loyal?" Jo demanded, her voice jumping up an entire register, as though it weren't night and the neighborhood around them weren't silent by comparison. "Don't you even want to know what happened?"

"Of course I do. But I already know I'm on your side."

Joanna stilled. "As I'm on yours."

On the stoop, Jo twisted so that their knees touched, and they faced each other, and then she laid her hand over his.

"I love you, Lorie."

His reply was a deep inhale that blossomed into a wide and handsome smile.

"I've known it all along, because I keep you with me even when you're not. And because you knew me from the start."

For once, he didn't answer back. She was glad he could accept her confession quietly, so that he did not have to perform its acceptance or distract from the hearing by trying to fashion something to say in return.

"And because you joined my family, and never tried to part me from it."

He shook his head, brows low in disapproval at the mere thought.

"I'm just afraid," Jo began, and her eyes fell. "That I don't love the way so many do. And that I'm keeping you from a better kind."

When she looked back, there was a dampness in Lorie's eyes.

"No," he said.

"No?" she echoed, smirking and mimicking the shaking of his head. "That's it?"

"That's it, Jo," Lorie said, and never broke her gaze. "There is no better kind."

XV

June 1866

WISDOM AND MEG WOULD HAVE LIKED TO HAVE HELD their wedding ceremony on the estate where they'd first danced, but the big house had been restored to its former owner and inhabitants. All things could not be reclaimed, of course, as the fine portrait in the entry had been kindling in the bonfire, and the many hidden treasures had been discovered and taken. Beth's sewing machine was forfeited back to the original family, only because she'd never elected to move it.

They held the wedding on the Roanoke shore instead, where there was space to set out blankets and where folks had easy access to the water as soon as the vows were exchanged and the broom was jumped.

"I want to wear this dress for the rest of my life, Beth," Meg said, fanning out the edges of the skirt. She and her three sisters were sitting on a quilt, with cushions beneath them, to identify that this was the designated space for the wedding party. "It must have been so difficult to make without the use of your machine, though."

Beth leaned toward the eyelets she'd handstitched for the summer wedding, and tucked a stray thread that only she had noticed.

"It wasn't difficult at all. I only had to keep imagining you in it, and the work flew by."

"That can't be so. I spied you working day and night these past months. And I adore it. I wouldn't have been married in anything but a dress my sister designed." And then, she turned to her youngest sister. "Don't pout, Amy."

Meg took Amy's hand, and as though it had begun an unspoken ceremony, Jo took Beth's, before Amy took Jo's, and, smiling, Beth completed the circle by taking Meg's. The four March sisters laughed, but did not release one another. It had been three years since they were all together, and not fellowshipping by way of ink and paper, and what they loved most was that in proximity, even silence could be shared.

"Anyway, Meg, I'm perfectly happy wearing the lovely dress I bought for you," Amethyst recommended the conversation after a short while, smoothing the white lace that spilled elegantly from a corseted waistline.

"One might almost suspect that had been her hope all along," Jo said, smirking.

"Expensive things look best on you, Amy," Meg reassured her. "I've worn my share, and I prefer to see them on you. You've worked so hard, and you deserve them." She hesitated then, but not because she was unsure what to say, only how to say it in a way that would keep her sister from becoming self-conscious. "I'm glad for you and Joseph Williams, as well. With all sincerity. You are the kind of high-society wife he will hopefully one day deserve."

"Thank you, Meg," Amy replied, bringing her eldest sister's hand to her lips and pressing a kiss into the back. "I knew you'd feel that way. But I'm happier now that you've said so."

"I want all my sisters to be as happy as I am today," Meg told them, looking at each young woman's face. "Whoever and wherever it requires."

They all looked to Beth now, and their joy mingled with a hint of sorrow.

"I hope you'll come and visit me, at least," Beth told them, embarrassed when she began to cry. "You can't very well sponsor such a trip, Amethyst, and not see the place for yourself."

The young women laughed at themselves, wiping each other's tears instead of their own, oblivious to the way their parents admired them from another spot on the shore.

"I hadn't wanted to tell you in my letter," Amy began. "Not until I was certain it wouldn't spoil the gift at all. Joseph has asked to sponsor you and Ella and Baby Fanny, in my place. He said he'd never gotten the chance to repay our hospitality, and I agreed."

"What an expensive way to repay a night of shad fish," Beth said, visibly astonished.

"Is it too much?" Amy asked, worried that she'd spoiled the excitement. "I shouldn't have said anything!"

"Of course it isn't," Jo interrupted before the young performer could get carried away.

"It isn't!" Meg insisted, to both Amy and Beth, whose eyes were leaping from one sister's face to the next, unsure. "We served him molasses apple pie, too!"

The four fell into laughter again, their happiness carrying so that all of the freedpeople joining them turned and smiled along with the sisters dressed in white.

"They'll always be happiest when they're all together," Lorie said to his company, and they agreed. He was standing with the Carter brothers, Wisdom and Honor, in finer clothing than he'd ever bothered with, when Joseph Williams joined them.

"For the bridegroom," Joseph said, and offered Wisdom a champagne coupe. He'd brought one for himself as well, and Honor eyed it.

"Careful," the young man said, as the sparkling liquid swirled with Joseph's movements. "You're likely to overflow. Not that I'd mind, since you've forgotten one for the best man."

"I regretfully have but two hands, Mr. Carter," Joseph answered. "And as for the overfilling, champagne glasses are regretfully shallow, and I did not want to return for another glass too quickly."

"One must remember his wedding decorum," Lorie snarked, to the Carters' amusement, only to find Joseph very unbecomingly hunched over the glass, lowering his lips to the rim, as though to raise the glass to his lips instead would invite disaster. "Oh, Amy will not have that," Lorie said, and all four of them laughed, Joseph almost spitting out the champagne he'd worked so hard to preserve.

There were too many of them to fit in Lorie's old boat, but after a few trips, everyone had crossed the sound, and stood on the shore of Manns Harbor.

Lorie, Wisdom, and Joseph mounted and secured the luggage on the two coaches Joseph or Amy had hired—they would not confirm which—and Alcott March looked on.

Ella sat close to the water, a sleeping Fanny on her lap, sweat plastering the little girl's dark curls to her forehead despite that her mother fanned her.

Mammy stood with her four daughters somewhere between the work with the coaches and the sleeping child, and the five March women created a ring when they joined hands.

"My heart might never recover, having to say goodbye to you all at once," Mammy said, and then she shook her head. "But I am so pleased that you're all departing together. I'm so glad we got to make one last memory in this colony of ours. This place we gave so much to."

"How long will you and Papa stay?" Jo asked.

"Until the end, I think," Mammy said, and then she nodded through a deep breath. "Until the bittersweet end. There are freedpeople petitioning for deeds, so that however much is taken back, perhaps we can save the house your father built. And all the ones you did."

"And do you think you'll succeed?" Jo asked.

All her children were women now, so Mammy could answer truthfully, except that she found the words too difficult to speak.

"Whatever happens," Jo spoke instead, because she knew her mother well. "You have so many places you can go. You can come to Raleigh and be with Lorie and me."

"And me!" Amy added. "I'll be in Raleigh a whole term, giving recitals and lessons at Raleigh Institute. I'll have far more leisure time than Jo, since she'll be enrolled as a student."

"I should like to see my girls at a university," Mammy said before the two could bicker. "Especially at one designed just for Black people."

"Or you could come to Mississippi, and be with Wisdom and me," Meg offered. "I know Beth and I have had more of you than Amy and Jo, but I will always want a little more."

"I don't expect anyone to cross the Atlantic very soon," Beth said, without a hint of offense. "But perhaps one day you'll come to Liberia, too, Mammy, and see me in my shop."

Mammy released Beth's hand so that she could cup the young woman's face, and then she let their foreheads rest together.

"Wherever my daughters are brave enough to go," Mammy said, eyes closed as though in prayer, "I will surely follow."

When the moment ended, the four men were facing them, still standing back beside the coaches so as not to interrupt. Ella struggled to stand under the sleeping weight of her daughter, and Wisdom rushed to help her.

"I suppose you must be off," Mammy said, smiling and tucking her lips inside her mouth as though she might swallow them along with any pleas for the young women to stay. "Take care of each other until Raleigh," she said, knowing their paths would diverge from that point, with the newly-weds taking a train to their destination, and Beth and Ella heading to their port.

"And ever after, Mammy," Amy told her. "We promise."

They hugged as one, refusing to embrace their mother in turn, so that they built a cocoon around her.

"Go on, my darlings," she said, while her daughters were still wrapped around her. "Be free."

Author's Note

In the summer of 2020, during the full weight of the pandemic and what one hopes was the beginning of a serious reckoning with the racist foundation of our country and all its brutal consequences, someone wrote that it isn't history people are trying to protect, it's memory.

When people decry the 1619 Project or don't want to remove terrorizing statues of enslavers and brutalizers, it isn't because they are protecting history. They're protecting their legends, their mythology, the things they've decided to believe or at least repeat, to the exclusion and misrepresentation of whatever really happened. In a country with an intentionally racist foundation and a recurring pandemic of state violence against Black Americans—which is always accompanied by the knowing deputization of white citizens to enact the same violence with little or no consequence—we who were never taught a dozen names of Black Americans before the 1960s know that we weren't taught "history" in the first place. We were taught propaganda, and it was and has been another dehumanizing campaign in the ongoing march of white supremacy.

So Many Beginnings is historical fiction. It's based on meticulously researched and collated correspondences and documentation, some of which I painstakingly searched through extensive endnotes in academic papers available on JSTOR. The lion's share of my treasure, and indeed the basis for the March family's life, is found in Patricia C. Click's *Time Full of Trial: The Roanoke Island Freedmen's Colony, 1862–1867* (University of North Carolina Press). It's a book I had never heard of and did not own prior to this project, despite being an American-educated adult with a university degree, and having had a partner whose undergraduate degree was in American Studies. That we could pass through more than fifteen years of education, with all its history components and requirements, and have had no instruction on something as distinct as the freedpeople colonies is alarming, to say the least.

This note is not to defend the historicity in *So Many Beginnings*, though. It's to challenge what we have accepted as history and acknowledge the roles that white supremacy and anti-Blackness play in that conception. For people woefully uneducated in the discipline, it's not adherence to canon that makes us challenge the validity of accents and diction and presence and impact; it is the mythology that we've ingested, and which has shaped our national imagination. For an audience supposedly unaware of the Tulsa Massacre and the brutality of sundown towns until recent television shows showcased them, it's laughable to assume resistance to historical truth is based on a breadth of knowledge. The sad truth is that any nation that would intentionally do the things ours has cannot be trusted to relay its doings. History must be searched out, and the people that myths have omitted or misrepresented restored. My deepest gratitude to the true historians doing that work, so that I can do mine.

Thank you for reading this Feiwel & Friends book. The friends who made *So Many Beginnings* possible are:

Jean Feiwel, Publisher
Liz Szabla, Associate Publisher
Rich Deas, Senior Creative Director
Holly West, Senior Editor
Anna Roberto, Senior Editor
Kat Brzozowski, Senior Editor
Dawn Ryan, Senior Managing Editor
Kim Waymer, Senior Production Manager
Emily Settle, Associate Editor
Erin Siu, Associate Editor
Rachel Diebel, Assistant Editor
Foyinsi Adegbonmire, Editorial Assistant
Kathy Wielgosz, Production Editor

Follow us on Facebook
or visit us online at mackids.com.
Our books are friends for life.

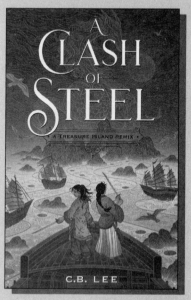